The Best
Bad Dream

Also by Robert Ward

Total Immunity
Four Kinds of Rain
Grace
The Cactus Garden
The King of Cards
Red Baker
The Sandman
Cattle Annie and Little Britches
Shedding Skin

The Best
Bad Dream

Robert Ward

The Mysterious Press
an imprint of Grove/Atlantic, Inc.
New York

Published simultaneously in Canada
Printed in the United States of America

FIRST EDITION

ISBN-13: 978-0-8021-2601-6

Mysterious Press
an imprint of Grove/Atlantic, Inc.
841 Broadway
New York, NY 10003

Distributed by Publishers Group West

www.groveatlantic.com

12 13 14 15   10 9 8 7 6 5 4 3 2 1

For
Celeste Wesson
and
Robbie Ward

Chapter One

They drove up Route 285 from Santa Fe as the sun went down, Michelle Wu and her younger sister Jennifer riding their matching metallic gray Suzuki B-King cycles over one hundred miles per hour.

"C'mon, sis," Michelle yelled as she cruised past her sister. "You're standing still out here."

Competitive since they were kids, Michelle expected Jennifer to shout back and speed by her. Instead, she just turned her head in a moody way and looked straight ahead at the dark road.

Michelle groaned. She'd thought getting out the bikes would cheer her sister up but it was obvious Jen was still furious with her. So maybe she could make it up to her by taking her to the Tewa Pueblo at Taos. At least Michelle prayed it would. Because when Jen got into a serious sulk it could last for days.

Michelle geared down and waited for her sister to catch up.

"Follow me. The next left. I'll race you there."

She shot ahead, hoping Jennifer would rise to the challenge, but it was no use. Her sister moped behind. What a waste of horsepower.

That it was her own fault made the whole thing even more annoying.

Ahead of her, Michelle saw the turnoff to the ancient pueblo. In the fading afternoon light it seemed an ancient magical place. Built a thousand years ago, the village glowed with a golden light.

But as they got closer, Michelle could see how barren and poor the pueblo really was. It was muddy outside the adobe walled buildings, and the Tewa people had to climb rickety ladders to go from the first to the second story, and from the second to the third.

Now Michelle worried that Jennifer, too, would find the whole trip a drag, and she'd be even more disgruntled than before.

There was a big Indian man standing at the base of the bleak dirt parking lot, selling tickets. He wore a cheap, torn, plaid cloth coat, and his pockmarked skin and big belly weren't exactly the romance novel idea of a native warrior. He looked exactly like what he was: a guy hustling his way through a tough, unforgiving life.

After they parked their bikes on a small side street, he sold them their entrance tickets and stamped their hands as though they were teenagers going to Disneyland.

Still, Michelle didn't want to be cynical. Two thousand people lived on this reservation in three-story adobe buildings. They warmed these rooms with fire, the old way, and raised their children with their grandparents close at hand. They made their own cornmeal, and sang the songs of their ancestors.

In a faked-up, bullshit world of fast food, McMansions, and jive there was something authentic and appealing about the pueblo, something even holy.

Jennifer walked slightly ahead of her, not yet finished being furious. Michelle wanted to poke her and say, "Snap out of it," but she knew her sister better than that. Better to wait until the rage wore off.

Then she could talk to Jen, explain what went wrong. It wasn't really her fault anyway. It was just the way things fell. You tried to do the right thing but sometimes—too many times—you ran into *ming*, or what Westerners called fate.

She had learned as a girl that *ming* often ran counter to puny human wishes and the way to deal with it was to forget it, and to act nobly anyway.

But Michelle wasn't really that much like her Chinese ancestors. She was American Chinese and wanted very badly to control *ming*, to make things work out. She could hear her dead grandmother laugh at such a thought.

"*Ming* is as controllable as the wind or the rain. How do you control either of them?"

She believed in *ming*, yes, but she also believed in happy endings. Happy endings achieved by any means necessary. Michelle had learned a long time ago that you had to cut corners to make things work. And when opportunities presented themselves you should strike and strike hard.

Surely Jen would understand all this. Though the sisters were different, they weren't *that* different. She'd understand it, and then they could get back on the right track.

The two of them climbed the ladders, walked hunched through the cramped adobe rooms, and Michelle wondered how anyone could stand living in so small a place. Smoke from the fireplaces gave all the rooms a deep musty odor that Michelle couldn't decide if she liked or not. Maybe if she got used to it.

As they went into a souvenir shop, she asked Jen how she had liked the tour but her sister rolled her eyes at her.

"In case you hadn't noticed, I'm really pissed at you."

Michelle took that as an opening and laughed.

"What's the matter, babe, you think I'm not sensitive?"

That got the smallest of smiles.

3

"I'm going to take a little walk, Michelle. I've got some thinking to do. They say the village's big religious room, the kiva, is down that way. Meet me there in, say, twenty minutes. Okay?"

"Okay," Michelle said. She wondered what she would do for the next twenty minutes. She was already getting a little bored. Michelle didn't dig history all that much. She had spent most of her life trying to live in the now. Her own family history was filled with remorse, drunkenness, and violence. She didn't want to remember it. But she knew that turning her back on her history was probably superficial and dumb. So she tried, even though looking at the past, hers or anyone else's, made her jumpy and nervous.

Now she watched as Jennifer left the little pueblo gift shop and headed down to the kiva, a couple of short, muddy blocks away. Michelle looked at a few Indian dolls—strange little things made of wood, feather, and bone—then checked the pocket of her leather cycle jacket.

There it was, a joint. Just what she needed to get through all this native culture.

She walked outside and climbed up to a second-floor balcony. Coming toward her was a tall, thin man with a black coat and . . . what was that . . . a white collar? A priest? The sight jolted her a bit.

She had suffered at the hands of priests when she was a girl, the beginning of a long series of betrayals.

As the man drew nearer she could see that he had Indian features, high cheekbones and a reddish color to his skin. He looked up at her, stared at her for a second, then walked on. He wasn't a priest at all, just a man wearing a collarless shirt.

After looking around to make sure no one could see her, she lit the J. She inhaled deeply a couple of times, then peered down at the burnt-orange valley and fell into a fantasy that she was actually an Indian maiden, living a thousand years ago. Hey, maybe she was wrong. When you were high, history became a lot more lifelike. The image was so interesting she felt as though she were a different person. She must have been a warrior woman, she was pretty sure. No sitting home waiting for the braves to come home shot up by the Spanish or, later, the Americans. She would go out with her own band of hand-chosen women and use their sex to ensnare the Spanish commandant. She could feel herself dancing wildly, mesmerizing the older man. Then, while making love to him, she'd stab him in the throat and be a heroine to her people.

The fantasy was so real that she indulged it again, and then a little wind came over the pueblo. She lay back on the cool adobe wall, her feet hanging over the ledge, and in seconds fell fast asleep.

When Michelle woke up, she looked down at the lonely pueblo street and saw only a few orange streetlights down by the big kiva.

God, she had gotten stoned and nodded off. Well, no wonder. The last few days with Lucky Avila had been totally stressful. The lying, cheating bastard.

She climbed back down the ladder and checked her watch. Oh man, she was ten minutes late. Not all that long in reality, but too long when your sister was already pissed off at you.

She walked down the creepy street to the kiva. Only two other tourists were there, a middle-aged man wearing an Ohio State football jacket and sweatpants and, at his side, a young, honey-blonde woman with eyes as blue and vacant as two plastic buttons.

Michelle started to look inside the round mound of adobe, the big kiva, but there was a sign on the wall that said, NO TRESPASSING.

She gave an irritated sigh, walked a block past the meeting spot, and came back but there was still no sign of her sister.

Finally, starting to worry, Michelle approached the Ohio couple.

"Hi, I'm looking for my sister. You didn't happen to see a Chinese girl around here a few minutes ago, did you?"

The man shook his big head and assumed a worried look.

"Chinese? No, ma'am. Nobody like that."

The woman made a face like she was sucking on a lemon.

"Naw, there was some Indians here. At least I think they was Indians, but they weren't Chinese, no way."

"Thanks," Michelle said, feeling a little uneasy.

She turned away and headed back to the parking lot.

As she left Phil looked at his wife, Dee Dee.

"She was a Chinese," the man said,

"So?" Dee Dee responded, fury in her voice.

"Well, it's just that I have some trouble telling the Asian races from one another. Like I was in line at Buckeye Noodles once in Columbus and there were people in the line who were, I am pretty sure, your Koreans and Japanese and maybe even your Chinese and I am somewhat ashamed to admit I could not tell them apart."

"Why am I not surprised by that?" Dee Dee said.

"Well, I suppose you can tell every damned Oriental from every other," he replied.

"Oh for Chrissakes, Phil. You are such a freaking hick."

Phil wanted to say something vicious back but he didn't have the heart for it. Instead he said, "You know what? I think I've had about enough of this Indian village. Why don't we get back down to the Blue Wolf? Must be around happy hour there now."

Dee Dee thought it was a good idea. But she wasn't going to give him credit. No way. She was sick of his jive, his ideas, and truth be told, pretty much sick of everything else about Phil, too.

She gave him a hard little smile, and they headed across the street toward their metallic gray Hummer.

Just outside the pueblo, Michelle walked past the adobe outer wall and turned onto the unpaved lot where they'd parked their bikes. She figured if Jennifer's bike was gone, then she'd just taken off and they would probably meet back in Santa Fe at their hotel, La Fonda. But if the bike was still there . . .

And it was. The two choppers were sitting there side by side, gleaming, ready to be ridden hard back down the starlit highway to Santa Fe.

But no Jennifer.

Michelle felt something turn in her stomach. Of course, Jen could still be wandering around the pueblo, but Michelle doubted it. No matter how mad the two sisters were at one another, it wasn't like them to play games. They had always been two against the world, even when they were young; each knew that she couldn't survive without the other.

She had to go back to the pueblo and look around some more. Maybe Jen had gotten lost in the dark streets.

Then she found herself doing a very uncharacteristic thing, yelling, "Jennifer, hey Jen, it's time to go, girl. Jen . . ."

But her words were lost in the cold, clear air. Only an old, wrinkled Indian woman smoking at the parking lot entrance looked her way, but she didn't say a word.

Chapter Two

As Jack Harper drove the seven blocks from his home toward Culver City High, he felt a great relief. No cases to worry about, no reports to write, no trials to attend, no lawyers to hassle with. No more office politics. For two whole weeks he would get to be on his own, relax. The thought was almost too much for him to take in. The only thing that bothered him was that he hadn't really mapped out any particular thing he wanted to do for his vacation. For the first day he'd beat up on himself for not making plans to go to Spain, or maybe down to Mexico to go sport fishing. But hey, he could always do the latter next week. It was easy to call and get a fishing boat at Baja, or, for that matter, he could always call his old buddy Will Lazenby and fly over to Hawaii for some marlin fishing.

The truth was he was almost relieved that he didn't have any plans. Maybe he'd just hang with his son Kevin for a while, like he was doing today. Watch the kid play lacrosse, go to the batting cages with him, or play some hoops down at the beach. That was something he really enjoyed and he needed to be with his son more. Kevin was a sophomore in high school now, and who knew where he would end up when he went off to college. Jack may not have been the best dad in the world, but the thought of not having Kevin around really shook him up.

He hoped his son would stay in town and go to UCLA, but Kevin was getting to be a great lacrosse player and might well get a full scholarship to an East Coast school. Scouts for the University of Virginia and Jack's old alma mater, the University of Maryland, had been hanging around his son's games.

If he ended up on the East Coast Jack would never see him. So he really ought to spend as much time with him as he could right now.

Jack stood on the sidelines with the other Culver City parents as Kevin cradled the ball in his midfielder's stick and made his way down the sideline toward the Brentwood goal. Jack was stunned by his son's speed. When he had played, Jack had been a good stick handler but wasn't all that fast. With Kevin the talents were reversed. His boy was blazing fast but he was sometimes a little careless with the ball.

Now Jack hoped that Kevin would see a wide open crease-attackman crossing in front of the goal. One good pass and a quick stick shot by Andrews, the attackman, and Culver City would win the first-round play-off game.

But Kevin was being dogged by a big defenseman and didn't see Andrews crossing and waving his stick high, calling for the ball. Instead Kevin tried a dodge, dropped the ball, and took a couple of steps cradling his empty stick, not realizing that the defenseman had already scooped up the loose ball and was heading to the other end of the field.

"Kev," Jack yelled. "Kev, the ball."

Kevin turned, looked at his stick, and Jack thought he could see his red face right through his helmet and mask.

For a second it looked as though Kev was going to hang his head and just stand there, but suddenly he lit out after the defenseman. The big guy was running in long strides but busy looking at opposing Culver City defensemen who were coming up to stop him.

He didn't see Kevin moving up behind him.

Now the Brentwood defenseman held his stick back a little, ready to make a pass to a lone attackman on his side. Which gave Kevin exactly the shot he needed. He whacked the big guy's stick so hard it fell from his hands, the ball rolled free, and Kevin scooped it up and headed back toward the Brentwood goal.

Everyone on the Culver bench was up and screaming as Kevin dodged one middie, then another, and ended up open in front of the Brentwood goalie. Two defensemen were closing fast on him and he barely had time to get off a low ground shot, which sailed to the left of the goalie's stick and into the net. Just as time ran out.

Immediately after the shot Kevin was decked by both defenders, a human sandwich. After the dust had cleared, he was up and being carried off the field by his ecstatic teammates.

Jack quickly joined him and the regular coach, Mike Mahoney. They pounded Kevin on the back as he was mobbed by mothers, fathers, and other Culver City lacrosse fans.

"Way to go, son," Jack said. "That was just awesome."

"Thanks, Dad," Kevin said. "Sorry I dropped the ball."

"Don't worry. You kept hustling and it paid off."

He tousled Kevin's black hair and felt a surge of happiness.

All around him parents were talking, chattering, and congratulating their sons for a great game.

Kevin stepped up to Jack and spoke in a low voice.

"Dad, I think I see the next Mrs. Harper checking you out."

Jack laughed. "You do? Where?"

"Look just off to your left. Slowly, don't be obvious about it."

Jack turned and looked across the green field to where he saw a brunette in her late thirties, wearing skin-tight Levi's and a form-fitting green sweater. And she had the body to fill it out. And those lips . . . even thirty feet away, Jack could see she had luscious, full lips. She smiled his way and he managed a half-smile back.

But then there was a nasty little surprise. A big, sandy-haired guy in his forties walked up behind her, took her hand, and they turned and walked away toward the parking lot.

"Well, there goes that fantasy," Jack said. "The next time you find me a new Mrs. Harper please see if she's married first, okay, pal?"

Kevin laughed and shook his head.

"Well, she looked like she was alone, Dad, and you gotta admit she was staring at you with that lean, hungry look."

"Yeah," Jack said. "But she's probably a team mom."

"Not for our school," Kevin said. "Must be for Brentwood."

"She looked too fancy for me even if she was single," Jack said. "Not my type."

Jack carried the lacrosse bag to the car and had just locked it in the trunk when his cell rung.

"Hello."

"Jackie, thank God it's you."

"Michelle? What's up?" It was his Michelle Wu, the most gorgeous and trickiest woman he'd ever met. Michelle specialized in hot cars. She worked with a gang who stole them, gave them to her to break down, and then resold the parts all over Mexico and Latin America.

Jack had busted her three years ago and recruited her as a snitch, but it had become a lot more complex during their last case. Michelle had risked her own life to save his.

Jack was uncomfortable being in her debt. And even more uncomfortable because he had feelings for her that were strictly taboo, given her line of work.

Now he tried to gauge the degree of panic in her voice. How much of it was real fear, and how much acting? Michelle Wu was a consummate actress and drama queen.

"I'm in Santa Fe, Jack. My sister Jennifer and I came here for a little holiday. We rode up to Taos to see the pueblo and got separated. Now she's gone. Someone has taken her."

"You sure she didn't just wander off, Michelle?"

"No way. She would never do that."

"You contacted the local cops?"

"Yes, of course. But they say they can't do anything for twenty-four hours. They gave me that 'most people come back on their own' bullshit."

"But they do, Michelle."

"Jackie, I would never ask you to do anything that interfered with your work, but please come out here. Please. I know this is bad."

"How do you know that, Michelle?"

"I can't talk about that on the phone, Jack. I can't. I'm at the La Fonda hotel in Santa Fe."

"Michelle, I'm sorry but I—"

"Jackie, are you going to make me say 'you owe me'?"

"You don't have to say it," Jack said. Jesus, he was already stressed out. His vacation had barely begun.

But it was true. He owed her.

"I gotta get some things together but I'll be there. By tomorrow, Michelle."

"Thanks, Jackie. I wouldn't bother you but this is freaky, man. Please call me as soon as you make your reservations. You can always stay with me in my room, Jack."

"No, thanks, Michelle. I'll get my own."

"I knew you would say that, baby," she said. "Thanks, Jack. This is really serious."

Jack hung up the phone and looked across the parking lot at his son.

"Hey, Dad, you want to hang out and get some pizza at the farmer's market with the guys?"

"Not tonight," Jack said. "Something's come up."

Kevin's face flashed severe disappointment.

"Oh, man," he said. "You gotta go? I thought you were on vacation."

"I was. I mean I still am. This should only take a couple of days."

Kevin shook his head.

"Yeah, right."

"I have to call Grandpa. He'll come down and stay with you. You'll have fun together."

Kevin sighed.

"I don't need Grandpa, Dad. I'm almost sixteen years old. I can stay by myself."

"No way," Jack said. "Hey, think of all that fried food he's going to make for you."

Kevin made a "gag me with a spoon" face and his shoulders slumped as he got inside the car.

"Kev, I'm sorry. But this is someone I can't turn down."

Kevin slammed the door and looked straight ahead.

Chapter Three

An hour later, Jack's father, Wade Harper, showed up in his battered 1965 Ford Mustang. Once dark green, the car badly needed a coat of paint. Gray primer showed through on both sides and the front bumper was cracked and about to fall off. The engine, however, was perfect, and Wade constantly claimed he was going to get the "old warhorse" cleaned up.

The joke between them, one repeated almost every time they saw each other, was that once the car was patched up, Wade would start showing it at Mustang shows, with all the other sixties guys who made a fetish out of the beloved model. Wade swore he would soon have the best-looking car at Bob's Big Boy's weekly classic car contest. But Jack knew better. If Wade actually fixed the car up and showed it at the old-car contest, that would be a tacit admission that he was sixty-four years old and that he had an "old guy" hobby. By not fixing the car up, he got to drive around like he was some kind of badass looking for girls and hot-rod races.

In short, Wade was having a lot of trouble admitting he was getting old, a lot closer to the end of the line than the beginning.

He lived in an apartment near the farmer's market and spent most of his retirement hanging out at EB's Wine Bar with a raffish assortment of roofers, welders, criminal lawyers, rockers, and wannabe actresses who enjoyed the camaraderie of beer, wine drinking, gossip, and occasional romances that flowered after a few too many drinks. Still good looking and fairly trim, Wade was dating a forty-eight-year-old ex-dancer named Billie Stone who taught elementary school at Carthay Circle. She was crazy about Wade, but he worried that she secretly thought he was too old for her. Whenever Jack asked him if was going to marry her, his father would say, "If I do she'll get all my money. I mean when we get divorced in two or three years. You know how that goes. Then what am I going to leave you and Kevin?"

"You could get her to sign a prenup," Jack said. But his old man just sighed and shook his head.

"Any good attorney can find ways to break one of those. Nah, I'm finished with marriage. Been there, done that. I'm fine living alone. Can't stand women more than three times a week anyway."

Jack laughed. Maybe being a fucked-up renegade ran in the family. Maybe the scientists were right. It *was* all in the genes and there was little you could do about any of it.

As Jack packed for his flight to Albuquerque, he went over the rules with his dad.

"I want Kevin in bed at ten. Not staying up all night listening to your stories."

Wade took a sip of Wild Turkey and laughed at Jack.

"You don't trust me to take care of my grandson, then maybe you ought to hire a professional babysitter!"

From the bedroom, Kevin gave a horselaugh.

"Yeah, like I'm a baby. I'll be sixteen soon, Grandpa."

"That's right," Wade said. "You gotta let the boy become a man, Jackie."

"All in due time, Dad," Jack said. "Ten o'clock bedtime for you, Kev. I'm not kidding."

"No problem," Kevin said.

"Yeah," Wade said, lighting a Marlboro. "And if he's five minutes behind schedule I'm going to go in there and spank his butt!"

There was a mocking laugh from the other room.

"Right," Kevin yelled. "I'll kick your butt, Granddaddy!"

"Hey," Wade said. "If you hit me and I hear about it, I'm gonna really be pissed off."

Jack laughed and shook his head. His dad had used the exact same lines on him when he was Kevin's age. It was comforting to hear the old saw, and Jack felt relieved that Kevin had laughed at the joke. Maybe he was feeling a little less furious at Jack for leaving.

He went into his son's bedroom and found him lying on his bed reading a manga called *Death Note*.

"Hey, Kev," Jack said, sitting down next to him, "I'm sorry I have to go right now."

"It's that woman you talk about sometimes, Michelle Wu, isn't it?" Kevin asked.

"It is," Jack said.

"Why do you have to fly off to save her butt? Isn't she a criminal?"

"Yeah," Jack said, "she is. But she also saved my life about two years ago."

"You told me already," Kevin said.

His tone was filled with doubt.

"It's true," Jack said. "She really did. I owe her."

Kevin put the book down and Jack took the opportunity to give him a hug.

"I'll get back as soon as I can, Kev," Jack said.

"I know," Kevin responded, "I just wish you had more time for me sometimes, Dad."

"I'll make time, Kev. I promise," he said.

But even as he spoke the words he felt as though they were a lie.

Chapter Four

Jennifer Wu felt as though she'd been hit over the head with a fifty-pound weight. Every inch of her skull was racked with a pulsating pain. Staved in by a . . . what? A gun barrel? No, something bigger than that. A big iron pole of some kind? Maybe, but that would make a huge lump, and as she raised her left hand and felt around her head, there was no lump, on either temple or anywhere else.

So she was wrong. There wasn't any pole used on her.

But why the terrible pulsating headache? Like with a migraine, her skull seemed to expand and contract with every beat of her heart.

Maybe . . . maybe she'd been drugged.

She felt herself waking up a little more. She blinked her eyes and saw a deep blackness in front of her.

God, she wanted to scream, and nearly did, but then she thought about it for a second. No, she wouldn't scream for help. Because it was obvious that she'd been kidnapped, and whoever had taken her had probably used drugs.

She realized that she was in some kind of cell. What else could it be? (Even though she could see nothing at all in front of her.) She had free use of her arms and legs. She could move around, and she didn't seem to be beaten anywhere on her body. So whoever had taken her hadn't hurt her, except for her head.

But why then? Why had they grabbed her out of the Indian pueblo and brought her here?

It didn't make any sense at all.

It wasn't as though she was a rich person whom they could ransom for big money.

Unless they thought that her sister would pay for her. She wasn't sure if Michelle was all that rich. Nobody quite knew how much money her sister had.

But maybe whoever had snatched her had thought Michelle was rich and would pay a ransom for her return.

She sat up and blinked. Gradually, her eyes got used to the darkness. Now she could see she was on a bed, that there was a toilet in the corner with a shelf where things had been laid out for her. Toothpaste, a toothbrush. A washrag, soap, a towel.

Yes, and toilet paper. How thoughtful.

But over on the other side of the room . . . just as she had suspected . . . prison bars. She *was* in a cell, somewhere.

Jesus, now she could see a hallway. She got up, and on shaky feet walked over to the cell bars. There was a small blue light down there somewhere, like a night-light.

Again, such a thoughtful touch. She almost laughed.

Then she had another thought, a weirder one. If she was in a cell block, then there might be other prisoners in here as well.

Which meant . . . which meant what?

That some lunatics or—or terrorists, yes, it could be terrorists—had picked up a group of normal Americans and were holding them for ransom.

But what kind of terrorists? Certainly not al-Qaeda. Not in an Indian pueblo. No, the weird thing was that the most logical terrorists would be the Indians themselves. Did Indian nationalist groups do this kind of thing?

She had never heard of anything like that before.

It made no sense whatsoever. But there were fights over Indian casinos. Maybe it had something to do with that. Because there was a big casino, the River Rock Casino, just three miles away from Taos. She didn't think it was Indian-owned though . . . wasn't it partially owned by a consortium of business people who merely used the Indians as a front? She wasn't at all sure. Could this be some kind of crazy part of a war between the whites and the Indians?

But as soon as she thought of such a thing the notion seemed even more absurd.

Native Americans weren't into kidnapping people.

But who was? One thing for sure was that she'd never be able to figure this out by herself.

She was dying to yell down the hall and see if someone else was here. But there had to be guards. And if she called out they'd come running and maybe they'd beat her.

Yeah, maybe this time they really would split her brain open with a club.

There had to be some way to find out where she was, and who else was down here.

Jennifer crept over to the left side of the cell and whispered around the corner, "Is there anyone over there? Can you hear me?"

There was no answer.

Okay. It was night (she thought) and they were asleep.

She tried again, a little louder. "Anyone? Anyone there?"

She jumped as she heard a voice whisper back to her.

"Yeah, girlfriend. Who are you?"

A woman with some kind of an accent. What was it? New York? The Bronx maybe?

"My name is Jennifer," she whispered. "Who are you?"

"Gerri. Gerri Maxwell. From the Bronx. Where you from?"

"I'm from Los Angeles. I'm just visiting here with my sister and we were touring the Indian pueblo in Taos, and somebody came up behind me and—"

"And shot you full of some kind of sleeping shit, and here you are."

"Yes, I guess so. I don't remember how it happened. I have the worst headache."

"Yeah, I know 'bout that, too. It lasts maybe three, four hours, then it goes away."

"But what the hell is going on?" Jennifer asked. "Why are we here?"

"I don't know. There was another person down here, too. Woman named Mary. But now she's gone."

"Gone? What do you mean?"

"I mean that this guy came down today and said they were letting her out."

"They did?"

"Yeah, that's right. They said she was getting sprung."

"Did they say *why* she was getting out?"

"No. He just said it was time for her to go."

Jennifer felt a cold chill up her back.

"Did he say exactly that?"

"What do you mean?"

"I mean what were the exact words the guy said?"

"Jesus, girl, how the fuck should I know? Does it matter?"

"Yes, it could. It could matter very much. Try to remember, won't you?"

"All right . . . The mother came in here . . . said, 'It's your turn.' Yeah, that was it, he said, 'It's your turn, sweetheart.'"

"Oh, Jesus," Jennifer said. "What did the guy look like?"

"Big guy, looks like a . . . what . . . like one of them bugs. A praying mantis. Dressed all in leather. With a mask. Scary son of a bitch! Man's a fucking hyena. He likes to punch you in the . . . inna private parts, if you get my drift. Anyway, when they come to get Mary, she changed her mind. All of a sudden she dint want to get out no more. Put up one hell of a fight, hanging onto her jail bars. The son of a bitch had to kick her around a little to get her loose. Then they had to use the needle on her."

Jennifer felt the chill coming again.

"The needle. Christ. Why, why do you think she had that kind of reaction?"

"Well, she told me she was real worried that wherever they took you next was going to be a lot worse than here."

"Like what?" Jennifer asked.

"Like nothing. She didn't itemize it, baby. Just 'worse.' But that don't make no sense. Look, the way I see it, we were put in here like for ransom or something. You know? The mantis-baby even joked about it once to me. Last week."

"How long have you been in here?"

"I don't know, you lose track of time. Maybe a week."

"A week?" The thought made her want to cry. She could barely stand another minute, much less a week.

"Well, I don't know about you, but I ain't lived a perfect life, so maybe they're having a hard time finding anyone who would want to go my bail."

Jennifer felt her knees weaken and her breath get short.

"Hey, Jennifer."

"Yes?"

"Don't worry. You seem like a nice girl. Somebody will pay to bail you out pretty soon. I'm sure of it."

"Yeah, thanks, Gerri."

"I'm going to sleep now," Gerri said. "We can talk more tomorrow."

"Yeah, good night, Gerri," Jennifer said, scarcely believing her own voice. This couldn't be happening. Not to her.

Jesus, what was Michelle doing?

Was anyone looking for her?

And what would happen when that hyena, Mr. Mantis, came to take her away?

Chapter Five

In Albuquerque, Jack rented a Ford Mustang and headed up the interstate to Santa Fe. He'd never been there before but knew that Hollywood movie stars and wealthy Los Angelenos went there to chill out. Also, an actress he'd dated a couple of years ago had told him that the town was filled with New Agers. The kind of people who scurried to that posh burg in the Sangre de Cristo mountains to find some deeper meaning in their lives. His partner, Oscar Hidalgo, who had been out there before, laughed at them for buying crystals, getting themselves rubbed down with "ancient stones," and taking two-day courses in meditation supposedly taught by some *curandero*, or witch doctor. Yeah, maybe old Oscar was right, but what Jack found funny was that Oscar actually believed in *curanderos* himself but only if they came from *his* town—Juarez. All of the *other* witch doctors were hustlers and cons.

As he pulled into Santa Fe and stopped at a light he saw the first sign of the kind of thing he'd been told about. There, in a little park just off the highway, was a group of older people being led by a white-haired man. They were all dressed in dark blue jumpsuits with a Blue

Wolf Lodge logo embroidered across the front pocket. Jack had done a little research on Santa Fe on the plane and knew that Blue Wolf was an exclusive lodge with a very wealthy clientele. The group he was watching now was elderly. Several of them must have been in their seventies. The white-haired man may have been even older. Yet they were all working out with incredible grace. They were doing what Jack knew were Tai Chi moves. He watched as they made graceful parabolas with their arms and hands. He smiled sympathetically as one of the older men kicked his left leg high into the air and came down on tiptoes, like a stork or a crane.

The white-haired man went around correcting their postures. There was one woman—a short, squat Mexican—who was having trouble holding her form. Jack watched as the older man worked with her. He was very patient.

She seemed to be explaining that her shoulder was frozen, or in pain. The older man nodded and rubbed it, and she tried again.

But the woman gave him a pained expression and it looked as though she was starting to get mad. She pointed at her shoulder again, as if she was saying, "This exercise is too much for me." Her teacher spoke to her in what looked like a kindly way, though Jack could hear nothing of what was said.

Jack found the little soap opera fascinating but was frustrated that he wouldn't be able to find out the outcome because the traffic light had changed.

Whatever the problem the woman was having Jack found himself impressed with the little band of old folks. It would be easy to laugh at them, but what the hell . . . they looked like they were dealing with old age in a graceful, and—dare he think it—healthy way. They weren't overweight like his dad, and they would probably live to a ripe old age. Jack had always had a sentimental love of the ravers and wild men, but he'd already known three federal agents who had died within a few years of their retirement. Why? Because they had nothing to do, no sense of community except the bar. He worried about his dad for the same reason. Maybe it would benefit the old man if he had a group that looked after one another, worked out together, though he strongly doubted that he would ever see Wade doing Tai Chi in the local park.

But it was kind of cool to see the old folks doing their thing. Maybe he was going to like Santa Fe after all.

And maybe he would find Jennifer Wu right away and he could hang out and do a little sightseeing while he was here.

He and his hot, illicit girlfriend, Michelle Wu.

He met her in La Plazuela, the restaurant on the ground floor of La Fonda. It was a stunning room full of turquoise-colored windowsills, *latilla* ceilings, and handcrafted chandeliers with birds, snakes and lizards painted on them. The floor was dark brown tile and at the end of the room was a brightly burning fireplace. The restaurant was filled with tourists, but when Jack saw Michelle Wu the room seemed to fade into a misty background.

Dressed in a white lace dress, her black hair radiantly pulled back, Michelle looked like a goddess. Jack blinked as he walked toward her.

He realized he'd never seen her dressed like this before. Usually she was under a car working on the brakes or fixing a leak in the oil pan. Her daily costume was a skintight Lakers T-shirt and even tighter black Levi's.

"Jackie," she said, smiling. "I can't believe you're here."

She threw her arms around him. Jack wanted to take her into his arms and kiss her. But he did the proper thing instead, pecking her lightly on the cheek.

He sat down across from her and looked into her green eyes.

"I wasn't sure you'd come, Jack."

"I said I would, didn't I?"

"Yes, you did, baby. But I thought you might blow me off. I know the bureau doesn't love you hanging out with me."

"Depends," Jack said.

"On what?"

"On why I'm hanging out. Why don't you fill me in?"

She nodded, but before she started a waitress arrived at their table. She laid down two menus for them, but Jack shook his head.

"Just coffee for me, thanks," he said. "At this altitude if I eat lunch I'll be sacked out in my room, asleep in no time."

Michelle ordered some guacamole and chips for them.

"I promise not to compromise you in any way, baby," Michelle said, reaching across the table and twisting her fingers through his.

Jack felt his neck tingle. Jesus, she was tough enough to ignore when she was dressed like a grease monkey but made up like this, in that lacy, form-fitting dress, it was next to impossible.

"Michelle, come on. No romance," he said, sounding like a parent talking to an unruly but adored child.

"Sorry, baby. I'm just so relieved to see you. I've barely slept a wink since Jennifer disappeared."

A couple of tears came to Michelle's eyes.

"Take it easy," he said. "And tell me what happened."

"For a long time I felt my sister and I were getting further and further apart. Of course, I understood that it was my fault, most of it anyway, leading the life that I do. Jen has always been a good girl. She was the one who went to UCLA, the one who had straight A's."

"And she was the baby you took care of when your parents split up, when your father went to San Quentin."

Michelle looked at Jack in a grateful way.

"That's right," she said. "But I'm no angel, huh, Jack?"

Jack didn't answer, only smiled. And thought, But, man, do you look like one.

"Anyway, I didn't want to lose touch with Jen altogether, so I thought I'd come down here to visit her. She's lived in Santa Fe for seven years. She's a nurse at the Blue Wolf Lodge. It's just outside town and it's an amazing place. They have every kind of therapy there, and there's a hospital, too. They do terrific things with older people. Anyway, the idea was for both of us to take some time off from work and just hang around—shop, maybe ride horses, see the sights. Just be sisters together, you know? That's what we were doing yesterday up at the Indian village in Taos. And look what happens."

Jack took his coffee from the waitress and sighed.

"That was the whole reason you chose to come here?"

"Yes, it was. And what does that mean? That's a real cop question. Like I had something to do with my sister being kidnapped."

Jack took a sip of his coffee and stared at her.

"Why do you think she was kidnapped?"

Michelle bit her lower lip and turned her head away from him.

"What else could it be? She says she'll meet me down at the kiva, and I fall asleep for just fifteen minutes and when I get there, she's gone."

"Were you and Jennifer having some kind of fight?"

"No way."

The way she said it, the anger in her denial, made Jack think that Michelle was lying.

"Not even a little disagreement?"

Michelle hesitated, and waited as the waitress came and made the guacamole for them. Jack ate a chip, trying to keep things relaxed.

There was something hinky going on. She wouldn't have called him here if she didn't want help. But there was something she wasn't revealing, something she didn't think she could tell him. He was sure of it.

"Why would you say that? I call you here to help me—I mean, I thought you'd want to go up to Taos to see where Jen disappeared."

Jack took another sip of his coffee, waited, then said, "I *am* going to do that. But I'm talking about you, now. It occurs to me that you aren't the kind of person who takes vacations."

Michelle snorted her disgust at this statement.

"What does that mean? That's absurd, Jackie. Maybe I should have called—"

"What that means is you're type A," he smiled. "With you, everything is about work. This is a wonderful place, obviously a cool town for people to kick back and relax, shop, get a nice massage . . . all that stuff. But none of that is you, Michelle. You wouldn't come here, or anywhere else, unless there was a deal to be made."

Michelle was on him, fast.

"Is that what you think of me, Jackie? You come all this way to insult me?"

"Don't make this about me," Jack said. "I know you."

"You *know* me? You *think* you know me? You come all this way to insult me?"

Jack smiled at her.

"You're good, Michelle. The best ever. But like I said, I know you. Here's what I'm guessing. I think you told me the truth about your sister. You did want to get together with her, so you called her up and arranged a visit."

"Yeah," Michelle said. "And?"

"And that was all very nice, because not only could you go to New Mexico and see your sister but you could also get some business done.

Maybe there's a chop shop down here and maybe you could expand your network while you were here. But something went wrong and you had a disagreement with your business partners. I don't know what it was, maybe they were pissed because you out-hustled them. So, possibly, they took your sister to show you how you can't just come in here and make them look like fools. How am I doing?"

"You think I'm just a hustler and a liar?" she asked.

"Not *just* a hustler and a liar," Jack said.

"You sit there acting so superior, so smug. I should scratch your eyes out, Jackie."

"But you won't," Jack said. "Because you need me to find your sister, and unless you tell me the truth, you know I can't deliver. Or maybe I can, but not in time."

She bit her lower lip again, and then shut her eyes.

"Can I rely on you, Jackie?"

"Come on Michelle . . ."

"All right," she said. "Then let's get out of here and take a walk."

Jack and Michelle strolled across the wind-whipped plaza.

"It's starting to get cold," she said.

"Yes, it is."

They sat down on a blue bench with a colorful lantern hanging over it. Nearby a father played catch with his daughter. Michelle sighed heavily.

"Well, you're right, smart guy. I did think it was okay to mix a little business with pleasure. See, up north a few miles is this old motel named El Coyote. A few years ago when I was riding my bike out there, I ran into this Mexican dude, Lucky Avila. He bought the motel and fixed it up. Built a kind of communal living place up there.

Very interesting guy. Kind of an outlaw but also a philosopher. And I think at one time he was an actor. Ran a street-theater group in Europe and New York. Very smart, and has this sort of following of bikers, runaways, and women. He dabbles in a lot of things, which I never asked about. It's possible, Jackie, that he makes meth. But I've never seen any cooking going on out there. One of his businesses is cars and choppers. He gets deals on a lot of stuff from the biker world. So I just do a little business with him when I come to town. Car parts, engines, skirts, lifters . . . all very legal."

"Right," Jack said. "I would expect nothing else from you. And what was your business this time?"

"Nothing much. He let me use the two choppers and when he comes to LA next month I was going to introduce him to some friends of mine who specialize in quality car parts. That was it. Nothing more."

Michelle Wu smiled at him in her warm/wicked way, and Jack felt his breath shorten.

"Anyway, Lucky and I always got along real well. We did some business, he was always a gentleman."

"Really?" Jack asked, feeling a pang of jealousy.

"Really," Michelle said. "You got nothing to worry about, Jack. You know you're always number one in my book."

Jack found his voice and laughed.

"Yeah, we'd make a hell of a couple," he said. "I can just see us tripping down the prison aisle together as I lock you up in your wedding dress. So tell me what happened."

"I don't know," Michelle said. "But if I had to take a guess I'd say that Lucky was using some of his own product."

"Meth? That's bad. That can screw you up real fast."

"I know. He used to be *muy guapo* but now he looks kind of haggard, older. And his temper is terrible. Plus, in the past he hit on me a couple of times but when I said 'No way,' he was cool about it. This time, man, he was different."

She shivered as they stood up and began walking across the plaza, heading for the St. Francis Cathedral, outside of which was a thirty-foot-tall Christmas tree. Next to the tree was a huge statue of St. Francis of Assisi feeding flocks of steel birds. Michelle crossed herself as they went inside.

They took a pew in the back, and looked out at the vast, silent church and the statue of Christ behind the pulpit.

"I didn't know you were religious, Michelle."

"There is so much you don't know about me, Jackie. But now maybe you'll learn more. 'Cause I am very loyal and I will do anything to save my sister."

"Tell me what happened."

She nodded and took a deep breath.

"Lucky was angry, too. Very angry, and paranoid."

"Sounds exactly like meth."

"Yeah, and so was his sex jones. Before he was cool, now he was all over me. Saying he wanted to do me right there in his shop. Then he started in about Jennifer."

"She was with you?"

"Yes. Lucky took one look at Jen and started making all these insinuations. Said he wanted to have a threesome right there. I told him to chill. He got angry, said we were just trying to play with him. Then he got into this other fixation. Said he heard I was planning to offer my engine parts to this rival gang of bikers, the Jesters. He accused me of trying to get a bidding war going between them, of betraying his friendship. I asked him how he could say that. I barely know those guys. But he said I was lying, you know? He came at me with a wrench, I couldn't believe it."

"What did you do?"

"I dodged out of his way, and took out a blade I keep in my pocket."

Michelle pointed to a small zippered pocket on her elegant white dress. Jack had to smile. He had seen that same pocket in every piece of clothing she owned.

"He lunged at me and I dodged the wrench by a hair, and then—it was just an instinctual move, Jackie—I sliced out at him and caught his right ear. I took off maybe a little piece of his earlobe. He began bleeding really bad and I didn't wait around to help him bandage it up. But as Jen and I were leaving, I heard him scream, 'I'll get you and your sister for this, Michelle.'"

Jack nodded and watched as a priest in a white robe lit the votive candles. On the altar in between the two pulpits were red carnations.

"So you think that's what happened? He grabbed Jennifer to pay you back?"

"Maybe. You've got to get a look at his place, Jack. He could have her imprisoned out there."

"And that's all you know? Really?"

"Yes, for God's sake, Jack. I don't know what you really think of me, but I wouldn't endanger my own sister."

Jack looked at her and nodded as though he believed her. And held her cold, beautiful hand.

"All right, Michelle," he said. "I'll get into it. Right now."

Chapter Six

After a highly successful West Coast swing ripping people off, Johnny Zaprado had come back to his old hang, Santa Fe. He'd done well in sunny Cali, oh, yes. He'd robbed four women's clothing stores, a retirement community in Long Beach, one in Newport Beach (big dough there), and one in Huntington Beach. Not to mention a gay bar called The Tunnel in West Hollywood.

He'd scored a lot of dough out there, and it had been a good time. But now he was back home at his ex-girlfriend's pad in Santa Fe and he was jonesing for some narcotics.

Which was easy enough to deal with. As soon as he'd taken a shower and changed into his black jeans and Metallica T-shirt, he went bopping down to the square, cruised by the Navajo and Ute Indians selling their "authentic tribal jewelry" (which they had shipped in from kid slave laborers in Hong Kong), cut down the alley behind the Historic Trading Post (replete with real Spanish artifacts made in a factory in Hoboken), and arrived at the office of his doc, Mike Franco.

Dr. Mike was away on vacation in Las Vegas, which meant that his mail—and the many free samples of narcotic painkillers—was dropped in the mail slot in his outer door. Which meant all Johnny had to do was stick his nail file in between the lock and the catch, jiggle it once or twice, and presto, he was inside the foyer and piling all the free sample goodies into his backpack.

He looked down at the nifty flat mailers.

There on the floor were three boxes of Vicodin and three boxes of Percocet, and then the pièce de résistance itself, the double big package of Oxy. Yes, Oxycontin, the very finest example of drugstore heroin.

All of these were headed for patients, most of them old-timers, with their cracked and withered limbs, but—sorry, geezer gang—these were going to the man his own self, none other than Johnny Z.

He strapped on his backpack, gently shut the door, and headed off down the alley.

A few minutes later, Johnny Boy was sipping a beer in the Turtle Bar and Grill with the out-of-work locals and five or six of the local independent villains, all of whom were his sometimes-friendly rivals. There was Lil Roger, the black hustler from Vegas who specialized in break-ins; Tommy Butler, the short-con artist; Violet and Luvleen Mc-Ghee, the twins who specialized in selling fake insurance; and Badass Billy Drexler, who was basically a stick-up artist. Though each of these fine citizens was an equal-opportunity bandit, they all liked working in Santa Fe because the people at the Blue Wolf Lodge and the River Rock Casino were mostly old folks who wouldn't give them any trouble.

After listening to his fellow criminals rave on about their latest conquests for a while, Johnny swallowed two Vikes and drank two shots of single-malt scotch. In no time he was feeling his heels lift off the Turtle floor and he was sailing above his fellow cons and thugs.

It was a great feeling, and he would have liked to hang in the bar all night feeding his high with a few more Vikes but, alas, there was work to be done.

The trouble with being a bad guy was that there was seldom a really big score that could set you up for months, much less years. No, you had to go on your merry way, finding victims whenever they presented themselves. You always had to stay where the action was, which was what Johnny was doing as he hot-wired a car and headed out on the highway toward Espanola and the River Rock Casino.

The River Rock had opened about ten years ago and it had made all the difference for Johnny. He actually thought of the whole Santa Fe area as two distinct time periods.

BTC and ATC. Before the Casino and After the Casino.

The BTC era was not a good one for a man in his profession. People came to town to get massages and to go into sweat lodges with a couple of peyote-wasted Indians in order to release their toxins and get in touch with their "Inner Buffalo," but they seldom carried great wads of money. So when Johnny Boy conked some blabbering counterculture moron over the head with his ceremonial Indian tomahawk (just for irony's sake), he was lucky to clear fifty bucks.

But After the Casino, especially out in the parking lot of said enterprise, Johnny Boy was in thieves' heaven. Oh man, it was bitchin'!

One night about a year ago, Johnny had conked out five guys and two chicks in one night and come away with twenty-three thousand freaking dollars.

That was a smokin' night, for sure!

And may tonight be just as profitable.

Johnny walked through the glittering lights and the *bling-bong* noise of the River Rock Casino. Old women sat at slot machines with huge baskets of coins. A lot of them knew one another and watched out for each other as they headed for their cars with their money. Big deal. He wasn't interested in their small change anyway.

He walked toward the blackjack tables. That could be a lucrative game, no question, but if you wanted to pick a winner there you had to do a Big Prey Number. And hang out for hours. And if you didn't want to be made as some kind of criminal yourself, you had to play the games, which meant you'd probably lose money before you even got a chance to club anyone.

And another thing: he didn't know why but blackjack players were mean sons of bitches. There had been a guy around sixty-five years old that he'd had a major battle with. In the end, of course, he'd staved his head in, but it was no easy task. Plus, the guy might have identified him if he hadn't croaked.

Thank God for small favors.

After that one, Johnny had ruled out blackjack players.

He cruised the big game room and found what he was looking for. His favorite game and the one that attracted the highest percentage of rich losers.

Yes, the craps table.

Johnny surveyed three different tables for a while and finally found the one he wanted to go with.

Table numero uno, the one with a skinny old guy wearing an Arizona Cardinals football shirt that said "Warner" on the back. This was the kind of guy he liked. Guy must have been pushing eighty, veins popping out of his fragile frame, wrinkles growing wrinkles, eyes half-closed from years of smoking, and there he was with five piles of chips. Serious dough. And the dude was on a roll. One of the "girls" who "just happened" to be standing next to him was Johnny's only rival. She was obviously a hooker and if she got the old duffer up to a room before Johnny could get him to walk to the car . . . well, that just wouldn't do. Not at all.

Johnny stepped up to the crowded table and began to root for the old guy, whose name he quickly found out was Les. People were screaming as Les made pass after pass.

"Go, Les, baby . . . do it, babe."

Everyone was betting with the old guy now, who took a drink from the girl next to him. She smiled and Johnny saw the lipstick on her teeth.

"You are the man, Lester!" she screamed in a baby-voice falsetto.

He looked at her and smiled. Tossed the dice and won again.

Johnny moved closer as a couple of people left the table. After the next winning roll he was right up next to Les.

"You have really got lady luck singing tonight, Les, man," Johnny said.

Les smiled at him and Johnny saw his upper plate jiggle a little. He won again, on a point six, and the crowd at the table went crazy.

"Bets, please," the croupier said.

But Lester pulled away from the table.

"Time to cash in," he said. "Never want to push your luck too far."

The girl next to him followed him away from the table. Johnny trailed along with them.

"Baby," she said, "with all that money, won't you buy me a little drink?"

He laughed and handed her a twenty.

"Here you go, darling," he said. "You take this and buy your own drink."

The girl pouted and stomped her foot like Betty Boop.

"Don't you like mama? If we go up to a room, I can show you a very good time."

"I don't think you can, baby," the old-timer said. "My thing don't work no more. Not even with a case of Viagra."

"Oh, that's what they all say until they roll with Shirl, babe."

The old man seemed to be enjoying the banter.

"Well, if I win some more moolah I might get me an operation to get the ol' woodpecker working again. Then I'll come and see you for sure, sweetie."

He gave her another ten and headed off to cash in his chips. She leered at Johnny as the old man headed for the door.

"How 'bout you, tough guy? You look like you need a good spanking."

Johnny gave her his semiwarm smile and said, "Can't think of anything better, baby, but I got a date with my wife."

"Unlucky you," she said and moved on.

Out on the macadam, Johnny Z watched as Lester limped toward his big Caddy Escalade.

"Mother is probably weighed down by all the cash on one side of his pants," he said under his breath, talking tough to himself so he could work up a little hatred for his new vic.

He slipped by some parked cars and was relieved to see that there was no one around. The old man opened his door and started to slide into the driver's seat.

"Hey, wait a minute, Les," Johnny said, in his most country-club friendly manner.

"What?" Lester said.

He turned his head, and Johnny pulled out the nice little black-jack from his coat pocket. He slammed it down on Lester's head and heard a dependable crack, the bones in his forehead breaking up like uncooked pasta.

Lester made a terrible noise and fell backward right into his car.

Johnny started to fall on top of him but was surprised by Lester's foot coming up in his groin. The pain was like an electric shock, and Johnny fell back on his ass into the parking lot.

"You fuck," Johnny exclaimed. "Fight dirty, huh?"

He started to get back up but was surprised to see Lester coming out of the car, swinging his big, bony fist at his face. Fortunately, the jack blow had caused blood to run down into the older man's eyes and his swings, though violent, were several inches short. As a result, Johnny thought, the old guy looked comical, like a cartoon Mickey Mouse fighting a giant.

Johnny got up, waited for a big swing to miss his face, then smashed the jack back toward Lester's mouth, this time splitting his upper lip and mashing his nose into a bloody pulp.

The old man went down next to his car and his head flopped over to one side.

Johnny approached him warily and when he was satisfied he was out cold, he rifled through his pockets.

He found the big wad of cash, stuffed it into his own pocket, and left Lester lying there in a rapidly growing pool of blood.

Seconds later Johnny was headed for the parking lot exit, seven thousand dollars richer.

Not bad for a night's work, he thought, though the pain in his balls told him a different story.

What he needed, he thought as he headed back down to Santa Fe, was a big one. One that would set him up for a good long while. He really was getting a little too old for this kind of work.

Chapter Seven

As they stood at the Piñon Bar at Blue Wolf Lodge, Phil watched as Dee Dee turned to speak to Ziko, the part Japanese, part Apache (or so he said) tennis instructor. A huge guy with black hair and a ponytail who had once been one of the top twenty players in the world, Ziko was sidling up to Dee Dee with something more than tennis on his mind.

Phil watched as Ziko put his arm around Dee Dee's shoulder and pulled her close to him.

"I bet you could really become a pretty player," Ziko said.

"Not as pretty as you," Dee Dee smiled.

Phil drank his vodka and tonic, and tried to act nonchalant.

"I'd teach you how to follow through on your shots. The thing is, you have to get down low."

"Like this?" the slightly bombed Dee Dee asked.

She knelt down in front of him in a way that no tennis player ever did.

"That's almost it," Ziko said, "but you'd have to bend your knees a little more."

Phil stepped forward and landed on Ziko's heel. Ziko squealed in pain.

"Ahhh," he whined. "You hurt my Achilles tendon!"

"Sorry," Phil said, in his most affable voice. "I must be some kind of clumsy oaf."

"You son of a bitch," Ziko cried.

Phil smiled as the black-haired Adonis hopped up and down on his right foot.

"Horribly careless of me, son," Phil said. "Guess I must have had a little too much of the old vino."

Dee Dee looked horrified. She put her arm around Ziko's wide shoulders and shook her head.

"He's just a drunken slob who don't know what he's doing, honey," she whispered.

"Christ, my heel. I have to teach."

"Seems like you were using your mouth, pal," Phil said.

Dee Dee looked at Phil and shook her head violently.

"Gee, drunk and out of control. What a shocker."

Ziko massaged his Achilles as Phil grabbed Dee Dee's arm and dragged her out of the bar.

They walked drunkenly down the hallway. Phil was hoping Dee Dee was all finished giving him shit but apparently she was just warming up.

"You made me look like a fool."

"You don't need me to do that, baby. You have that down all on your own."

They wandered on down the corridor, unable to speak at all for fear of sounding like angry fools.

On the elevator, Phil began to feel a slight tinge of remorse.

"Baby, how did it ever come to this? I thought that when I sold the business we'd be free. Man, I even remember a time you got nervous if I was twenty minutes late coming home. And now look at us."

Phil sighed, overwhelmed with melancholy. But Dee Dee only scowled at him.

"Well, maybe if you'd give me a little freedom instead of trying to put me in a freaking cell all the time it would be different."

Phil shook his head.

"Freedom? I used to know what that meant. Or thought I did. Let's just go back to the room, baby."

"Great," Dee Dee said. "You wouldn't want to miss a chance for another of your three-hour snore-a-thons, would you?"

Phil had a sudden impulse to grab his wife by the throat and start choking her. He barely managed to restrain himself. He felt a rage that shot through his body and seemed to singe what was left of his brain.

This was it, he thought. Getting older, a success, and these were going to be the highly touted golden years.

Christ, Christ, Christ.

Chapter Eight

Though he missed his dad, Kevin didn't mind having his grandfather around. First of all, Wade was great fun, telling stories of his wild youth and letting Kevin eat whatever he wanted. But mainly he liked having Wade around because he was a lot more lenient about what time Kevin had to be back at the house. He could tell Grandpop that he was at the local library studying and the old man would believe it. Well, it was practically the truth.

He was, after all, at the Culver City library. And he had been *trying* to read the lousy book.

When something amazing had happened.

He was about to put the damned thing down and head home, when he saw her. Right across from him, at the librarian's desk.

He couldn't believe it. The woman who had stared so long at his dad at the last lacrosse game. The woman he'd kidded Jack about, calling her "the next Mrs. Harper."

They had both thought she was a Brentwood mother but instead it seemed she was the new librarian right at Culver City's brand-new library.

And man did she look hot!

She had on a tight black sweater and an even tighter skirt, which emphasized her trim hips.

She had blue eyes and blonde hair. Wow, if Dad was here right now he'd be thinking it was time to go over and ask her something about how the new computerized library system worked.

Kevin felt his penis get hard. Oh, my God . . . he couldn't stand up, that was for sure.

But the really weird thing was she seemed to be staring over at him, really staring at him, and he got an odd thought. Maybe . . . maybe that day at the lacrosse game she hadn't been staring at his dad after all, but at him.

That seemed crazy to him but he'd heard of crazier things.

That woman in Seattle who had a thing for her eighth-grade student, Mary Kay something or other. She had an affair with him and they ended up getting married.

Nah, that couldn't be happening here. She was just looking in his general direction and he only thought she was staring at him. Of course, that was all there was to it.

Except now she seemed to be coming around the side of the desk and, oh, man, she was walking right toward him. And looking right at him. And the way she walked, with her hips swinging. She looked like a runway model on one of those reality shows.

Even if at this closer vantage point, Kevin could now see some crow's feet around her eyes and a couple of deeper lines in her cheeks.

Not that it mattered. She was smoking hot.

Kevin's heart seemed to be beating about eight hundred times per second and his mouth was getting dry. Sounds in the library—chairs squeaking and people scuffling around—all seemed magnified.

Oh, Jesus, she was heading right for him.

"Hi," she said to him in a voice barely above a whisper. Like a sexy actress in a commercial.

"Hi," he croaked back at her. Then he cleared his throat. Man, he had to do better than that, for God's sake. He sounded like a bullfrog with a throat infection.

"You're Kevin Harper, right?" she said.

"Guilty," he said. He'd heard somebody cool like a spy on TV say that once, and it had sounded so, what, suave? But when Kevin said it, well, it just sounded . . . literal, like, "Yeah, you caught me. I'm guilty even talking to you." He tried for a cool smile then but felt like only one corner of his mouth had turned up, which probably made him look like a retard.

"I'm Vicki Hastings, the new librarian. I saw you playing lacrosse the other day."

Kevin knew he was supposed to come back with something sort of modest, yet hip, but all that came out of his mouth was, "Oh."

Now Vicki Hastings leaned down on the table on her elbows, which accentuated her wonderful cleavage. He told himself not to look but it was impossible, and he found himself staring down at the two most beautiful adult woman breasts he had ever seen. Okay, they were the only *live* female adult breasts he had ever seen, but so what? Christ, her skin was so creamy, so smooth, and he could even see the top of one nipple. Man, he was harder than ever.

"You scored the winning goal," she said, smiling at him with the whitest teeth he could imagine.

"Just got lucky," he said. (That sounded better.)

She smiled even wider and her eyes danced as she stared into his.

"Uh-huh," she said. "I saw the whole play. You lost the ball but instead of giving up, you went back after that guy, a much bigger guy than you, too, and you took the ball back from him, and then dodged, what was it, three guys? And then you scored. That was amazing."

He could feel her hot breath in his face, and he could see her breasts, and hear her voice, and it was all like being drunk, like the first time he had ever gotten loaded driving around with his buddies, hanging out at In-N-Out, drinking beer and whiskey shooters, and then all of a sudden he was goofy and happy. Yeah, it was sort of like that but it was better than that, because of the breasts and the breath, and the way she was now reaching over and touching his hand.

"*You* were amazing," she said.

"Thanks," he replied, letting her hand rub against his own.

"Thank you for making the game so great," she said.

"You a lacrosse fan?" he asked, suddenly finding his stride. If he could talk about sports he'd be okay.

"Oh, yes," she said. "I played in college. Of course, girls lacrosse isn't like the real thing. You can't check sticks like the boys do. You can't throw body blocks at people's legs, either."

Kevin smiled.

She looked at him and her tongue flicked at the edge of her lips.

"What is it?" she asked.

"Nothing. Just thinking how sexy girls look in their lacrosse uniforms. The short little plaid miniskirts."

Now she smiled in a way that made Kevin suck in his breath.

"Really?" she said. "You like that, do you? How about the leather gloves and the sticks themselves? When they cradle the ball, don't you find that kind of phallic?"

"Yeah, I guess so," Kevin said.

Oh, Jesus, if he'd had any doubts before about where this was going that phallic bit pretty much ended them.

"Where'd you go to college?" Kevin asked, his voice breaking again.

"I went to Amherst," she said. "It's in New England."

She slipped into a chair and was now sitting across from him.

"That must be a great school," Kevin said.

"Oh, it was a good school," Vicki Hastings said. "But kind of boring, too. They said it was a serious place but I found it to be a lot of suburbanites. People who had money, and whose parents played it safe. Most of them will end up being middle managers."

She said "middle managers" as though she was saying something obscene. And Kevin found himself agreeing with her, though he wasn't quite sure what a middle manager was or what one did. He got the idea though . . . scared little people who lived harried little lives. Nothing like his dad, who put himself on the line for his country, and nothing like him either, he hoped.

"I hate people who don't go for it. Don't you, Kevin?"

"I guess so, yeah," Kevin said.

"That's what appealed to me so much about the way you play lacrosse. When you lost the ball you didn't just sulk, you reacted like . . . like . . ."

Kevin found himself leaning toward her now, intoxicated once again by her smell and the hazy, sexual look in her eyes.

"Like what?" he asked.

"Like an animal," Vicki said. "You went after him with the ferocity of a cat, a leopard maybe, defending his turf."

Kevin laughed.

"You're very dramatic, aren't you?" he said.

She blushed and looked a little shocked that he'd called her on it.

"I guess I am. But I can't help it. I feel like it's the only way to be. I mean, if you're not, you just turn into some, some . . . old person."

"That will never happen to you," Kevin said.

She smiled and pursed her lips.

"That's sweet of you to say," she answered, "but I'm getting older every day. I look around this library and see all the gorgeous young girls and I feel ancient!"

"No way," Kevin said. "That's silly."

She reached over and lightly touched his cheek.

"That's so sweet, coming from you, a man of action."

Kevin felt heat in his cheeks. A man of action. He'd never thought of himself as a man at all. In fact he had started to worry during the last few years if he would ever become a real man. Like his old man or Grandpop Wade. They were real men. He remembered the story about how his grandpop had been in a freighter that sank; he was out in the water with sharks, and everyone else panicked, but Wade kept everyone cool by singing songs and making jokes until the Coast Guard came and fished everyone out. And, of course, Dad . . . the things he'd gone through were amazing. And he never ever bragged about it. Like those actors and phony athletes on TV, talking about hitting a homer, or catching a pass . . . God, Dad did things that made those guys look like the egotistical jerks they were.

Both Wade and Dad had had so many women come after them. And unlike Kevin, they knew just how to handle things, the right things to say, and how to hold your body so you'd look cool. Like exactly the opposite of the way he was holding his body now, all stiff and goofy looking.

A man of action. That was a laugh.

And yet she was staring at him now and there was something in her eyes, something overwhelming, like . . . like what he'd heard about in movies and on TV. Desire. He could see it. Feel it.

Unless . . . unless this whole thing was a joke. Maybe that's what it was. The guys on the team had set this all up with her and a minute from now they were all going to run out and yell, "You're punked, Kevin. We gotcha!" That was it, had to be.

"Hey, it's been good talking to you, Ms. Hastings," Kevin said, "but I gotta go now."

"I know," she said. "But I'll be done here in a few minutes. Why don't I give you a ride home?"

"Hey," he said, "I wouldn't want you to go out of your way or anything."

"It's not out of my way. I live just a couple of blocks from you."

He stopped then, turning away from her so he could hide his erection by pulling his shirttail out.

"You know where I live?" he asked.

She smiled.

"Don't worry," she said. "I'm not stalking you. I happen to drive by your house every day on my way here. I've seen you outside, too, when I'm coming home from Ralphs with my groceries. You might as well come with me. We can talk some more."

"Yeah," Kevin said. "Okay, if you don't mind."

She smiled at him in a way that told him that she wouldn't like anything better. Then she went back to the librarian's desk.

Her car was out in the parking lot, in the corner near a big ficus tree. The branches hovered over the hood of the car, a ten-year-old Thunderbird, bright blue, with porthole windows and a sleek low look that reminded Kevin of an era he'd only read about, the world of the fifties and early sixties when America was the greatest power in the world and no one would have dared send planes into our buildings.

"This is such a cool car," Kevin said as he opened the door and slipped inside, onto the cool leather seat.

"I know. I love it," she said. "And I got it cheap just two months ago."

"From where?" Kevin asked. Here in the two-seater car he felt overwhelmed by their intimacy. It was like the car was a magical carriage and they were going on some kind of fantastic journey together. He told himself not to think that way, that she was a librarian, for God's sake, and that she was an adult and probably married to the guy in the leather jacket he'd seen at the Brentwood game. But just the same, here in the car, with her perfume and her body so close to him . . . He was only inches away from touching her . . . his left hand had to maybe move three inches to touch her breast . . .

"I got the car from a friend, a fellow librarian, believe it or not. An older man who is sort of an admirer of mine . . . nothing sexy, just a friend, if you know what I mean."

"What about your husband?" Kevin asked, feeling a sudden panic cutting through his chest.

"What about him?" she countered.

"Doesn't he get jealous if some guy is giving you a car?"

"Oh, no," she said. "You misunderstand, Kevin. I paid for the car. It's just that my friend gave me a very good price on it. My husband liked that very much."

She smiled and turned the key and the engine roared to life. She hit reverse and backed out fast, then slid a little as she turned to head to the street.

Kevin laughed.

"You drive like a teenager," he said.

"I know," she said. "Watch this."

She stepped on the pedal and the T-Bird shot forward down Culver Boulevard. When she got to the light she made a sharp turn and hit the pedal harder; by the time they'd hit Venice Boulevard they were doing seventy-five. Then, without warning, she hit the brakes and the car skidded to a perfect stop at the red light.

"Wow," Kevin said, "you really know how to handle it."

She took a right and suddenly turned into a darkened parking lot at an abandoned hamburger place called Ruby's.

Then she downshifted, and drove the car slowly behind the restaurant, under some electric wires.

"Where are we going?" Kevin asked.

She stopped the car, and in a husky voice said, "Come here, Kevin. And be very quiet. No talking in the library."

She turned to him and kissed him with those pink lips and Kevin put his arms around her and seconds later his tongue was in her mouth.

She ran her hands through his hair and moved her mouth to his neck, biting and kissing him, driving him crazy.

Then she put his right hand on her breast and told him to pinch her nipple, hard. He did it, in a daze, stunned out of his mind.

She groaned and put her hand on his cock, squeezing it and making some kind of animal sound he'd never heard before. And then her head was down in his lap and she was unzipping his Levi's and Kevin felt as though he would burst. Not only his cock but his brain, his heart . . . all of it would burst, be blown apart . . . and he heard himself making noises similar to hers, groans of pleasure that sounded as though they came from outside of him.

And then her head was rocking back and forth on his cock and Kevin held her head in his hands and felt totally mad for her and knew that he could never, ever let this stop.

Never.

No matter what.

Chapter Nine

Was it the next day? The same night?

In her cell, Jennifer didn't have a clue.

She had finally fallen asleep, then wakened, then slept again . . . for who knew how long?

The truth was, she was in shock. It was just too hard to believe. She couldn't be here, she just couldn't . . . but the sounds of a rat running across the floor at the end of the hall convinced her it was all too real.

She was caught, trapped, and could think of no reason why. Maybe a lunatic had done it. Yeah, what was she thinking? Of course, it had to be a lunatic, and she knew the one. That Lucky Avila. Of course. He was pissed at Michelle and her because they wouldn't let him have his way with them. That had to be it.

Jesus, the guy was off his rocker on methedrine. That was the deal, had to be. He was going to keep her here, scare the shit out of her . . . and maybe . . . God, maybe rape her.

And if he raped her, then he could never let her go. He'd have to . . . God, she didn't want to think about it. Shit.

Do not panic! Do not freak out!

She took three deep breaths and let the air out slowly as she had been taught when studying yoga.

Chill. There had to be a way out.

And though part of her just wanted to lie there and cry, she wouldn't give in. Oh, no, she was going to battle. If it *was* Lucky Avila, he was going to be in for the fight of his life.

The first thing she had to do was find out if there was a way out of the cell. How did they do it in movies she had seen? Try to remember . . . Oh, right, the hero always looked up in the ceiling and found a loose tile. Then he climbed up there and got into an air duct and cruised right along until he found a way outside.

Jennifer got up and looked at the ceiling. It didn't take long before her hopes in that direction were dashed. There were no loose tiles because there were no tiles, period. The ceiling was concrete. She'd have one hell of a time getting through there. Maybe . . . maybe she could take the leg off of her bed and whack at the cement. Yeah, and maybe the guard would hear her and come down and dash her head against the wall.

What else? The toilet . . . wait, didn't she see a movie about a guy who dug out under his toilet and created a trench, which led to sewer lines?

No, that was wrong. She was conflating two movies. One was the *The Great Escape,* where they dug under the fence at the prison camp, and the other was *Trainspotting,* where a junkie dove into a toilet and swam into a cesspool.

Who was she kidding? She was a nurse. She knew nothing about how to escape from jail. Jennifer burst into tears. She was no heroine. She wasn't going to escape. She was going to die.

It was the first time she had let herself think that thought. Now she said it out loud, to convince herself of its terrible reality.

"You are going to die," she said, and the sound of her own voice, low and trembling, was a shock to her.

It was true, wasn't it? She was going to die. They had brought her here to kill her.

Why?

She shed a few more tears, and then a strange calm came over her. She began to think, rather than panic.

Okay, she wasn't going to be able to go up into a handy air shaft, and she wasn't going to be able to dig a tunnel, either. She wasn't strong enough. And she probably didn't have enough time, even if she'd been built like a lady weightlifter.

But she was smart.

And so the thing to do was think. Think . . .

For example, if they were bringing only good-looking women here, then you would assume they were some kind of sex slave traffickers. Yeah, and they had to wait to take them away because . . . uh, because they had to set up the various houses of ill repute they were sending them to. Some girls would go to Asia, and maybe some to South America or Mexico. And that took time, and boats, and payoffs to authorities.

Maybe that was it.

But sex slaves? Didn't that mean really young kids? Maybe not. There were all kinds of people who wanted all kinds of sex.

She was twenty-four years old and she looked great in a bikini, and maybe some sick fucking drug czar wanted a good-looking Chinese girl that he could fuck until she was half-dead.

She began to feel her skin itch.

She had to talk to Gerri, figure out why they had been marked and if it was Lucky who had done it. Hadn't he mentioned to Michelle that he used to frequent some whorehouse? What was it called? The Jackalope Ranch, that was it.

Maybe she was there now. Maybe she was waiting her turn to be thrust into a life of prostitution.

She got up from her bed and moved back over to the corner of the cell door.

"Gerri," she whispered.

No answer. Gerri must be sound asleep.

"Gerri," she cried out now. "Wake the fuck up!"

"Huh? What—"

"It's me, Jennifer."

"Geez, girlfriend, it's the middle of the night."

"You can sleep when you're dead, Ger."

"What the fuck? All right, what is it?"

"I want to know something."

"Yeah, fine, we've established that. So, like what?"

"Are you . . . a hot chick?"

There was an outraged sigh.

"For this you wake me up inna middle of the fucking night? What you want to do, have some sex talk?"

"No, Gerri," Jennifer said, forgetting all about whispering. "Sorry, not interested. I said it wrong. How old are you?"

"Twenty-four, baby."

"And do you have a nice body?"

"You sick girl. We are in deep shit and you want to play lesbo games."

"No, I want to know if you and I could be candidates for sex slavery."

There, she had finally said it.

"Shit, I hope not," Gerri said.

"And Mary, was she young, too?"

"Yeah, she was. Very young. Christ, maybe that's it. They sending us off to some foreign country to be whores."

Jennifer sat down on the edge of the table in her cell.

"It could be that. It's the most logical thing."

"Yeah, but I thought they did that mainly with little Asian girls. Like ten or twelve years old."

"Yeah, me, too," Jennifer said. "But in our new world of sexual diversity anything is possible. Besides, I'm Asian."

There was a long silence from Gerri, and finally Jennifer heard her start to cry.

"I'm sorry," Jennifer said. "I'm just trying to find some reason for all of this. Maybe if we find it we can somehow use what we know to get out of here."

"Yeah, I get it, girl," Gerri said. "But if they are really all about having us be sex slaves, there ain't nothing we can do. They got drugs, baby. I seen 'em before. They knock you out and they rape you. And you ain't got a thing to say about it. And when they all done with you, they cut you up and throw yo ass away."

Jennifer shook her head, and went quietly back to her bed.

She remembered something she'd heard in college. Knowledge shall set you free. Well, not all the time, baby. Not all the time.

Chapter Ten

In the morning Jack headed up to Taos and spent two hours talking to the people of the pueblo. The pueblo was an interesting place, and the round kiva prayer building was a spot he wished he could spend time in. Unfortunately, the Taos Indians gave him no answers. Not one person had seen anything. That is, they hadn't seen anything of Jennifer. An Indian sculptress named Rada Mankiller had met a couple from Blue Wolf. She even had their card, and she gave it to Jack. On it were the names Phil and Dee Dee Holden. They were from Columbus, Ohio. They had come up to look at the art but found it too expensive. Rada Mankiller said that they had told her they loved her pots but they could get a "pot for a lot cheaper at Target in Columbus. It was even Indian, sort of . . . anyway, it had an arrow on it and it only cost 29.95, plus tax."

Jack thanked her and headed back down the hill. He needed to get to Blue Wolf and find the Holdens. But it so happened that he still had to pass right by the doors of Lucky Avila's El Coyote. He found a spot in the hills just across from the converted motel and watched the action at Lucky's place for a while. He had done some research on him in the morning, and found that Lucky was a kind of renaissance crook. He had robbed Good Humor trucks when he was a kid, sold porno pictures of his classmates at Sacramento High School, and blackmailed his minister at the Faith Catholic Church. All the while he had been playing lead guitar in a heavy metal band called Headripper and had been known to have four or five girlfriends whom he kept at a commune he called the Playpen.

Now he was loaded with dough and flying high. Lucky was the Scarface of the Southwest. He had fast cars, gorgeous (if mentally challenged) women, and boats to pull along behind his massive SUVs. He'd also built a barn and several other residences behind the main house at El Coyote. These cabins were where his gang members lived.

His Achilles' heel, as Michelle had said, was that he apparently dealt meth. And like most meth dealers he couldn't resist using his own product. The word Jack got from reading old police reports about him was that he'd become even more mercurial and violent than he'd ever been.

He sounded sick enough, Jack thought, to take Jennifer Wu.

She could be held prisoner right now in one of the outbuildings that Jack was observing through his Hasselblads.

Still, he doubted it. Anyone who went to all the trouble to kidnap someone surely wouldn't be dumb enough to hide her right on their own grounds.

Jack watched for three hours before anything happened.

He saw Lucky Avila lead a group of six fellow Sons of Satan out of the gate and down the highway.

Jack followed them.

Two miles down the road, Jack watched as Lucky and his boys pulled into the parking lot of a local restaurant, the Red Sombrero.

Jack waited until they'd been inside the restaurant for five minutes, then parked and went inside.

As he entered the Red Sombrero he saw the Sons of Satan standing by a back door. They were complaining loudly to the Mexican waiter, a little man with a ratty moustache.

"You have it wrong, sir," Lucky said, in a mocking way.

"I do not have it wrong," the waiter said. "The back patio is already booked, *sir*." He wanted to show he wasn't intimidated by six assholes dressed in black leather jackets, with faces like Visigoths and attitudes to match.

Jack moved between two other diners and got closer to the bikers. They didn't notice him at all because they were busy staring with venomous hatred at the short, bald keeper of the gate.

"Yeah, you're right about one thing, asshole," Lucky Avila said. "The room is already booked. It's booked by us, dickhead. Who the fuck is out there now?"

The waiter sighed and looked down at his schedule.

"That would be the group from Blue Wolf Lodge," he said.

Lucky Avila looked as though he would gag.

"Hey, fuck those dipshits," Lucky said. "Tell 'em to shove off."

"I'm sorry, sir," the host said. "They use the patio every year for their council meeting."

"Yeah?" said Lucky. "And when does the freaking council get their asses out of our seats?"

"I'm afraid they've reserved the room for the entire night. They'll be out there until ten thirty, or perhaps even later."

"No," Lucky said. "They won't be."

The other Sons growled at the little man, and one of them, a short, wide guy named Zollie who looked like Yosemite Sam, knocked a painting of a black bull standing in a sea of flowers from the wall.

"I think we should, like, trash the Sombrero," he said.

The other Sons mumbled agreement. But Lucky Avila only smiled, shook his head, and then pushed the waiter out of the way. He kicked the door open and crashed the festivities on the patio.

Jack eased around behind the gang and watched the collision. Bikers versus New Agers.

The first thing Jack noticed was that the Blue Wolf crew was the same aging group he'd seen when he first came into town. The ones who had been so surprisingly nimble as they worked out in the park.

Jack felt his hair bristle. If this was going to be a physical conflict the Blue Wolfers were going to lose, and lose badly.

Surely they must know this. But they didn't seem at all intimidated.

"Look who we have here," said the white-haired leader who sat at the head of the table. "If it isn't the great outlaw himself, Lucky Avila. You're looking well, Lucky. Let me introduce myself. I'm Alex Williams, the president of the Blue Wolf council."

The older man's hair was still thick, his voice strong.

"Like I give a shit who you are," Lucky said. "Listen up, Williams. You guys have to leave. And I mean now!"

The old folks at the table looked up at the outlaw king and seemed amused. They smiled as if Lucky were joking with them.

"Really, and why is that?" Williams asked.

"Because," Lucky said. "Me and my guys, we had the place reserved for two months."

"Well, I'm afraid I've got you there," Williams said. "Because we reserve the room one year in advance for our council meeting."

"Fuck your reservation. We have an important dinner and business meeting scheduled for tonight, so I think you better take your little crew here and buzz off."

"Sorry," Alex Williams said, "we haven't even eaten our appetizers yet. But I do admire your aggressive stance, Lucky. Very manly."

Williams thrust his hand toward Lucky, steady and strong, and Lucky seemed compelled to shake it. Jack watched as the older man's fingers enveloped Lucky's. The gang leader grimaced and tried to pull away, but found the old man's huge hand held him firmly in his grasp.

Panic crossed Lucky's face. He pulled backward as hard as he could, and then Alex Williams let go, catching him off guard. Lucky fell back against the wall, hard. He slid down it like a drunken cat.

The Sons of Satan looked stunned. They seemed lost, unable to make a move without their leader.

Jack watched as Lucky's face turned bright red.

"That was funny," he snarled at Williams as he got up. "See how you like this."

Contorting his face in anger, he raised his massive fist. But before he could strike the aged Blue Wolf president, Jack grabbed him and, a second later, had twisted his arm behind him and shoved his face up against the wall.

"We're gonna kill your ass, mister," a huge biker named Terry said, moving toward Jack.

"Oh, yeah, you are one dead mother," another biker, Popeye, added.

"That wouldn't be smart," Jack said, releasing the pressure on the leader's arm a little. "I saw the bartender call the state police about two minutes ago. They're undoubtedly on their way here now. You haven't done anything chargeable yet. But if you hit Mr. Williams here you'll end up in jail, probably for a long, long stretch."

"Yeah, but you twisted his—"

"It's all right, Terry," Lucky said. "He had to do that to stop me. Mister, you just did us a big favor. What's your name?"

"Jack Morrison," Jack said, using his undercover name. "Don't like to see a brother take a fall when he don't have to."

"Who you ride with?" Lucky asked.

"Gypsy Jokers," Jack said. "Out of Portland."

"Come see me at the Coyote," Lucky said. "We might do some business."

Jack gave Lucky a little salute, and the biker turned and looked at Alex Williams.

"You were real lucky just now, old man," he said.

"Sometimes it's better to be lucky, Lucky," the old man said.

"Funny. But I got a feeling your luck ain't gonna hold," Lucky added. Then he motioned to his men. "Out of here. Now."

He nodded to Jack again and they all cleared out, like a pack of wild dogs.

Back at the patio, Alex Williams and the other Blue Wolf oldsters raised their glasses to Jack.

"To our benefactor and friend," Alex said. "Thanks, Jack. We owe you one."

"Nah," Jack said. "Looked to me like you had the situation well under control."

"Not at all. If Lucky had landed that blow he would have probably broken all the bones in my face."

The others at the table nodded in agreement. Alex Williams introduced his dining partners.

"Jack, this is Ellen Garcia, one of the founders of Blue Wolf."

Jack looked over at the white-haired Mexican woman whose right arm was in a sling.

"Nice to meet you, Jack," she said. Though her face was lined, her blue eyes shone with intelligence and clarity.

"Good to meet you, too," Jack said. "What happened to your arm?"

"Old age happened to it," Ellen said. "But we've got some terrific new methods at Blue Wolf, and before long it's going to be just like new."

63

Jack smiled and nodded, but wondered silently if she was just kidding herself. Still, he reminded himself, there were amazing new things happening every day. What did he really know about any of it?

"And this is Nigel Russell," Williams said. "He's our program developer."

Jack looked at the heavyset man with the big back brace, and smiled.

"Nice work, Jack. I thought for a second I was going to have to take the jerk out myself."

The table howled at that, and Nigel gave Jack a mischievous grin.

Jack was then introduced to a woman who was all hunched over, Sally Amoros. Sally was the head of something called Ancient Ways.

"They gave me that post because I'm so fucking ancient," she said. The group at the table cracked up, including Jack.

Jack then met the man with the cane, Desmond Phillips, and the man with the eye patch, Jerry Hoffman. Hoffman was an architect, and the head of new building for Blue Wolf, and Desmond Phillips was the comptroller of the corporation. They, like the others, were witty and completely free of self-pity.

"You really saved the day, Jack," Hoffman said.

"No problem. Maybe you people need some security."

"Thanks, but we have it," Williams said. "Anyway, these things rarely happen. Blue Wolf is a spa vacation spot and a deeply spiritual world. If we're involved in physical ugliness . . . well, it just isn't good for the resort's image or Blue Wolf's stockholders."

"Not to mention our souls," Sally Amoros said, and several other members added, "Amen."

Jack nodded.

"You know, we don't usually get bothered by the bikers because they're busy hating their rivals, the Jesters. About twice a year they war and kill one another."

The old man laughed a little as he said it.

"More entertaining than HBO," said Sally Amoros.

"But seriously," Jack said, "those are some dangerous guys. What if they come back? How will you deal with them?"

"Oh, positive energy forces, meditation . . . there are many ways, all of them nonviolent."

"Yeah," Jack said, "that's all fine. I have a lot of respect for nonviolence myself, but do the things you're advocating get through to the morons and the haters, the guys like Lucky who are born predators? I mean they see something, they take it if they can. Can people like that be influenced by . . . whatever you call them . . . good vibes?"

"A good question," Alex said. "And one I don't take lightly. But at Blue Wolf we're working on much more than just good vibes. Come up and I'll give you a tour."

"I'd like that very much," Jack said.

He felt warmth toward the old man, and thought of his own dad.

"What are you doing down here, Jack?" Alex Williams asked.

Jack reached into his shirt pocket, pulled out the photo of Jennifer Wu, and handed it to him.

"I came down to see a friend, Michelle. She and her sister Jennifer were sightseeing the other day up in Taos and Jennifer disappeared. And the funny thing is, I was intending to come see you later today. Because Jennifer Wu works for you, as a nurse."

"I know Jennifer," Ellen Garcia said. "Terrific nurse."

"So do I," said Phillips. "Nice girl."

"Yes, I've seen her around as well. Disappeared?" Williams asked. "What do you mean?"

"I don't know. Wandered off. Or worse."

"Kidnapped?"

"Possibly, yes."

"You think Lucky Avila might have something to do with it?"

"I don't know," Jack said. "But Jennifer's sister Michelle knows Lucky and they had a very unpleasant run-in a couple of days ago."

"I see," Alex said. "Well, he's a bad sort, no doubt. But I never heard anyone say he was into kidnapping. Anyway, I'll duplicate this photo and circulate it up at the resort. If she's anywhere near there, we'll find her."

"I'd appreciate that."

"Meanwhile, please come up and ask around if you want to. And you're more than welcome to use any of our facilities."

"Thanks," Jack said, and shook the older man's hand. Like Lucky, he was surprised by Alex's strength. The old man might have a lot of wrinkles, but he was still as strong as a man half his age.

Chapter Eleven

Phil sat in the apartment drinking his tequila, furious. The thing was, he wasn't some old guy. Hell, he was still in his forties. And he had made fifty mil in his business.

But now that he had the money, the sad thing was that his wife Dee Dee wanted younger men. Phil wished he had never started this swinger thing.

It had been fun for a while, sure. But now the bitch couldn't get off unless she had some new young guy in bed with her.

She craved, absolutely craved, sex with as many men as possible.

Now she was out fucking Ziko. Of course.

Well, two could play that game. He'd get himself down to the bar and see who he could round up.

Yeah, he'd find a hot new chick. There were some women who were more loyal, and some people who would think of a man in his forties as desirable.

Yes, sir.

She'd see, and in the end he would leave her and not give the bitch a dime.

He laughed and combed his hair straight back. Looked cool, like a young, prefat Brando.

Fuck feeling bad. What he needed was a little bar action.

Chapter Twelve

Though he felt guilty for interrupting Oscar's vacation, Jack called his partner at seven in the morning.

"Hey, amigo," a sleepy Oscar said. "You having fun in Santa Fe?"

"Not exactly, "Jack said. "See, the case has taken a couple of weird twists, and it's more than one gringo cop can handle. Now if I had a really smart Latino to help me out down here, somebody I could trust . . ."

"I must be going deaf in my old age," Oscar said. "I just had an auditory hallucination that you asked me to give up my vacation to come down there and help you and your completely untrustworthy criminal girlfriend in a kidnapping case. I'm telling you, Jackie, I think I need to go to the ear doctor."

Jack started laughing.

"There's nothing wrong with your ears, Osc. The next Southwest plane leaves at ten o'clock."

"Oh, Jack . . . I don't believe you're doing this."

"Okay, Osc, you don't have to. You enjoy your vacation, which you wouldn't be having anyway if I hadn't saved your ass that time in Cartagena."

"I can't believe you're bringing that up."

"I know it's a cheap shot, but that's how desperate I am."

"Shit, amigo. That is so low of you. But I'll be there. You bastard."

"Love you, too, Oscar."

Jack hung up, ashamed of himself but greatly relieved. He had half the day before Oscar arrived, and there was a lot he wanted to see at Blue Wolf.

The Blue Wolf Lodge was a slick place, with modern steel and glass buildings and a medical wing where celebrities and CEOs got face-lifts and tummy tucks while they looked out at the mountains.

As Alex Williams showed him around the place, Jack saw people getting treatments called Adobe Mud Wraps, green-tinted Turquoise Facials, Cornmeal Wraps, and Volcanic Clay massages. Other people, mostly older women, were having their feet pummeled gently by so-called Mystical River Stones, and still others were having their lymph glands massaged.

The whole deal seemed like a giant hustle to him, and he wasn't getting any closer to finding Jennifer Wu.

"Look, Mr. Williams," he said. "I appreciate your showing me around. But what I really need is to find the Holdens. Phil and Dee Dee."

"Of course," Alex Williams apologized. "Sorry, I got a little carried away."

"No problem," Jack said. "I wish I was here on vacation."

"No, you're right. I'll get you to them right now."

They walked across the "campus," as Williams called it, and Jack saw the vast and otherworldly cactus gardens and the Desert Rose Meditation Center. Finally, he and his friendly host wandered out to the parking lot, where tour bus after tour bus arrived with old couples in them. They came with crutches, canes, walkers, fancy wheelchairs, and oxygen tanks. Soon they had formed a line and were trundling along to check in at the Soul and Spirit Center.

"Let me guess, my friend," Alex Williams said. "You're a little skeptical about all of this?"

Jack laughed and admitted that he was. "I see a lot of desperate people, closer to the end of their lives than they would like to admit. They come to these places for some kind of mud-wrap miracle."

Williams shook his head.

"No," he said. "We don't promise them that. Just renewal. It can be long-lasting or it can be short-term, depending on how serious they are."

"Or how much money they spend?"

"Yes, that, too. Healing doesn't come cheap. Nor do the therapies we use. People study years and years to learn the disciplines we teach here. A great native healer, for example, has to undergo a long apprenticeship under a licensed medicine man from his tribe. It's no less than the kind of education taken by a Western practitioner."

Jack smiled as a stunning pair of pearl-colored clouds moved overhead.

"Well, let's just say I'm more of a fan of Western medicine than you are."

But Alex Williams wouldn't give in.

"You're wrong there, too. I have a medical degree from Harvard. What we try to do here at Blue Wolf is integrate both traditional Western practices and the best of all the other traditions. Remember, Asian, Mexican, and Indian cultures were all around thousands of years before we were and know many things we've yet to discover."

Jack nodded his head, though Williams had scarcely convinced him.

As the older guests trudged past him to check in, Jack felt that he could see the desperation on all of their faces, and a terrible fear in their eyes.

They must know, Jack thought, that all this nontraditional, spiritual "medicine" was jive. Wasn't it obvious that having their legs pummeled with rocks from ancient stream beds wasn't going to do a damned thing for their failing hearts and crummy circulation? And didn't they know that having their skin exfoliated, and their imaginary third eye filled with some kind of fancy, heated olive oil, was going to mean absolutely zero in a fight against cancer? They must know; but they did it anyway. They had mud baths and Cornmeal Wraps, and ate lizard skins ground up in capsules, and they knew that at least some of the staff was laughing at them behind their backs while they accepted their over-the-top tips, but they went on with it, because "what if?" What if it somehow worked? What if the Cornmeal Wrap broke through some kind of molecular twenty-first-century fucked-up dying-cell cancer, and somehow stimulated youth in them? What if it worked in spite of their cynicism? What if there was some particle of truth to it all and it made them young again? Even if just for a month, or a couple of weeks or, for that matter, one weekend?

Why not give it a shot?

They found Phil Holden at the Piñon Bar. He was standing at the bar downing a margarita. He wore a green silk shirt with blue parrots on it and white pants. He looked like an eighties refugee from *Miami Vice*.

Alex Williams introduced Jack, who noticed that Holden's face was bloated from alcohol.

"I understand you were up at the Tewa Pueblo yesterday," Jack said. "Did you happen to see this girl?"

He showed Holden a picture of Jennifer Wu.

"Yeah," Phil said, as he picked up his drink. "Yeah, I guess I did see her. She was standing over by the big round structure they got there. What's that thing called?"

"The kiva," Jack said.

"Right, me and Dee Dee—that's my wife—we just come out of there and we saw this Chinese girl talking to some people."

"What did they look like?"

"I don't know. Three or four guys. Not Indians, I don't think. They seemed to be asking her for directions. She kind of walked away with them . . . and she was pointing, you know, south, I guess. Like they were asking directions to Santa Fe, or someplace south of Taos, anyway."

"You sure of this?" Jack asked.

"Yeah, I am."

"Well then, yesterday, when the second Chinese girl came up and asked you where her sister went, why did you tell her you hadn't seen her?"

Phil shook his head.

"I don't know why I said that," he blushed. "I just smelled bad news coming and I didn't want any part of it."

"What do you mean, bad news?" Jack pushed. "We think that this girl, Jennifer Wu, was kidnapped and maybe you could have stopped it."

"Yeah, I see that now," Phil said. "I do. But I didn't know anything about that yesterday, right? I mean, for all I know, those Chinese girls coulda been in cahoots with the bikers. They get us to go somewhere with them and the next thing me and Dee Dee know is we're out in the desert somewhere, our money gone, and bullet holes in our heads."

Jack sighed.

"You see what kind of rides the bikers had?"

"Couldn't be sure. Harleys maybe."

"License plates?"

"Well, they were New Mexico plates, that's for sure. But I didn't get any of them."

"Could you physically identify any of the guys who took her?" Jack asked.

"Not really. I didn't get that close and, you know, it's dark up there. Only moonlight. Now, if you guys don't mind, I'm going to order another drink and then take a nap."

"Yeah, sure," Jack said. "That's just fine. But I may want to talk to you again. Okay?"

"Sure," Phil said. "Most exciting thing that's happened to me since I been here." He took another sip of his drink and turned away from Jack.

"Does that help you at all?" Alex Williams asked, looking concerned, as they walked outside.

"Well, it confirms one thing. That Jennifer was taken by bikers."

"Very unsettling, Jack," Alex said. "Do you want to talk to any of her coworkers?"

"Yeah," Jack said. "Anyone she worked with in the nursing department. Speaking of which—what kind of a nurse is she?"

"Surgical nurse and a damned good one," Alex said. "I'll work up a list of all her coworkers. You can tackle it after lunch."

"Thanks for all your cooperation, Alex."

"The least I can do. First, you saved me from a beating, and second, this is one of our own. We think of Blue Wolf as an extended family. What happens to one of us happens to all of us."

"Y'know, I'd like to see Jennifer's room, if that's possible," Jack said.

"Of course," Williams said. "She lived on the fourth floor of the medical building, in the dorm rooms. I took the liberty of getting you a key. The only thing is, I can't allow you to ask questions of the guests on the first and second floors. Many of them are well-known people who pay quite a bit of money to have their treatments with maximum security."

"Really?" Jack asked. "But what if she worked with some of them?"

"You can talk to the surgeons she worked with. But not the patients. We wouldn't be open for a week if word got out that our privacy rules had been violated."

"All right," Jack said. "You're the boss."

Alex smiled and warmly shook Jack's hand.

"Now I've got to get back to work. I want to thank you again for standing up to those bikers. That took real courage. I won't soon forget it. And I'm sure you'll find Jennifer. The only thing is . . ."

"What?" Jack asked.

"I'm about ninety-nine percent positive she isn't around here. And if one of the cycle gangs took her, maybe you should be looking at them and their brothels. If they grabbed her right off the street, well, they could be hustling her out of the state right now."

Jack nodded. "I know. Trust me, I'm on it."

"Good," Alex smiled. He waved good-bye and headed across the parking lot.

There was a separate door that led to the dorm rooms on the third and fourth floors of the medical building, and a skinny, pock-faced guard who sat at a desk ringed with cameras. On hearing Jack's name he let him in at once and pointed to the elevator to the fourth floor, then went back to playing his computer game, Dr. Dinky's Death Camp.

Jennifer's place was a one-bedroom apartment, neatly kept. There was much more of an Asian motif than Jack had seen in any of her sister's merely functional apartments. There was a Qing Dynasty red Suzhou cabinet. It must be a knockoff, Jack thought. The real thing would be ridiculously expensive . . . unless, of course, it was stolen. Michelle had always maintained that her little sister was straighter than straight, but one couldn't really believe much of anything Michelle said. For that matter, Jack thought, as he opened the doors of the chest, Michelle herself could have stolen the chest and given it to her sister.

With Michelle Wu and any of her friends or family, pretty much anything was possible.

He looked at a golden ceremonial robe on the wall and a floor screen with cranes and pines on it.

Jennifer was much more into her Asian heritage than Michelle, who veered from punk rock to super goth depending on her mercurial moods.

In her bedroom he found a jade-inlaid desk, which Jack guessed was made in Shanghai perhaps a hundred years ago. He looked at the wood—elm—and then tried to open the drawer, but it was locked. Jack took out his lock picks, and within two minutes the desk was open.

Inside were piles of papers and receipts wrapped with rubber bands, and a book of photographs of Michelle and Jennifer when they were young and a woman who might have been their mother. She had the girls' good looks, and was wearing shorts and a halter top. Very rare for a Chinese woman of that era to show so much skin. Jack found himself forgetting why he was here as he leafed through the pictures. Just seeing Michelle's photos did something visceral to him—one part protective, one part desire.

Reminding himself why he was in this room, he looked under the bed, then in the medicine cabinet, and found nothing.

Then he saw it. The outline of dust on the desktop where a laptop computer must have been.

Whoever took Jennifer had also been here and found her computer.

Which could mean only one thing . . . she knew something, something that could be bad news for her captors.

In all likelihood, Jennifer's kidnapping was not just a random crime, nor was it a simple, impulsive revenge play by Lucky and his crew.

Lucky was probably involved, though, in some way. Maybe Michelle and Jennifer were in cahoots after all, and they were threatening Lucky's enterprise. Jack was walking back toward the front door when he heard someone in the hallway. He quickly ducked back into the bathroom and waited until the footsteps subsided. Standing there, he saw a pack of matches that had fallen behind the sink.

He reached down and picked it up. The Jackalope Ranch. Interesting. He put them in his pocket and quickly headed toward the front door.

Outside, Jack was walking around toward the back end of the medical building, trying to figure out a way to get inside, when he saw a blonde he'd noticed earlier that morning as she had been taking people around the grounds. She was a stunning-looking thirty-something woman with a terrific body, a fantastic smile, and intelligent eyes. She wore tight blue jeans and a Blue Wolf T-shirt.

"Hello," she said, as they crossed paths, "my name is Kim Walker. I do publicity for Blue Wolf."

"Jack Morrison," he volunteered.

"I know," she said. "You're the talk of the lodge. You saved Alex last night."

"Maybe," Jack said. "But he's a pretty tough guy. I bet he could have handled Lucky all by himself."

"I doubt that,"she said. "Where are you heading, Jack Morrison?"

"Need to grab some lunch," Jack answered.

"Why don't you eat with me here at the Piñon?' she offered. "We have great food, and maybe I can help you with that girl you're look-ing for."

"You heard about Jennifer?" Jack asked.

"Of course," Kim said. "And I've got my own little theory."

"Really?"

"Really. Come along, Jack. I think you'll be interested in what I have to tell you."

As they waited for their food, Jack smiled and looked hard at her. Her skin had an almost luminescent shine to it and her eyes actually twinkled when she spoke.

"Okay, here's the deal. Lucky Avila lives in an old converted motel not far from Blue Wolf. Just below us, actually. Fortunately, there's no road between his place and ours, but every once in a while some of the drugged-out bikers and other lowlifes who live there like to drive their cycles up to our property line and hassle our guests. This all started about five years ago. It was irritating at first but Alex decided to ignore them. That worked for a while, until one day about three years ago, a teenaged girl named Ellie Kozack went missing. The cops were called in, then the FBI. For a while, maybe two weeks, there was nothing, not a trace of her. Then a witness stepped forward, an old guy named Charlie Huff who was out of it on various prescription drugs, so no one knew whether to believe him or not. Anyway, he swore he saw Ellie getting on the back of a cycle. He said the driver looked like a gang member. He also said they were headed down to El Coyote, Lucky's place. The police came and looked all around but didn't find anything. Which, of course, means nothing. Whoever took her had her for at least three days before the search at Lucky's place. They could have all raped her, slit her throat, and buried her out in the desert by that time. Trust me, Jack, people disappear in the desert all the time and are never heard from again. Just about the only way they can be found is if animals dig them up and somebody, a hiker or someone like that, happens to cross paths with the body before the animals devour it."

"So you think maybe the same thing happened to Jennifer?"

"I don't know. From what I heard your missing girl was up at the Taos Reservation but Lucky and his boys do a lot of business up there. Selling speed to the Indians. They could have bumped into her, got her to take a little ride . . ."

"No," Jack said, "she was not the kind of girl who'd take a joy ride with bikers. If they took her they must have knocked her out."

"Sounds more and more like Lucky," Kim said. "He might do it on a whim. The guy is very impulsive."

Jack looked at her with a thoughtful expression.

"What?"

"I don't understand why Alex didn't mention this."

"That's easy. The case is closed, and Lucky would love to sue Blue Wolf. He's the most litigious person on the planet."

"I see," Jack said.

"You want my advice, I'd say get a search warrant and some help from the sheriff's office and go over Lucky's property with a fine-tooth comb. Before Jennifer Wu ends up like Ellie Kozack."

"Not easy to get a search warrant based on hearsay evidence. I imagine if Avila is like many other motorcycle gang leaders he's got some big-shot lawyers representing him."

Kim Walker shook her head and picked at her salad.

"That's bullshit. That girl could be on his property right now. Maybe she's still alive, but if I know Lucky Avila she won't be for long, and once she's dead no one will ever find her bones."

She dabbed a speck of blue cheese dressing from her mouth.

"I have a feeling about you, Jack. You seem like a very capable man who wouldn't let a technicality like a search warrant stop you from saving a girl's life."

She smiled warmly at him and Jack felt it deep in his bones.

Chapter Thirteen

Kim was right, Jack thought, as he left his car on a mesa top and looked down at Lucky Avila's spread, El Coyote. The place was situated under Blue Wolf, but a range of hills hid any sign of the spa from Lucky's old motel. There was a small guard shack in front of Lucky's place. Whatever went on in there, it was obvious Lucky wasn't interested in having people pop in to say hello.

Jack drove by and saw two beefy guards carrying rifles and sidearms. He wouldn't be entering anywhere near there.

What he did find about a mile down the road was a dirt trail that ran adjacent to Lucky's property. There was nothing to stop someone from parking on the trail and then crawling on his belly under the barbed-wire fence that bounded Lucky's land.

Which was what Jack did now, snaking his way under the fence, then running low across the land, hiding behind trees and cacti until he saw Lucky's back barns and small cabins. This, according to what he had learned from Kim, was where his men lived, but he saw no sign of them.

Perfect. He would start with the barn, then move to the cabins and see if he could find any sign of Jennifer Wu.

* * *

Jack slid down a dusty hill, hunched over, and made it to the faded red barn. The door was open and he slipped inside.

It really was a barn. There were horses, a hay loft, and some pigs who wandered through like they were looking for a friend.

Jack moved through the barn, looking for trapdoors that might lead to an underground cell. He had once read a study of kidnappers, and something like 78 percent of them put their victims underground. Many people's ultimate fear was of being buried alive. It made the kidnapper feel that much more powerful.

Jack smelled a particularly noxious odor in a stall near the barn door and looked in. There was a huge javelina pig with tusks that could tear a man's stomach apart. The pig stared up at him, and there seemed to be something shining and sinister in his eyes.

"Nice piggy," Jack said. He started to turn around and head back the way he had come in, when something hit him in the back of the head.

He saw a few blue lights, and then hit the hard ground, out cold.

Jack dreamed that he was snorting like a hog. He could feel his nostrils turning hogesque and his legs mutating into hog feet. He could feel himself getting hog angry and ready to charge an interloper who was interrupting a nice sexy dream of a sow, who was giving him a lap dance.

Jack opened his eyes and looked into the sun. At first blinded, he then squinted hard and realized that the hog he had just been dreaming about was staring at him for real. He and the hog were no longer in the barn, but outside, with only a battered wooden fence between them.

He struggled to a kneeling position and saw how massive the animal was. It snorted and stared into his eyes.

Jack reached for the fence for support, but someone slapped his hand away.

Zollie, the heavy biker from the Red Sombrero, was standing over him. In his hand was a pump-action 500 Slugster shotgun, which he pointed at Jack's head.

"You waking up, hero?" the big guy asked menacingly.

"I could use a drink of water," Jack said.

Zollie turned to his right to look at the great hog and Jack noticed he had a walleye and a cauliflower ear. Jack took him for an ex–club boxer, the kind of guy who inflicted a lot of damage but took twice as much.

Jack started to get to his feet, but Zollie pushed him back down with the gun stock.

"Why you messing around in our business, mister?"

"I'm not. I just didn't like seeing you guys beating up on old people."

Zollie slammed the gun stock into Jack's forehead, knocking him back into the mud.

"Don't you try to bullshit, me, pal. I know exactly why you're here."

"Listen, big guy. I'm trying to find a woman. That's all. A woman named Jennifer Wu."

"Bullshit," said the big man, his face reddening in fury. "You're here to take Ole Biggie, my pet pig. I knew you was a pig stealing mother ever since I laid eyes on you at the Sombrero."

Jack looked at the pig, who made another grunting noise as though he were in complete agreement with Zollie.

"I do not want your pig, Mister," Jack said.

"Bullshit," Zollie said again. "I know exactly what you aim to do with Ole Biggie, too. I've seen your kind before. I betcha you go green when you take a crap. But it's fine if you steal my pig and do some work on him, huh?"

Jack wondered which lunatic asylum Zollie had escaped from.

He looked back at the pig, who eyed him as a possible appetizer.

"I might jest let Ole Big here eat you up," Zollie said. He walked over to the pig and petted the animal through the fence slat. The pig purred like a car revving at a stoplight.

Jack managed to pick up a handful of mud as he got to his feet.

"You think you can fool ole Zollie 'cause you got a college diploma. But you ain't about to."

Jack walked toward him and the big man moved backward, keeping the shotgun on him, chest high.

"Don't get any ideas about running for it. Lucky told me he wants to talk with you but if you try and run I should do my thing. He wants to question you but that's all bull. 'Cause I know why you're here. Yessir, I do."

He nodded his head up and down as if reassuring himself that he had Jack nailed.

Jack laughed and shook his head.

"I think I understand why you feel such a close kinship with that ugly, hairy, fuckface motherfucker and that's because you look just like him. Except he's a little better looking, warthog head."

"That's the end," Zollie yelled. "You're all done here, buddy!"

He reached down to a sheath on his belt and took out a big hunting knife. He came toward Jack, the blade thrust frontward. Jack waited until he stabbed at his midsection with an upward slice, then dodged to his left and caught the big man on his neck with a well-aimed forearm punch. Zollie fell hard against the fence, and Jack quickly reached down, grabbed his head, and rammed it into a fence post. Zollie collapsed at his feet. Jack quickly rid him of both knife and shotgun.

The hog, as if annoyed at all this commotion, backed off and fell into a mud hole. He emitted a great, long, contented fart and began a dream of sows.

Jack dragged Zollie into the cow pens and tied him up with the fat man's own shirt. For a gag, he pulled off Zollie's socks and stuck them in his mouth.

Jack looked up at the main house. There was a light on inside and someone was listening to the Rolling Stones song "Ruby Tuesday."

He knew he should get out of here now, but he had to check the ranch first. The other backhouses were quiet. It seemed like everyone in the gang was gone for now. This might be the only chance he would get. He picked up Zollie's shotgun and moved toward the first house, running low.

In the next forty-five minutes, Jack picked the locks of five of the six cabins. Inside he found drugs (coke, pot, and pills, especially Vicodin and Percocet), guns, porno, all manners of knives, and even a few hand grenades, but not one thing that related to kidnapped girls, sex slaves, or Jennifer Wu.

Nor did he find any signs of a meth lab.

As he headed toward the sixth cabin he noticed a slight movement on his left, about fifty yards away. And it wasn't an animal because animals didn't glint in the sun. No, that little flash could only come from the barrel of a gun. So he was being watched now by someone who would probably be waiting for him when he came out of the last cabin.

Jack went inside, speedily looked through the cabin, found nothing, then waited, and waited some more. Waiting was one of his strongest attributes, just as it was one of the weakest in most criminals, who were usually people who acted on sheer impulse.

This time was no different. After waiting and watching for twenty-one minutes, whoever was outside lost his patience and headed for the door. He opened it slowly, poked his head inside, and Jack clubbed him with the stock of Zollie's gun.

The man fell to the ground, unconscious. Jack turned him over and was surprised to see that he wasn't a man at all but a mere kid.

At least Jack thought he was a kid. Though he appeared youthful, the boy's skin was crepe colored, like someone who has a terminal disease, and his eyes were bloodshot and yellowed, the pupil about as small as a period at the end of a sentence.

He looked wasted despite looking so young, an altogether disconcerting image.

Jack took the man/boy's rifle, then shook his shoulder and woke him up.

"What the hell?"

"I knocked you on the head, pal. But it looks like you survived," Jack said.

"Shit," the kid said. "I was supposed to take you up to the house. Now Lucky's gonna be all over me."

Jack pulled him up and dusted him off.

"You make a lousy guard," Jack said. "What's your name, son?"

"Tommy Wilson," the kid said. "I didn't used to be so obvious. It's my nerves or something, they got all fucked up since I been here."

Jack pulled out the picture of Jennifer Wu.

"You know who this is, Tommy? Look familiar?"

Tommy looked at it for a few seconds, then rubbed his lip.

"Seen her somewhere," he said. "Maybe up at Blue Wolf once."

"So you know her?"

"Yeah . . . not by name or nothing but I seen her."

"When was the last time?"

"I don't know. Couple of weeks ago. My memory ain't too good 'cause some fucking guy hit me in the head."

He looked up at Jack and smiled in a clever way. Jack smiled back.

"You think about it, Tom. You think hard, okay? 'Cause this girl is in trouble, and anyone who helps is going to get a very nice reward."

"Izzat right?" Tommy asked. "Hey, that would be great. Look, you do me a favor?"

"What's that?" Jack asked.

Tommy smiled again, and his facial skin was wrinkly, as if he were a human shar-pei. It made Jack wonder if he was a child or a coot.

"Gimme back my gun, okay?"

"How come?"

"So I can look like a successful guard. You can take the bullets out if you don't trust me."

Jack laughed, unloaded, and handed him back his gun.

"This is a first," he said.

Jack moved toward the main house with Tommy behind him, the empty gun in Jack's back.

"I sure appreciate this, Jack. This will keep me from getting demoted to latrine duty."

"Anything to help the youth of America. By the way, how old are you, Tom?"

"I'm nineteen years old. If you're referring to my skin it's called Manlinger's Syndrome. My skin is aging before its time. It's weird, huh?"

"Yeah, a little," Jack said.

"I might look like a rhino neck before long," the kid said. "But it's okay. I'm drinking some good stuff now. D-35. Gonna shape me right up."

"That's good," Jack said. "They sell you that at Blue Wolf?"

"Yeah, and it works, too. I ain't half as wrinkly as I was when I started guzzling the juice."

As they approached the house Jack could see Lucky through a side window. The bandito was sitting at his desk, writing something on his Vaio computer. It looked odd, the bandit with the bandage on his right ear, wearing his badass beard and hand-stitched boots, sitting in front of a laptop like a young professional.

Jack wondered what he was doing. Shipping drugs to some other part of the country? Keeping track of his sex slave market? Instant messaging with other perverts?

There was only one way to find out, so Jack and the kid cruised around to the back door, walked into the kitchen, and quickly moved through the hallway to Lucky's little den. He was only inches behind him when Lucky turned around.

"Hi, Lucky, working late?"

The biker pulled out his ear buds, and smiled.

"Jack? So you escaped Zollie's clutches, eh? But I see young Tom caught you. Nice work, T."

"Thanks, Mr. Avila," Tommy said. "I found him snooping through the cabins."

"That right? You find any evidence of misdoings and malfeasance, Jack?"

"Plenty, but not what I was looking for."

Lucky laughed and signaled for Jack to sit down on a cozy-looking couch on the other side of the room. It was covered with a colorful Indian blanket.

"I hope you didn't hurt ole Zollie too bad," Lucky said.

Jack was starting for the couch when he saw Lucky reach under an Indian blanket that was spread over a kitchen chair. Before he could react Lucky had a large red gun trained on him.

He pulled the trigger and sprayed Jack with a shot of water.

Jack was stunned, confused. "A Super Soaker?" he questioned.

Lucky cracked up.

"I know it's juvenile, but when I was a kid I always wanted one. My mother was antigun, though, and wouldn't let me have it. I was in Target the other day and saw it and just couldn't resist. Guess I'm just trying to reach the old child-within, you know what I mean?"

Jack shook his head. "Yeah," he said. "I guess so."

"You think it's silly, huh? Guess it is. But the older I get the more I want to go back."

Jack shook his head again.

"You ever heard the phrase, 'You can't go home again'?"

"Sure," Lucky said. "A great book by Thomas Wolfe, right?"

Jack was stunned that Lucky knew the novel.

"Yeah, right. And the title's the truth. Once childhood is over, the door is shut, pal."

"For most people," Lucky said. "But I've lived all my life like a child. A child with vision, though. Everyone knows the kid years are the best, so why not relive them, *pal*?"

"If you so say so, Luck," Jack said. He knew the motorcycle leader was used to having the final word, so why go any further with him on this dumb tangent? Lucky put the toy gun down and signaled for Tommy to leave.

"Go untie Zollie," Lucky said.

"He's in the barn," Jack said. "If his hog hasn't dined on him yet."

The kid nodded, and when Lucky looked away he winked at Jack, then left.

88

"Truth is, Jack," Lucky said, "I owe you one for bailing me out of that mess at the Red Sombrero. So why don't you just tell me what it is you're looking for?"

"Trying to find someone," Jack said.

"And who might that be?"

"That would be Jennifer Wu, the sister of Michelle Wu."

"Jennifer? Well, why didn't you just say so in the first place? I know Michelle and her sister. I just had a delightful lunch with them two days ago."

"Not the way I heard it," Jack said.

"Really?" Lucky asked. He arched his eyebrows as if surprised and troubled by this slur on his social graces.

"Really," Jack said. "In fact, Michelle told me you were stoned on speed and that you suggested they both jump in the sack with you. And when they refused, you said you'd make them pay for their lack of interest."

Lucky laughed as he took out a gold toothpick.

"I'd had a little too much to drink, I'm afraid. I might have to get back to AA. It's just damned embarrassing, though. A motorcycle gang leader, the scourge of the tristate area saying, 'Hi, I'm Lucky and I'm an alcoholic.' But wait a minute, here . . . what are you suggesting? That I got so darn infuriated that they wouldn't play house with me that I kidnapped Jennifer? Or that I'm using her for some kind of poke machine? After which I'll . . . let's see . . . kill her and bury her body in the desert?"

Jack felt an eerie chill. That was the exact scenario Kim Walker had laid out for him. Was Lucky just playing with him?

Before Jack could respond, Lucky cracked up and pounded his computer table.

"Really, man, that's too weird. I'm a businessman. Okay, I got a little wasted and overzealous. Santa Fe is kind of like a hipper version of Vegas. People come down here for freedom, you know? They do wild things sexually under the name of 'self-discovery,' whereas in Vegas it's just out-and-out lechery. Personally, I like the more honest approach, but I couldn't live in Vegas."

"Why not?"

"Too many guys with string ties," Lucky said. "Also, girls with fake lips. I don't mind fake tits, but the big fake lips phenom is really too weird for me. Women who come to Santa Fe have kinder and gentler surgeons. The lips might be chemically aided but the doctors make it look organic. Anyway, I thought the girls might want to experience something cool. Sister ménage. I mean, that way you get two modes of self-discovery at once. Two-in-one, sex and incest. Anyway, that was my little rap, but they weren't buying."

"When was the last time you saw Jennifer?"

"Right then. At the ill-fated lunch," Lucky said.

"Where was this lunch held?" Jack asked.

"At the Red Sombrero. Right after we finished eating they said they were on their way to Taos to check out the Indian village."

Now Lucky got up from his seat and began to walk around, like a professor lecturing a class.

"Wait a minute," Lucky said. "Something just occurred to me. There were three other people at the Sombrero that day. Man, you should have come to me right away about this and I bet we could have solved the whole mystery in one fell swoop."

"Who were they?"

"That's the thing. They were three members of the the Jesters. Mexican mothers who were seated only a few feet away. The thing about them that I remember is they were all eating salads of endive and sliced pear with a sprinkling of walnuts. Their leader, Pancho Flores, made them all take physicals last year so they could get cheaper bike insurance, and most of them flunked. So now the whole gang is on a diet. Low carb, high fiber, and they drink white wine instead of tequila."

"A Mexican biker gang drinking white wine and eating salads?" Jack questioned.

"Oh, yeah, and they talk about their public reach-out, how they give breakfast to the poor and indigent Indians down on the square, how they help Latino sculptors and artists sell their wares. They make themselves sound like Mother Teresa. But what they're really into is whores, dope, and sex slavery. They kidnap women and send them off to Mexico. Down to Juarez or Nuevo Laredo. To the Papagàyo. But I happen to know they only ship them three or four times a year. They keep the girls penned up somewhere. I'm not sure where their jail is but a good place to start would be the Jackalope Ranch. I hear tell that's their jumping-off point."

The Jackalope. That was the name on the pack of matches Jack had found at Jennifer's place.

"Thanks for the tip," Jack said. "But why are you being so helpful?"

"First of all, we don't kidnap people. We find that scumful. Second of all, the Jesters are a nuisance. They can't really compete with us but they can get in our way sometimes. I'd be less than honest if I said I wouldn't like to wipe them out."

Lucky threw his head back and laughed out loud and a black tooth fell out of his head and into his hand. He tossed it into a candy dish on the coffee table.

"See, I have lots of businesses around here. Mainly the car biz."

"Really?" Jack asked. "I heard your main business was meth."

"You hear all kinds of things," Lucky said. "Meth is so last year. The stuff I'm into now, it's twenty-first-century stuff. Lucky Avila is all about the future. I'm investing our bankroll in genetic meds. That and tourism are the future. Illegal, renegade shit is for losers."

"I thought that's what you guys were," Jack said.

"Again, so old school. See, what we, the third generation of bikers, realize is that we don't want to terrorize the street . . . well, a little bit, once in a while, for nostalgia's sake . . . but really, what we want now is to *own* it. All the rest—the bikes, the colors, the badass attitude—that's just show business."

Lucky laughed happily, a black-leathered, scar-faced, soon-to-be-toothless entrepreneur.

Jack didn't quite buy it. That tooth falling out seemed very much like a symptom of rampant meth use, but the rest of it sounded pretty good. The mob, after all, did the same thing. And the ones who stayed in the dope business for too long ended up in prison for life, or wrapped in bailing wire.

"I'm telling you, it's the Jesters," Lucky said. "You want to find Jennifer Wu, look there. But be careful. Unlike us, the Jesters have been very slow to evolve. They might *really* cut your dick off and feed it to the hogs."

Jack nodded and looked around.

Lucky looked at him and smiled like a mind reader.

"Your car is right out front. We took real good care of it for you." Lucky laughed, and spit out another tooth.

"It's been fun, Jack. When you find Jen, tell her the offer is still open. With or without Michelle."

He flicked the second tooth into the candy dish as Jack went out the door.

Chapter Fourteen

Kevin couldn't get his mind off her. He'd get a hard-on just thinking about her body. The way her breasts looked, her hard nipples, her flat stomach. Man, he couldn't believe it. And her ass . . . that was too much. Really. It was so compact, so hard, and when she opened her perfect long legs, he could see the triangle of hair and her wet, waiting pussy.

Just today, someone threw him a pass and he missed it altogether, something he *never* did. He wasn't the best player on the team but he was known for his reliability.

Or at least he used to be. Now the ball just zipped right by him. Another time there had been a loose ball on the field, and Kevin had just sort of forgotten to go after it.

His coach, Jerry Schmidt, went nuts.

"Kevin, what the hell you doing out there, jerking off?"

Kevin almost wanted to yell back, "As a matter of fact, yeah. That's exactly what I'm doing. If you ever saw Vicki Hastings open her legs with her silk stockings still on, you'd be jerking off, too."

Of course he said nothing at all. Just ran after the next ground ball and was glad that he was wearing a protective cup so no one could see what a hard-on he had.

He couldn't stop thinking about her. Not at lacrosse, not at home, not talking to Grandpa. No way.

He couldn't wait for school to end.

Tonight, Friday, only two days after they had first done it, was no different, at first.

He left practice, picked up his books, and headed over to the library about ten minutes before closing.

She came out, walking so sexily in the sodium lights, across the dark parking lot. Even from a hundred yards away he knew that walk, those white legs.

Why didn't she hurry? He couldn't wait to touch her, to kiss her mouth, then her throat and work his way down . . .

She smiled at him and got into her car.

He got in after her and leaned toward her.

"Wait," she said. "I have a surprise for you."

"What?" Kevin asked. His voice cracked when he said it.

"I want to show you how to really make love. And the first thing we need is a bed."

"Yeah," Kevin said. "But what are we going to do, go to a motel?"

"No, baby, I have a better idea."

"Where?"

"My house."

"Great," Kevin said. "I gotta feeling your husband might not go for it."

"My husband is out of town," Vicki said. "For three days. At a business meeting in Chicago. We have the whole house to play in."

"But your neighbors," Kevin said.

"They won't see you. Trust me, you won't be sorry."

She reached over and squeezed his cock, and he almost came right there.

"It's the next house," she said, as they drove down the dark block. "You keep hunched down back there, okay?"

"Yeah, I can't get any lower."

"Okay," she said. "I'm turning left now."

In the back, hunkered down on the floor, Kevin felt the bump as they headed into the driveway. Then he heard her click the remote and the garage door started to rise. Slowly, the car moved forward, and then they were inside. Behind him the door went back down.

She got out of the car, then opened the back door and looked down at him, huddled on the floor. She laughed.

"C'mon," she said. "Let the games begin."

He was naked, wandering through the dark upstairs hallway. And he was *sooooo* stoned. She'd brought out some weed and, at first, he didn't want to smoke it. His father was an FBI agent and here he was taking drugs. Man, that was worse than anything else he had done. But she wanted him to, and he couldn't turn her down. He didn't want to look like some young punk.

So he'd smoked the stuff, held it down like she told him to, and then, man, it was like the top of his head was gone. Really. He could imagine there were these little hinges on his scalp, and they unlatched, and then they sort of disappeared, and then the top just floated off and he had exposed brain pan in there, and it was okay because he couldn't feel it anyway, and also the walls were shimmering and his eyeballs were rolling around and his cock was hard and he was crawling . . . was he really crawling, yes . . . across the floor toward the bedroom, where she was hiding, and he had to find her or she would have to punish him. He thought that was the game anyway. She would punish him in some "terrible way," she said.

And here he was crawling along with this huge hard-on, totally naked, and laughing and saying in a sort of growling voice, "If I find you I am going to fuck you."

Which seemed stupid but also kind of funny, and he was laughing, hearing this hollow "hahaha" sound coming out of his mouth, but disembodied from it as well.

Hahahahahahaha.

And then he was in the master bedroom (but the master wasn't there, haha), and he crawled to the bed, and looked under it, and saw only darkness, but put out his hand and felt around. Nothing.

He crawled over to the closet and opened the door and there was no one there, either, and he felt like he was going to freak out he was so excited. Then he saw a tall wardrobe on the other side of the room and he crawled over the bed, laughing some more. And he said, "I know you're in there. Come out and plaaaay."

And then he grabbed the knob and swung open the door, expecting her to pop out into his arms.

But nothing. Nothing at all.

He was shocked. Where the hell . . . and then he saw the cedar chest in the corner of the room, but before he could really give it his full attention, she leapt out of it, scaring the living shit out of him.

She gave a wild, terrifying yell and lunged at him, pointing a handgun at his face.

"You evil fucking child," she screamed. "Give me your cock!"

Kevin fell back, horrified, as she jumped on him and aimed the barrel of the gun at his head.

Then she broke into wild laughter and pulled the trigger. Kevin heard the click and felt his heart stop for a beat. She laughed again and began to kiss him and hug him.

"Whoaaaa," Kevin said.

"I love you so fucking much," she said.

And she reached down and put his still-hard cock into her and began to ride on top of him.

The weed, the fun of the game, and the fear put Kevin into a whole new place, something he couldn't even name. He was inside her, and she was tight and she was kissing and biting his neck and what if Granddad saw it, but the hell with Granddad. He was inside Vicki and he was madly, wildly in love with her, and nothing else in the world mattered one damned bit.

But after it was over and he felt they had become one, a single thing, had actually melded into one another, she did a strange thing.

She sat in front of her mirror and looked at her face, running her fingers along the wrinkles on her cheeks and the little crow's feet by her eyes.

And she began to cry.

Kevin was out of bed at once and got up behind her, patting her cheeks and kissing her head.

"What's wrong, Vicki?"

"I look soooo old. God, my mother was so beautiful. Much more beautiful than I am. But in her forties she just fell apart. Wrinkles everywhere. She tried every cream they make but none of them really worked. She was the belle of the ball, as they used to say, but poof, like a fairy tale, it was all over."

"That won't happen to you," Kevin said. "That will never happen to you. And even if you do get some wrinkles, I'll never leave you, Vicki. You can count on that."

She half turned and looked up at him with tears in her eyes.

"Are you sure?" she asked.

"Of course," Kevin said. "I love you, Vicki, and no matter what I'll never, ever leave you."

"Of course," Vicki said. "You're my good, true boy. My sweetheart. I know I can always trust you."

He kissed her and his heart almost burst with emotion.

How he hated to see her suffer. He would do anything to prevent that from happening. Anything.

Chapter Fifteen

Jack sat in the little park behind La Fonda. It was cold. Snow was in the air. But he was watching something that stunned him. Ellen Garcia, the woman he had seen with her right arm in a sling the day he had arrived in Santa Fe, was now standing in the park with a young trainer. And she was doing pull-ups.

That seemed beyond remarkable. It was almost spooky.

She seemed to have healed via the promise of Santa Fe: come here and expect a miracle.

Jack watched as she did one, two . . . three. She stopped at six. Okay, not that many, but she had looked almost completely out of it, not forty-eight hours ago.

He got up from his bench and walked toward her.

"Hi, Ellen, how are you?"

"I'm fine, Jack," she said. "Jack, I want you to meet my trainer, Rich Carlson."

"Nice to meet you, sir," the young man said.

"Same here," Jack responded. "Just the other day you couldn't even lift your arm. How in the world . . . ?"

"Shots," Ellen said. "D-35, developed at Blue Wolf. All new. And unlike some of the stuff you get, this doesn't wear off. Not if you ex-ercise with it."

"I see," Jack said. "Do the patients use it, too?"

"Yes, some of them. But you have to do the rehab afterward. If you don't, the formula doesn't really have a chance to work."

"What the hell *is* D-35?" Jack asked.

Ellen and Carlson both smiled.

"Well, if we tell you that, we'll have to kill you," Carlson said, still smiling.

Ellen did another chin-up. And one more, which she held for a few extra seconds.

"D-35 does many things for the body, but one of the most im-portant is that it allows superfast healing after injury." Carlson said.

"Amazing," Jack said, smiling, but thought "steroids." The only sub-stance he knew that promoted fast healing and simultaneous muscle growth was steroids. Of course, they caused heart attacks, impotence, and tumors, as well, but perhaps people at this age—their late fifties and up—didn't worry about that so much. The risk might be worth looking and feeling ten years younger.

Saying good day to both of them, Jack headed back to the hotel.

When he arrived at his room the door was already open. He took out his Glock and went inside. He looked around, the gun out in front of him.

Then he heard a cough from across the room.

Michelle Wu was sitting in a chair, looking down on the now-snowy square below.

She was wearing a pair of tight jeans and a blue and red plaid shirt.

"You going out to the Jackalope?" she asked.

"As soon as Oscar gets here," he said.

"Good," she parried. "Maybe he can keep an eye on you."

"What's that mean?"

"That means, Jackie Boy, you and Kim Walker."

"You're kidding," Jack said. "I had lunch with her to find out about your sister."

"I know. Of course. It was all business. Right!"

"It was. I can't believe you were watching me."

"I wasn't," Michelle said. "I happened to be up there, asking questions, and I saw you in the dining room. I nearly walked in on you."

"You're nuts, Michelle," Jack said. "I came down here, risked my career for you, and you're following me around? That's just too lame."

"Listen to me, Jackie. My sister is missing. You don't have time to have a love life."

"I was trying to learn things from her, Michelle. And I did."

"Yeah," Michelle said. "I'm sure you learned plenty. You fucker."

She picked up an ashtray and hurled it at him. Jack ducked as it slammed into the wall behind him and crumbled into pieces.

"Cut it out. You don't have any idea what's happening."

"Oh, yeah I do, Jackie. I know."

She ran at him and raised her fists. Jack put his arms up to defend himself and felt a rain of blows.

Then, when she was out of breath, he grabbed both of her arms.

"What the hell are you doing?"

"You bastard. You hustler," she said.

Then Jack found himself pulling her close to him. Her lips parted and he kissed her deeply.

"You son of a bitch," she said when they were done. "I hate you."

She kissed him again, and somehow they moved across the room to the bed.

"I fucking hate you so much," she said, as she unzipped his pants. He unbuttoned her shirt and a second later his mouth was on her breast.

They mashed together, furious and mad for one another. Jack had never felt anything like it before.

Though he never wanted it to end, it was almost unbearable.

He was inside of her and holding her perfect tight ass with his hands, and he felt as though he would explode.

He felt such an overwhelming fullness that he wanted to cry out in pain.

And why? For fear that it would end, though that was something he could barely acknowledge to himself.

They exploded together, both of them crying out.

Afterward they lay back on the pillows. Jack felt his entire body humming. He had heard an old friend once tell him that his ex-wife made him "nuts in love." Jack laughed now. That was it.

He was pure "nuts in love." It was terrifying and joyous and he doubted anything could ever compare with it again.

"God," she said, turning to him. "I am yours, Jack. You hear me?"

"Yeah," Jack said. "I hear you."

He kissed her again and his entire body shuddered in absurd happiness.

Later, as they dressed and tried to reassemble themselves, Jack held her at the door.

"I love you," he said. "I love you so much it kills me."

"I know," she said. "Me, too."

"Don't play me, though," Jack said. "I know you, Michelle. I know you and if you play me, I don't know what I'll do."

"I won't, Jackie," she said. "No matter what. We're together. But we have to hurry. I'm so afraid for Jennifer."

She kissed him deeply again, and Jack ran his fingers through her thick hair.

Then she opened the hotel room door.

"Tell me what happens at Jackalope," she said.

She smiled seductively, twitched her perfect ass, and walked away from him into the hall.

Chapter Sixteen

Oscar Hidalgo wore a black Rodeo King cowboy hat, jeans, and an ancient pair of rattlesnake boots that he had inherited from his Mexican sheriff grandfather. With his new black moustache, he looked downright scary.

They drove out into the desert dark, the road illuminated only by fierce moonlight.

Jack was dressed in black denim, and wore black leather boots.

"Man, you make a great cowboy," Jack said. "We oughta take a picture of you and me like this and send it to the Great Supervisor, Watt."

Oscar almost laughed.

"No, man. We don't want to irritate him any more than he is already. If he wasn't so busy with the Homeland Security guys he'd be keeping tabs on you. If he finds out we're going rogue down here he'll be all over your ass."

"What are those Homeland Security guys up to?"

"They want to see all our records. They want to run every investigation. The only agency they treat worse than us is the D.E.A. They got the power right now and they are kicking ass and taking names, bro."

"Good," Jack said. "That'll keep the boss busy for a while. Which is just what we need."

"You really think Jennifer Wu is out here?"

"That's what I've been able to learn so far and it fits. Jennifer has probably been kidnapped by these Jester assholes. She could be drugged and forced to 'work' out here or they might have sent her to one of their other places."

"That makes more sense, doesn't it?" Oscar said. "I mean they take her off the streets and put her out here, someone is going to recognize her."

"Yeah," Jack said, as he hit a jackrabbit head-on. The thing made a sickening slushy sound and blood and a little fur came flying up onto the windshield. "That does make more sense. But according to Lucky Avila they could be keeping her out here until they make their shipment to Mexico."

"And you trust this Avila dude?"

"Not hardly," Jack said. "He's a weird kind of New Age redneck. Like Merle Haggard meets Deepak Chopra."

"That *is* weird," Oscar said.

"Yeah, he seemed eager to lead me out here."

"And you searched his whole place?"

"Yeah, I did. Maybe he has some kind of secret room, but I couldn't find it."

"But if he did kidnap Jennifer to punish Michelle he'd make some kind of demand, a ransom or something?" Oscar wondered out loud.

"I know. And so far he hasn't asked for a thing. And yet . . . I feel like he's involved somehow. I know Michelle thinks he is."

"Well, we'll check this place out and see what we can learn. Maybe it'll be simple after all, compadre. We bring her back tonight and we're heroes."

"That would be nice," Jack said. "I could use an easy win right now. Man, I'm supposed to be on my free time, hanging out with my son."

"How is that rascal?' Oscar asked, smiling.

"He's fine," Jack said. "Staying with my dad."

"Good," Oscar said. "I like your old man. Even if he is a dog sometimes."

Jack laughed and gunned the car down the moonlit road.

Jack had expected the place to be a dump, but it turned out that the Jackalope Ranch was a big stone house at the foot of a mountain. There was a wide front porch with comfortable-looking rocking chairs. Some of the girls for hire sat out there now, one of them dressed in supershort cut-off Levi's and a tank top that barely covered her breasts. Another wore a lacy party dress and a sports bra, and a third wore spandex so tight Jack wondered if she could ever peel out of it.

They parked in the nearby lot, and as they walked back to the gate Jack saw three big Mexican guys wielding shotguns. As he and Oscar approached up the stone pathway to the porch, one of the girls welcomed them to the Jackalope in Spanish.

That was the cue for the other girls to surround them, giggling and playfully touching them. The spandex girl took Jack by the hand and pulled him through the screen door. The girl in the party dress nabbed Oscar.

"You are *muy guapo,* senor," she said, with a fake, bashful smile.

Inside there was a big living room with a long bar. Behind the bar was a sexy woman busy making margaritas for two couples who were laughing and eating chips and salsa.

On the walls were some of the same pictures that Jack had seen downtown at the local galleries. Blue dogs, wise roosters, and more O'Keeffe rip-off blue flowers.

The chairs were comfortable and filled with more girls and some tired-looking Mexican ranch hands.

As Jack and the young girl headed toward the bar, they were cut off by a wide man in a Brooks Brothers suit and a rep tie. Though he had longish hair and a big moustache, he looked like a broker at Smith Barney.

"*Buenas noches,*" he said. "I am Pancho Flores. The owner of the Jackalope."

"Jack Morrison." At the first sight of Flores, the girl had dropped his hand and suddenly become busy talking to another girl who was getting some appetizers at the bar.

"I have not seen you and your friend here before," Flores said.

"That's because it's our first time," Jack said. "But you have a very good reputation."

He looked across the room and saw Oscar and his girl drinking margaritas.

"That's good to hear," Flores said. "You are from where?"

"Los Angeles," Jack said.

"Ahhh, the city of Lost Angels. Now, what drink can I buy you?"

"I'll have tequila on the rocks."

"Excellent," Flores said. "I see you have a nice girl already. But if you like something a little more special, we can always accommodate that, too."

"Really?" Jack asked.

"Yes. Whatever your taste in escorts, we have them all. Though some of the more rarefied women are available only if you are a club member."

"I see," Jack said. "And what are the benefits of membership?"

"Your wildest fantasy—any fantasy—comes true."

"Sounds interesting," Jack said.

"Yes, time catches up with the most beautiful of women, senor," Pablo said. "And to be honest, with men, too. But some day, maybe soon, we will beat time down."

"Yeah," Jack said. "If we just drink enough tequila we can pretend that we're still young."

Flores laughed but shook his head.

"No, senor. There are new paths to take. I am thankful I live in the center of consciousness, senor. All the battles for cosmic consciousness in the sixties were forgotten in the commercial eighties and nineties. All except in Santa Fe and a few other enlightened places."

"I see," Jack said. "And do you think running a bordello takes cosmic consciousness?"

"Oh, yes, senor. This is all part of the new movement. Pleasure goes mainstream, the breaking down of the old Puritan ethic. Do you know the DVDs we make here have more effect on consciousness all over the world than a thousand plays by Shakespeare? And soon, senor, what is called porn now will be seen as the liberation it really is. That and new scientific breakthroughs will make a whole new world. Instead of hiding our sexuality in a basement we will put it front and center in the world, where it ought to be. God and religion will trade places with it. If you say you believe in God you will be laughed at. And rightfully so. Sex, youth, and vitality will replace the invisible despot in the sky. The judgmental tyrant who starts wars. The hippies were right when they said 'Make love, not war,' but they didn't take it far enough."

"But you charge people for sex," Jack said.

"Yes, because they are so unliberated they think only if they pay can it be worth anything. But in the coming Utopia, my friend, we shall all be young and we shall all be free of money. We shall be drenched in the earthy sperm of perfection, senor."

Pancho Flores looked at him with a malevolent twinkle. Jack thought for a second about showing Flores a picture of Jennifer Wu, but then thought better of it. After all, if he had her out here, penned up somewhere, he wasn't going to admit it.

Then Flores patted him on the arm in a fatherly way and drifted off to talk to another patron.

A second later, the attractive young girl who had met him at the door found her way back to him.

"You met Pancho. I think he likes you very much. I am Maria. You want buy me a drink?"

"Sure," Jack said. "What's your pleasure?"

"I like margarita. Strawberry," she said laughing.

"Whiskey for me," Jack said. "Jack Daniel's."

"You want to drink in here, or go back to my room?" she asked. She batted her eyes in a silent-movie-actress kind of way. Jack laughed and she grabbed his hand again.

"I think maybe you want to go to the room first. We can order drinks and have them brought back there. You like that?"

"Sounds great," Jack said.

Maria looked at the bartender and rapped twice on the bar. He nodded and she led Jack off down the hall.

The guitar player started singing "Wasted Days and Wasted Nights." That seemed odd to Jack. He had just been thinking about Freddy Fender, and now they were playing the very song that had been rolling through his mind. He had the strange sensation that whoever was running things around the Jackalope could read his thoughts. He knew it was an absurd idea, but this wasn't his usual low-grade paranoia. It was as though he had ingested some speed and could feel it tweaking his mind.

They knew what he was thinking. They knew he was going to come here, and they also knew he was with the FBI.

They knew all about him. They were playing with him. Like Lucky had played with him back at El Coyote.

He shook his head as though physically trying to shake out the spooks.

They don't know a damned thing, he silently reminded himself. They think you're just a friend of Michelle's. Relax.

As they headed out back, the porch door opened and Jack saw that his partner had added another woman. Now one was hanging from each arm. Oscar looked at Jack and cracked up.

"A man's gotta do his duty," he said.

Maria took Jack to what looked like a motel room, just across from a broken fountain and a smaller service bar being tended by a spectacular-looking transvestite with a pink and gold D.A. haircut. They got their drinks from him/her, and Maria unlocked the door to her room. The bed was made, but just barely, and she left the lights out and lit an incense candle.

She smiled at him, sat down on the bed, and took off her top. The move was about as erotic as a child undressing a doll. Rather than being aroused, Jack felt protective of her. He hadn't really looked at her closely outside. But now she seemed about fifteen years old. Her breasts were small and there was a scar under one of them. Where a knife had sliced her, Jack thought.

"You pay me now?" she asked, timidly. "One hundred fifty dollars."

"Sorry," Jack said. "I only have a hundred."

He took the bill out of his pocket and handed it to her.

"You a cop?"

"No way," Jack said.

"You want something? Blow job?"

She reached for Jack's crotch and before he could do anything she had squeezed his soft penis.

"You not hard. You a fag?"

"No, what I am is a *hermano*."

"A brother?"

"That's right," Jack said. "A brother who is looking for his adopted sister."

He sat down on the bed next to Maria and took out the picture of Jennifer and showed it to her.

"She disappeared two days ago. You seen her anywhere around here?"

She looked at the photo and shook her head.

"No, I don't think so." But her whole manner had changed. She was frightened, her hands shaking.

"I think you're a cop. You going to take me to jail?"

Tears rolled down her face and she had begun to shiver. Jack took her hands softly in his.

"Now listen," he said, "I'm not here to hurt you."

She looked up at him with doubt in her eyes.

"Maybe you take me away. Maybe you feed me to the beast."

"The beast," Jack said. "What are you talking about?"

"You don't know? Really?"

"Really. Tell me, Maria."

She bit her lower lip. Jack tenderly wiped the tears from her eyes.

"All the girls know. There is a man, wears black, he may not even be a man. May be the devil . . . He comes up to people on the street or even in their homes and he takes them to some place where he has . . ."

She could barely continue.

"Where he has a beast. A . . . how you say, a—"

"Monster?"

"*Si*. Monster. Terrible thing, weighs many pounds, and will chew up the girls. He gets strength from their hearts and brains. He is like a divinity. Can never die."

"Where is this monster?"

"I don't know. Some people say he is at the Satan's place."

"The Sons of Satan?"

"*Si*. A monster they feed girls who try to get away. In underground."

She must be talking about Ole Big, the hog, Jack thought. But why would the Jesters have him eat people? Unless it was like a goodwill gesture between two nation-states. The Sons sold meth, the Jesters sold women. A little business between them made it possible for them to coexist; they might even do each other favors.

It sounded like something that sick creep Zollie would do.

But would Lucky be involved? It was possible. If a girl had seen too much in either camp she could put the whole operation at risk.

He thought of Jennifer, half-drugged, being fed to that horrible hog.

He looked at Maria again but she looked away and played nervously with her hair. He was struck by another possibility.

"Do you know of any girls who have disappeared?"

"No . . . I am not sure," she said. "But maybe . . ."

"You know," he said, "you're pretty good, kid. I gotta hand it to you. You send me away from here, back to the Sons of Satan."

Her face hardened.

She'd run her young-and-helpless routine for him and he'd bought it wholesale. He'd gotten sentimental over a young whore. He wasn't the first or the last guy to make that mistake. But it pissed him off anyway.

Jack grabbed her arm and twisted it behind her back.

She emitted a little bark of pain.

"Now, you tell me. Have you seen this girl? And if so, where the fuck is she?"

She turned toward him, her face twisted into a snarl. The innocent kid who had been so abused by the world was gone, replaced by a braying hyena.

"If I scream the guards will come and beat your gringo ass to death."

"If you scream I'll cut your fucking head off before they get here."

Jack reached into his boot and took out his hunting knife. She looked down at it and began to tremble in fear.

"Okay," she said, "I don't know for sure, but in the back beyond the houses there is a barn. And in there they have the Acts Speciales . . ."

"Like what?"

"Girls with animals. Horses, dogs . . . for people bored with regular sex. Sometimes they put girls in there for a while. Then the girls, they disappear. But you dint hear this from me."

"Have you ever seen my sister back there? Answer me."

"No, but that means nada, senor. They bring in new girls every day in a black van. None of us who works in the front ever sees them. They take them off the street and they bring them in a back entrance. And the girls are blindfolded. Then they take them to the cellar."

"The cellar? In which building?"

"There is a white building behind the barn. They store stuff for the bar and *restaurante* there. The girls in Acts Speciales live beneath it. Outside, to the left."

"Today? Did you see the van come up today?"

"Yes, I think it was the one. But I only see it drive in. I dint see your sister."

"I want to see the place, right now. You're going to take me there."

"No! They catch us, they kill us!"

"You don't take me I'm going to cut you up right here."

She looked at him, and spat on the floor. But then she got up, put on her top, and led him to the door.

They walked around the fountain as they headed toward the end of the Jackalope's land. Jack looked around for Oscar but he was nowhere in sight. He tried his number on his cell phone but there was no reply.

What should he do? Find which room his partner was in, and maybe call attention to the fact that he was wandering around a part of the ranch that was off limits? Or just go in?

What the hell? If she was in there, he'd get her out and hook up with Oscar when he was done.

They walked into darkness for maybe fifty yards. Then Jack saw it, near the chain-link fence in the back, a low white building that looked like a bunker. It had blacked-out windows.

"The entrance is around the side, I think," Maria said. "I never been in there."

She stiffened as she spoke and Jack had to prod her with the knife to keep her going.

They came to the side of the building. There was no guard there but there was a metal door with a large padlock on it.

"Down there?" Jack asked.

"*Si.* They keep them here, sometimes for days, until they decide whether to use them in the show or get rid of them."

"And if they don't want them, then what?"

"I don't know, senor. Maybe they send them to another bar in Arizona, maybe to Texas. Or maybe they feed them to . . . the beast."

Her voice was high and she looked terrified.

Jack reached into his pocket and took out his handy little burglar's tools: a pen and a straight pin. He took the pen's shirt clip off and bent the end so that it was straight up. Then he put it in the bottom of the lock. After turning it twice he knew that he had to turn it right to open the lock. But first he had to work on the pins. There would be five or six of them in a lock this large. Keeping the pen clip taut against the bottom of the lock, he inserted the straight pin and slowly found the first tumbler, which he pushed straight up. He heard a small click inside and then proceeded to do the same thing to the other four pins.

Within seconds he had pushed all four pins up inside the lock. Then he turned the pen clip all the way to the right and the lock sprung open.

"Come on," he said to Maria, "we're going in there together."

"No way. You leave me out here."

"So you can run and tell the Jackalope security boys? I don't think so."

They walked in slowly and saw a storeroom floor covered with boxes of all kinds. To the left of the boxes was another door, this one also padlocked, leading to the basement.

He looked around the room and saw some rope and a pile of old rags. Within a few minutes he had Maria bound and gagged, and he left her tied to a radiator.

Then he started working on the lock to the cellar door. Seconds later the door opened and he slowly swung it open. He had his Glock in his hand.

On the left was a wall switch, but when Jack flicked it with his forefinger it failed to turn on the lights.

He reached back into his jacket pocket, pulled out a small pocket flashlight, and started down the steps, pistol in his right hand, flashlight in his left.

He lit up the steps in front of him and saw a filthy dirt floor and smelled the odor of rotting flesh.

When he got to the basement floor he looked around the room and saw rotting old magazines, piles of them sitting on a blond wood table. Over in the corner were an ancient television set and a flower vase with a couple of dead sunflowers drooping out of it.

Was this the living room for some poor girl who had been chosen to be the queen of the Acts Speciales? Jack felt such a deep hatred for the Jackalope and all the rot that it stood for that he half hoped someone would come out of the back, someone he could shoot full of holes.

But there was no one. Not yet, anyway.

He walked down the dark hallway. Slowly, carefully, he worked his way through three rooms, but all of them were empty. Finally there was one last door, and just before he opened it he thought he heard something. Crying? Yes, crying. A high-pitched voice crying . . . sobbing now, long, wrenching sobs. Was it Jennifer?

He readied his gun, opened the door, and then kicked it open, hard.

The dim light from the hallway barely lit up the room but there was enough to see a moldy old bed with something lying under a filthy sheet. Jack shone his flashlight on the sheet and saw that it was not really dirt he was looking at, but something greenish blue, something that shimmered, and then he saw what it was: a thousand filthy roaches that had been feasting on whatever the hell was under the sheet. The light made them scatter, and they scurried away from him in a mad race to the cracks in the walls.

What the hell was in the bed?

The stench was overwhelming . . . a rotting corpse? He moved toward it, barely able to breathe.

Then he became aware of a closet door opening on the other side of the room. He swung his light toward it, expecting someone to walk out, but there was no one there.

Jack turned his attention back to the foul-smelling bed. He reached down and slowly pulled back the filthy sheet.

What he saw was unbearable. It was a corpse all right, but not of a man. It was a hideous dead pig, its snout blown off by what looked like a shotgun blast. The roaches had gotten into its eyeballs and were streaming out of what was left of them. He looked closer and saw that the dead hog was covered with a kind of light green dust.

Jack gasped and stepped backward.

"Christ," he said. "Jesus."

But there was something else. He shone his flashlight on the animal's body and saw what seemed to be surgical cuts in its side and under its belly. He forced himself to look again and then held his breath as he stuck his hand into the wound. Bile came up in his throat as he felt around. There was blood and gore everywhere but he could tell that the intestines and liver were gone.

Someone had operated on the hog. He pulled his hand out, barely able to stand, and wiped it off on the bedsheet. What the hell was going on? Was this some kind of really weird fetish at the Jackalope? Not only watch a whore screw a burro, but kill and operate on (and screw!) your own pig?

Big fun at the Jackalope tonight. Have hot sex . . . with . . . with Ole Big?

Jack now realized that this wasn't just any hog, but Ole Big himself. He recognized the cloudlike markings and the odd hump in the hog's back.

Who the hell did this? And why?

While Jack was pondering this, he heard something. Out in the hallway. The sound of footsteps.

He quickly ducked behind the open door, pressing his body flat against the wall.

Heavy, loud footsteps were coming toward the room.

The footsteps came close, closer . . . and then a man walked through the door. Jack leaped out from his hiding spot and pushed him hard in the back. There was a cry of terror as the big man fell onto the bed, on top of the body of the dead hog.

He turned and looked up at Jack, who shone his flashlight into his face. It was Zollie, lying there on Ole Big. His shirt was also covered with an odd green dust. Like fairy dust, Jack thought. Fairy dust on an idiot giant and his pet hog.

"I'll get you, you son of a bitch!" the big man yelled.

He made a mighty attempt to rise to his feet but Jack pushed him back down and took out his gun. He was about to arrest Zollie when he heard other men somewhere behind him.

Time to leave.

Jack ran out into the hall and headed up the steps the way he had come. Seconds later, he heard someone coming down the steps. He was too late, and there was no place to hide. He reached for his gun but his flashlight beam landed on Oscar.

"Jack! There you are! I bribed one of the bartenders to tell me where he thought Jennifer might be."

"You lost your money, pal. She's not back there," Jack said. "But you wouldn't believe what is."

They heard what sounded like a large group of men running toward them, talking loudly in Spanish.

"Too many of them," Jack said. "Time to retreat, Osc."

They turned to head out the back way but Zollie came running out of the room, saw them, and started to lift his gun. Oscar ran into him, knocking him backward. The voices grew louder behind them and shots rang out.

Jack and Oscar ran across the desert toward the parking lot with Zollie and the guards in pursuit. Jack heard another shot and a bullet whizzed by his head.

They kept running until they got to the gate, ran through, and scrambled into their car.

Jack looked back and saw Zollie at the edge of the parking lot. In his fat hands was a shotgun, which he aimed at them and fired.

They peeled out and turned left, barely avoiding getting their brains splattered all over the access road.

The two agents drove out into the moonlit desert, careening down the highway.

"It was very dark," Jack said. "I tied Maria up down there. Went down into the basement. Then the guy I told you about, Zollie, came in. On the bed in there was this hog . . . the same hog I saw at Lucky Avila's ranch. Except he was dead and it looked like someone had cut out some of his organs."

"The big guy, Zollie, did it?"

"I don't think so. The sick fuck loves that animal."

"Then who?" Oscar asked.

"I don't know for sure," Jack said. "But I'm starting to get an idea."

His voice trailed off as he looked up at the lunatic moon.

Chapter Seventeen

After saying good night to Oscar, Jack went back to his own room at La Fonda. He was dazed, exhausted, and more than a little confused. He fell on the bed and drifted off into a twilight dream in which young Mexican girls were morphing into giant hogs. They chased him down back alleys and through the hallways of Blue Wolf. Nurses in white dresses appeared in front of him and then they, too, were suddenly great snorting hogs, racing toward him.

He lashed out at them with his hands and saw his fingers being chomped off. He screamed and fell to the floor as the hogs closed in, their little eyes as determined and mindless as a Muslim militant's.

He woke up with a start, his heart pumping wildly.

What was Ole Big doing in bed at the Jackalope?

Who had operated on him?

Jack got up and walked obsessively back and forth across the room like it was a crime scene. He felt like a criminal himself. He should report this, get the whole agency involved. But that would put Michelle in a compromising position. He couldn't bear to think of her in jail.

There was something finally happening between them. Jack had been to bed with many women over the years, but nothing had ever been this intense.

It was real. Had to be.

He looked out at the square, at the snow blowing.

He had to find Jennifer. Not only for her sake but for Michelle's, and for his own.

Or was that what Michelle wanted him to think?

Was he getting caught in her trap?

But she had saved his life before, and she was here with him now. She loved her sister and wouldn't endanger her.

Michelle was a criminal but she was the most amazing woman he'd ever known.

But what about his son? How could he be involved with a woman like Michelle and look Kevin in the eyes?

Maybe she could get straight. Maybe . . . maybe she wanted to. Maybe this was all part of that.

Maybe when he saved her sister she would get her head straight and see that he loved her and that she had to turn away from the dark side.

And meanwhile, what *about* Kevin?

Jack picked up his cell phone, dialed.

When Jack was away Kevin had a knack for getting himself in trouble. Jack had always assumed that the kid was just sowing his wild oats, but what if Kevin's rebellious behavior was the precursor of some deeper craziness?

The phone rang five times before Wade picked up.

"Hey," Jack said. "How you doing there, Pop?"

"Just fine," Wade said. "Everything's just as fine as Christmas here."

"Kev's all right?"

"Sure is," his dad said. "Couldn't be any better. Things are great. Only thing is I had no idea how much homework he got in high school. Really changed since my day."

"What do you mean?" Jack asked.

"Well, he's been really late the last couple of nights. Got these term papers he's gotta do. One for English and one for history and one for civics. I don't see how they can give 'em that much writing to do in one semester. Heck, we had one paper for the whole year."

"Yeah," Jack said, "but he's getting back home in time to get plenty of sleep, right?"

"Oh, yeah. Latest he stayed out was ten o' clock or maybe it was eleven one night."

Jack ran his hand through his hair.

"Eleven. That's entirely too late, Pop. Gotta be in the house and in bed by ten thirty. He's only fifteen, for God's sake."

"Yeah, but the library closes at ten. He stops to get a soda with a friend, and then he comes home."

"Friend," Jack said. "What friend?"

"The lady librarian," his dad said.

"He gets a ride home with the librarian?" Jack asked. "Well, that's a relief. I thought you meant he was out riding around with hoodlums."

"You're getting him mixed up with you, son. Kevin's a good boy. I know he had that little fling last year when he was cutting school, but he's all done with that. Yep, he said he and the lady librarian had lots of nice talks about ideas and books, stuff like that."

Jack smiled and shook his head in wonder.

Maybe his son was finally growing up after all. He'd always had a good brain; maybe he was starting to use it. To that he said a whispered, "Thank God. He's all right." What was he thinking? Kevin wasn't going crazy. Neither was he. He was just tired, too much pressure for too long.

"Is Kevin there now?" Jack asked.

"Yeah, but he's in his room, asleep. Got back around ten and looked completely worn out. Gotta figure he had a long day. School, then lacrosse, then all that library time. Poor little guy looks all beat up. But I'll make him some pancakes in the morning and he'll be as good as new."

Jack smiled. His dad had always been a great fry cook and pancakes were his specialty.

"Okay, Dad, just checking in. You okay?"

"Not bad for a guy who's lame and half-blind."

Jack smiled again. He'd only been making that joke for forty years.

"You okay, son?"

"Yeah," Jack said, "I'm fine. I might be down here a little longer, though. This is some case."

"That's fine, Jackie. I know you'll get your man. I got things battened down here so don't you worry at all. Love you, Jackie."

"Love you, Dad," Jack said, and hung up the phone. Well, he thought as he let out a sigh of relief, at least things were okay back home. Thank God for old Wade. Dad was a lifesaver.

Now if he could just figure out what the hell was going on here in Santa Fe. What the hell was Zollie doing in that house with a hollowed-out pig?

Then he remembered the crying he'd heard. High-pitched. Yeah, he'd thought it was a woman, but it wasn't. It was Zollie. He had been in the bathroom weeping over his dead hog.

He also remembered Zollie worrying that Jack was going to steal the pig. So he'd been worrying about that before Jack got there.

But why would anyone want to steal Ole Big and operate on him? What possible reason could anyone have?

Unless a doctor was doing some kind of experiment on the animal. But why? For what purpose?

Exhausted, Jack fell back on his pillows and quickly fell asleep.

But not for long.

There was a knock on the door. Not so much a knock as a scraping. He was sure he'd heard it.

He took his Glock out of his holster on the bedside chair and crept lightly across the room.

"Who's there?'

"Kim," the voice said. Jack could barely hear her.

Still not sure if he was being tricked, Jack kept the gun out and opened the door a crack.

Kim Walker, the beautiful publicist from Blue Wolf. But she wasn't beautiful now. Her face was bruised and beaten, her left eye blackened, and her lower lip split.

"What the . . ."

She fell into his arms. Jack held her close and half dragged her across the room to his bed. She fell on her side, whimpering.

"Jack, help me."

"What the hell happened?" Jack asked, as he went into the bathroom and ran cold water over a washrag. He got two ibuprofens from the bottle, then went back to Kim and held the rag to her swollen right eye.

She jerked as the cold compress hit her flesh.

"Take it easy," Jack said. "It's going to help. Can you tell me what happened?"

"I was taking a walk just outside the compound. There's a desert trail there. It was a gorgeous night, and I was trying to decompress from a busy day . . . and then . . ."

She began to cry pitifully and Jack held her.

"They came . . . they seemed to come right out of the desert. They beat me down, then they kicked me and hit me over and over. When I woke up they were gone. I wandered down to the highway and flagged a ride with a trucker."

She sobbed and Jack used the washcloth to wipe her tears away.

"Did you see who it was?"

"No, they wore masks."

"Masks? What kind?"

"Halloween masks. There were four of them. One was a demon of some kind and one was some kind of gargoyle. The other two were . . . I don't know. I can't remember."

"Did they . . . ?"

She shook her head.

"No, not that. They didn't touch me. But the one with the demon mask said, 'You should beware of the friends you make. The next time it won't be so much fun.'"

Jack shook his head. "The Jesters. They must have been watching us when we talked. Then when Oscar and I went out there . . ."

Kim nodded and put her arms around him.

"I thought I could help. But this could be either Lucky or the Jesters. He might have seen us and told them. They'll do anything to keep their business alive."

Jack gently held her head up and made her swallow the two pain pills with sips of water.

"You never saw them?'

"No."

"We should get you to the hospital," he said.

"No," she said. "I'd have to explain a lot of things and I might end up getting bad publicity for Blue Wolf. I'll be all right. Now that you're here."

Jack nodded and pulled the covers up over her.

She was soon asleep and stayed that way for several hours. Late in the night she awoke and cried out and Jack held her and gently lulled her back to sleep.

In the morning Kim seemed much calmer, though her pain was much worse.

"Jack, thank you so much," she said. "I don't know how I would have made it without you."

Jack, who had slept next to her, smiled at her now and started to get out of bed. But she pulled him back.

"Can I convince you to give me a little massage first? I ache all over."

"Why not?" Jack said.

She rolled over on her stomach and Jack straddled her, trying not to put pressure on her back.

He started lightly but she groaned and asked for more.

"You were lucky the sons of bitches didn't kill you."

She turned her head, and Jack lay down beside her and held her in his arms.

"You've got quite a shiner," he said, smiling.

"Maybe you can kiss it and make it better."

Jack sighed and shook his head.

"I'd like to. But . . ."

"You're with somebody?"

"Yeah. At least I hope so," Jack said.

"Bad luck for me," Kim said. "Can I tell you something?"

"Sure."

"I think you're a pretty terrific guy, Mr. Morrison."

"You, too, Miss Walker."

They kissed but then Jack, surprising himself, got out of bed.

"There's something I want you to know," she said. "If you ever do get free I think we would make a terrific couple. And trust me, Jack, I haven't said anything like that to anyone for a long, long time."

Jack smiled and looked at her terrific body. He was suddenly struck with a deep regret. What was he doing falling for Michelle? Here was an unencumbered woman, the right age, and perfect for him.

But still, he thought, if it was ever going to work between himself and Michelle Wu, he had to play straight with her.

And hope against hope that she loved him and would do the same.

Kim refused to see the doctor, saying she felt much better. As she showered and got dressed, Jack called Oscar and told him what had happened.

"We must be getting close out there, bro," Oscar said. "They're freaked out. If they have connections in Juarez, I want to know about it. Let me call some friends in my old city, hey?"

Jack agreed. If a Chinese girl had showed up in one of the whorehouses in the City of Death, Oscar would find out about it.

"I'm going to take Kim back to Blue Wolf," Jack said. "And as long as I'm there I'm going to try and see one more thing. The medical building. "

"Good idea," Oscar said. "You notice, bro, that everyone seems to want us to look at the Jackalope?"

"Exactly," Jack said. "Which is why we're going to go the other way before we call in for backup."

"Yeah," Oscar said. "After all, that's what Sherlock Holmes would do."

"Right," said Jack. "And we're at least as smart as him."

With Kim in the passenger seat Jack had no trouble getting by the guard at Blue Wolf. But after he had dropped her safely at her condo, he still had to figure out a way to get into the medical building.

What he needed was a clever diversion and he thought of one right away. One he had used ten years ago but, what the hell, there was no reason why it shouldn't work again.

Just to the right of the loading platform at the back of the medical center was a wooden guard shack with a uniformed guard inside. And about twenty feet away from the building was a fairly dense stand of bristlecone pine trees. Jack situated himself in the middle of the stand. In his hands were the matches he'd found in Jennifer Wu's apartment.

He pulled down two low-hanging pine branches and struck a match. In a few seconds they were sending up glorious spirals of smoke.

He hid behind the trees and watched as the skinny, long-nosed guard in the shack stared out at the grounds.

Any second now he would see the smoke and come out to inspect it. Jack, meanwhile, would be at the other end of the stand and be able to sneak into the building without the guard seeing him.

Jack waited for the guard to notice the gathering smoke. But the guard simply stared, without moving.

What the hell? He *seemed* to be looking right at the fire. So why wasn't he racing out to see what the hell was going down?

Then Jack realized what the problem was. The guard wasn't really staring out the window at all. He was staring down at his cell phone, no doubt playing a video game of some kind, or texting his girlfriend. Goddamn it. You couldn't use old-fashioned diversions anymore. Though there were video cameras everywhere, no one was actually watching the outer world. Instead, people were hypnotized by the latest app on their latest high-tech gizmo. It made Jack feel depressed and old.

The dependable old fire trick was now as useless as smoke signals.

Which, by the way, didn't stop the fire from burning higher and higher. Soon some of the trees would actually catch fire and his clever little diversion would be a blazing furnace that really *would* catch onto the building and burn the whole fucking place down. That would be perfect. If by some miracle Jennifer Wu was being held prisoner inside she could be charred beyond recognition by the very man who meant to save her.

Not to mention the doctors and patients.

Meanwhile, Jack would be caught and imprisoned for life as a mental patient.

He looked back at the guard, who was now looking out the window and scratching his head.

Finally! Jack saw him stick his goddamned phone in his pocket and actually open the door to the shack.

Needle-nose shouted, "Hey, fire!" in a weak voice, like the whole thing was kind of an embarrassment, then ran toward the half-incinerated tree.

Jack crept to the other side of the copse of trees and headed along a retainer wall toward the back entrance.

As he slipped inside he looked back and saw the guard running around the fire like an Indian doing a Hopi spirit dance. The guy had taken out his gun, as if he might try to shoot the fire to death.

A few minutes after he had entered the medical wing, Jack found the laundry room and borrowed some doctor's whites. Then, surgeon's mask in place, he moved along the floor, looking into every room in the place. Nurses and doctors walked by him and nodded, apparently suspecting nothing.

There were patients in practically every room, but none of them were Jennifer Wu. At the end of one hall was a meeting room. Thinking that this looked promising, Jack tried the door, found it unlocked, and went inside.

The space was decorated like a club room, with a wet bar, decent-looking leather furniture, and walls painted a pleasant shade of green with large blue wolves baying at an orange moon.

Jack looked everywhere, tried every closet door—there were three—but found nothing unusual.

Back out in the hall he came to a circular stairway that led up to the second floor. As he went upstairs he looked out the window and saw four firemen running around out back. The guard was still pointing his gun at the burned tree, like he was personally offended by it.

On the second floor, Jack walked down the hall, looking in every doorway. Most of the patients were sleeping. Many of them were heavily bandaged but it was obvious from their physiques, hair coloring, and skin tone that none of them were Jennifer Wu.

He was near the end of the hall and about to give up his search when he heard someone behind him. Jack turned and saw an old woman peering out of her room. She had wrinkles on her wrinkles, but her eyes were lively and sparkling.

"Dr. Carlson?" she asked.

"Yes?"

"Can you come in a minute, sir?"

"Certainly."

Jack quickly accompanied the old woman into her room. She moved toward her bed in a herky-jerky way, like a toy solder marching out of sync. She sat on the side of the bed and pointed to a chair across from her. Jack sat down.

"Hey," she said, squinting at him. "You're not Dr. Carlson."

"No, I'm taking his rounds tonight," Jack said. "I'm Dr. Pillas."

"I see," the old woman said. "Well, I'm Mary Jo Thatcher from Baltimore, Maryland, and I hope you don't think I'm a nut! But you look kind of furtive."

Jack smiled.

"Yeah, well, you are very observant, Mary Jo," Jack said.

"That's right, I am. And I am not a nut at all," Mary Jo responded. "Though I am from Baltimore and we do have a lot of nuts living there."

"Does Dr. Carlson think you're a nut?"

"He does. He thinks I am a great, big nut. Thinks I'm senile. That I have the Alzheimer's. Do I sound like I have the Alzheimer's to you?"

"Not at all. Why do you think he says that?"

"He says I lost my memory is why. But he's all wrong. I have never had a bad memory. In fact, along with my breasts, when I was younger, my memory was my best feature. You could say I had two really good attributes. My memory and my mammaries."

She laughed in a contrived, hearty way, like it was a joke she had told a thousand times before.

"That's good," Jack laughed. "Why does he think you're losing your memory?"

"'Cause he promised me something, which I remind him of, and then he says that I misunderstood his promises."

"And what would that be?"

"Well, he said I would be . . . here, wait . . . look at this."

She slowly opened a drawer in the table next to her bed. Then she took out a photo and handed it to Jack.

The old photo was of a strikingly good-looking girl, maybe in her late teens. She wore a tight V-neck sweater that showed off her figure to great advantage. She was smiling and leaning against a tree.

"That was taken by my boyfriend Jimmy," she said. "Jimmy died ten years ago. I wish I had married him but this other guy came along, Herbert, who was wealthier and drove me around in his Buick. I got blinded by all the chrome in the Buick. I mean *on* it . . . and . . ."

Jack reached over and gave her back the photo.

"I'm sorry, but what has this to do with your memory and Dr. Carlson?"

"Plenty. It has plenty to do with it. See, I got old. I don't look like this anymore, but Dr. 'Fake-o Promises' Carlson said I could look this young again if I paid him a lot of money and came down here."

"Really?" Jack asked.

"Yes, really. And it cost a lot of money. But then why am I telling you this? You work here, too. You must know all this."

"No," Jack said. "I'm new here. I'm an assistant. I haven't learned all of the ins and outs yet."

"Well, you will, buddy. They tell you they're going to make you look and feel young again. They give you this juice and these D-35 injections and for a while it works. You look and feel a lot better."

"But then it wears off," Jack prompted.

"Yeah. I think they just give you speed and some other stuff to make you feel high. That's all. I should have realized they were all crooks but it sounded so good."

Jack nodded sympathetically.

"Let me ask you something," he said, pulling the photograph of Jennifer Wu from his jacket pocket. "Have you ever seen this girl?"

Mary Jo looked at the picture, squinted, and nodded her head.

"Sure I have," Mary Jo said. "That's Jen. She used to be my nurse. Till she disappeared."

"You have any idea where she is?"

Mary Jo looked at him in a suspicious way.

"I have a very good idea what happened to her but I don't know if I can trust you."

"Come on," Jack said, looking at her in his most sincere manner.

"Okay . . . see, it all goes back to Rachel."

"Rachel?"

"Yes. She was another patient here. A young girl who shared this room with me. She was only about twenty-three, and she was getting a breast job. She told me she wanted to work as a model but they said she needed bigger boobs. That was why she was getting her breasts enlarged. Anyway, the next thing you know she decides she doesn't want to do it after all. She doesn't want the boob job."

"Why was that?" Jack asked, moving over to sit on the side of Mary Jo's bed.

"I don't know. But she talked to someone, her girlfriend or somebody on her cell phone, and she got this terrible scared look on her face."

Mary Jo Thatcher made a "terrible, scared" look.

"What happened then?"

"I fell asleep early one night. I swear I think they put something in my food. And when I woke up, she was gone. They said she went home. But it was all sudden-like and we were very close and she didn't even say good-bye. I tell you, something was all wrong about that, and I wasn't the only one who thought so."

Her mouth twisted in excitement.

"You mean Jen . . ."

"That's right," Mary Jo said, her eyes almost bugging out. "She thought there was something wrong, too. She was kind of close to Rachel and thought it very strange that she didn't say good-bye to her, either. And not only that, she left a couple of her blouses in the closet."

"She did?"

"Yes, I saw them. Listen here, Doc. This girl didn't have a lot of money. She wouldn't leave perfectly good blouses hanging in there."

"Hmmm," Jack said.

"'Hmmm' is right," Mary Jo echoed. "Hmmmm and double hmmmm. And that's where the Alzheimer's and Dr. Carlson come in again. I told him that I saw the blouses hanging in the closet after she left and he tells me that's not true. He then opens the closet door and it's empty. But it wasn't before. I told him so, too, and then he tells me he thinks I might be losing my memory. You see?"

"I do," Jack said.

"I think they did something to her, which is so sad because she was turning her life around."

"Had she been in some kind of trouble?" Jack asked.

"Yes. She told me not to say anything but I have to tell someone. She had come from a terrible family and her father had done unspeakable things to her and she had so little self-esteem that she had become a prostitute and a thief for a while. In Dallas. But she had moved here to get herself straightened out and she wanted to be a legitimate model . . . until she didn't anymore, and then they took her away. Oh, it's awful, and this Jennifer you're looking for, she agreed with me that something was funny, and I heard her talking to Dr. Carlson about it kind of loud in the hall one day and then . . . boom, two days later *she* disappears. You see what I'm getting at?"

"I do," Jack said. "Sounds like—"

"Foul play," Mary Jo Thatcher finished his sentence. "You were going to say 'Sounds like foul play,' weren't you? I love it in old books when Sherlock Holmes says that to Watson."

Two seconds earlier, her mouth had been twisted in fear, but now she was smiling like a happy lunatic.

"They're taking everybody away who knows anything," she said with a melodramatic hiss. "I think I could be next!"

She grabbed the neck of her nightgown and crushed it up against her chin in a nineteenth-century version of girlish terror.

"That is most interesting," Jack said. "Do you have any idea where Jennifer and Rachel are?"

"I sure do," she said. "I think they're somewhere under a rock! Or more than one rock. A big pile of rocks out there in the mountains because of what they knew."

"Ah," Jack said. "And what might that be?"

Mary Jo looked around as though she was sure they were being spied on by minicameras, and then twisted up her mouth again.

"I think they were both killed because they might spill the beans that the treatments here aren't real!"

Jack nodded his head.

"I see," he said. "I think you've discovered a real mystery, Mary Jo."

"Thatcher," Mary Jo said. "Mary Jo Thatcher. From Baltimore. Actually, from Roland Park in Baltimore. I knew I should have never left, to come down here with all these Mexicans and Indians. I'm afraid I'll be next."

"I don't think so," Jack said. "They're too afraid of you to hurt you. After all, you're Mary Jo Thatcher of Baltimore."

"Roland Park," she said. "The finest neighborhood in the whole world. And believe you me, once I get back there I am never going to go past the driveway again."

"That's a good idea," Jack said. "If I was you that is exactly what I would—"

"Hey," said a voice at the doorway. "Who the hell are you?"

Jack glanced up. The man speaking to him was about six foot four and looked like a professional wrestler. He had muscles that popped from his forehead like turnips from the earth.

"I'm Dr. Perry Pillas," Jack said. "I'm new here."

"Where's your badge?" Turnip Head asked.

"I forgot it. First week, ya know?"

"Yeah, I know all right," the man said.

He moved toward Jack in a way that bespoke serious disbelief. He reached his stubby fingers for Jack's lapels.

"You're coming with me, Pillas," he said.

"That's out of the question," Jack replied.

He reached down, picked up Mary Jo's glass of orange juice, and threw it into the attendant's face. When the big man blinked he kicked him hard in the shins, then grabbed his lapels and head-butted him in the nose. Blood sprayed out all over the floor as he fell.

Mary Jo laughed nervously as Jack stepped over the fallen man and quickly moved toward the door.

"I'm going to look into this for you. Don't worry about a thing, Mary Jo," he said. "Go home to Baltimore as soon as you can."

"I plan on doing exactly that," she said. Then fell back on the bed with a little sigh.

Jack quickly moved into the hall and sprinted toward the steps.

Chapter Eighteen

After a speedy drive back to Santa Fe, Jack and Oscar went to breakfast at Pasqual's on Don Gaspar Avenue. Jack had a cheese omelet
with black bean sauce and Oscar had a breakfast burrito with cheese,
chicken, and green sauce. The food was terrific but Jack was too
frustrated to enjoy it.

As he finished up his summary of his morning with Mary Jo at
Blue Wolf, he shook his head.

"It doesn't add up," he said.

But Oscar interrupted him.

"I don't know," he speculated, "maybe that old senorita up there,
Mary Jo, had it right. They sell capital-letter Youth and Vitality and
maybe this girl knew it was all a bunch of jive. So they got rid of her."

"No, no, no," Jack said. "Look, resorts like Blue Wolf are all hype
and everyone knows it. People come here to play at restoring their
old batteries and everyone agrees not to mention that nothing works
for very long. No one really believes they're going to get young again.
They just come here to pretend and get pampered."

"Wait a minute," Oscar said. "This Mary Jo believed it. You just
said so."

Jack shook his head again.

"Nah. I don't think even she did. She's one of these rich older women who like to go someplace and find a mystery. She's playing at being Miss Marple. She doesn't really believe that they would kill girls to prevent them from telling the world that they hadn't discovered the fountain of youth."

Oscar finished his breakfast burrito with gusto and took a gulp of his black coffee.

"I know the kind of woman you're talking about. My aunt Sharon is like that. She gets on a ship and two seconds later she thinks she's in some kind of Agatha Christie novel. She loves doing that. Makes the whole trip seem exciting."

"Exactly," Jack said. "She liked getting me involved in it, too."

"But wait a minute," Oscar said. "There's something she said that bothers me. She felt really, really good. From some shots they gave her. Too good, if all she had was B-12 or a few yoga classes. And they didn't want to admit that the girl's clothes were left in the closet."

"If they even were," Jack said.

"*Sí*. She could have imagined it," Oscar said. "But that part of the story . . . I mean the way you told it to me . . . it sounded like not only she believed it but *you* also believed her, amigo."

Jack couldn't suppress a smile.

"You got me there, Osc. I did believe it."

"So maybe her conclusion—that they're trying to hide the fact that they don't really do much for people—is off, but what she noticed, maybe that is for real. Maybe, for example, they're using speed to make people feel better, or shooting them full of some other kind of dangerous illegal drug. Maybe Jennifer and the other girl, Rachel, were going to report them, so they sold them off to the guys at the Jackalope to keep them from talking."

"Yeah," Jack said. "But there was no sign of them out there. And I checked every room. Did you get anywhere with your phone calls and e-mails to Juarez?"

"Nada. No sight of any Chinese girl. And I talked to some people who would know."

"And then there's this other thing. How do the fat boy, Zollie, and his hog fit in?" Jack wondered.

But before Oscar could answer him, Jack's cell phone rang.

"This Jack Harper?" a tense voice asked.

"Yeah," Jack said.

"It's me, Tommy. From Lucky's. I gotta talk to you."

"Sure, kid," Jack said. "What's up?"

"Can't talk long now. I think I know what happened to that girl you're hunting for."

"You do?"

"Yeah. But they'll be walking in here any minute. You know the Red Sombrero? I can meet you near there. If Lucky don't catch me first. There's a big butte near the Sombrero. You take Dark Moon Road. I'll be back along there. Can't go in the restaurant. They'd find me."

"I don't know the area."

"Pull off at Dark Moon and drive north on the dirt road. When you get to the high rocks, wait. I'll signal you. Don't bring a bunch of cops, though, Harper, or I'm a dead man, and maybe you, too. Shit, they're coming. I gotta go."

The phone clicked dead, and Jack turned and looked at Oscar.

"Man, this is getting weirder by the minute. That was Tommy, the kid from Lucky's gang. Says he knows where Jennifer is."

"You believe him?"

"I don't know. But he sounded for real. And scared shitless."

"Which makes him the perfect person to send us right into an ambush."

"Yeah, I know."

"We could use some backup," Oscar said.

"Kid says we bring in backup, he dies."

"I knew you were going to say that," Oscar sighed. "Guess we play it down and dirty then, hey, amigo?"

"Guess so. I mean, why should this time be any different?"

He pulled out his wallet, laid down some bills, and they took off.

Chapter Nineteen

Jack and Oscar drove like lunatics toward the Red Sombrero. As they got near the place, Jack looked up and saw an overhanging butte just north of the restaurant. Hawks soared by on thermal wind gusts. Otherwise, the area looked deserted.

"That's gotta be it."

"The only big butte around here."

"Where's the road?"

They drove parallel to the butte, until Oscar spotted it.

"There, that's it. The sign says Dark Moon Road."

Jack turned the car off the paved road, and seconds later they were headed down a dusty, bumpy road toward the rocks. There was a curve ahead and Jack slowed down.

Oscar felt adrenaline coursing through his chest.

When they got closer to the butte, Jack pulled over and Oscar got out, rifle in hand.

"Be careful, partner," Oscar said.

"You, too. And make sure you cover my ass 'cause if they shoot me I'm going to come back and haunt you."

"Just as I would expect, gringo dog."

Oscar scrambled up the hill to the south side of the butte as Jack drove slowly down the road.

A few hundred feet farther he pulled the car into a natural parking space below the rocks. He looked up and saw what looked like a ledge, and suddenly a light flashed in his eyes. Tommy was signaling him with a mirror. Jack wished he had a mirror on him to signal back but he'd thrown his away when he stopped hanging out with coke dealers.

He looked to his left and prayed that Oscar was making his way toward the adjacent ledge. He started up the steep trail, making his way over massive boulders and along tricky paths that were mere sand and gave way when he put his weight on them. At one point he had to climb up by grabbing a half-dead cactus that threatened to come out of the ground. The needles stuck in his hand.

Finally, Jack climbed to a level spot and there, in front of what looked like a cave entrance, was Tommy, dirty, and frightened.

"You made it," he said.

He reached down behind a boulder and pulled out a pistol.

"Come on, kid," Jack said. "You must be really afraid of something. Suppose you tell me what it is."

"Can I trust you?"

"I thought you already made that decision."

"Yeah, I did, but now I'm not so sure. I don't really know you."

"So you're taking a chance," Jack said. "But one thing's for sure. You do know Lucky and his pals. They've got Jennifer, right?"

Tommy got up and walked back and forth in front of the cave.

"It's not that simple," he said. "I need assurances, Jack."

"Come on, Tom, we're wasting time."

Tommy stopped, looked at him, and then shook his head and started pacing again.

Jack noticed something familiar about him, but couldn't place it. Then he knew. Tommy was covered with the same green dust that had been on Ole Big and Zollie back at the Jackalope. And there was something about his vocabulary. It was that of a different person than the kid he'd met at the Red Sombrero. Would a teen-aged kid use the word "assurances"? Jack wondered again about his skin, which seemed somehow different than it had been only a day ago. There was something gray about it, like the skin of a friend he'd seen years ago, a friend who died of alcoholism. Before he died his skin had become gray and pouchy, like popped Bubble Wrap. There were blisters on Tommy's neck, too, and some kind of weird rash on his forearms.

"What kind of assurances?"

"Look, Jack, I already figured you must be some kind of cop. I need to know that whatever happens I won't be prosecuted. If you can't offer me that, get somebody who can."

Jack looked at him and Tommy looked away, at the ground, as though he was ashamed of even asking for immunity.

"I can't promise you that until I hear what you're offering," Jack said.

Tommy laughed in a hapless way. "I knew you were going to say that," he said. "You're a cop, right?"

"Yeah, I am. Tell me what you've got and we can make a deal of some kind." Jack said.

"They're going to kill me if I talk to you," Tommy said.

"I can protect you," Jack tried to reassure him, "but you have to tell me everything."

"I don't know where to begin, man," Tommy said.

Then the kid glanced down at his blistered arms and began to cry.

"Look at me," he said. "Look at my fucking skin. I look like a fucking dingo."

Oscar fell down in the sand. Sand he had assumed was a solid rock but which somehow gave way the second he stepped on it. His ankle twisted under him and he grunted with a flash of pain.

"*Madre de Dios,*" he said.

He made his way forward slowly. He saw the ledge above and across from him, still pretty far away. But he could see Jack and the kid up there, silhouetted against the sky. He looked to his right and left, saw nobody. So maybe it wasn't a setup after all. Maybe the kid was for real.

He stood up and the pain in his right ankle was so intense he nearly cried out.

In agony, he climbed farther, the pain almost unbearable.

He staggered on, suddenly terrified that he would be late and that his partner and best friend, his real true amigo, would die because he couldn't climb for shit.

Tommy sucked in his breath, looked at Jack seriously, then made his decision.

"Okay, a lot of this is nuts, but I'm just going to tell you the part you need to know first. What's happening to your girl. Okay?"

"Yeah."

"All right. I heard Lucky talking to this guy who came by the other day. They sometimes talk right in front of me 'cause they think I'm some kind of fucked-up retard who doesn't know anything. They said they had another 'lamb for the slaughter.' Said it like it was a joke, you know? But it wasn't any joke. Trust me. "

"What did they mean?" Jack asked, suddenly feeling sick.

"They were talking about the night of rebirth. They said that the big night was the winter solstice, you see? I looked it up. It's December twenty-first. That's tomorrow night."

"Go on."

"They mentioned Jennifer Wu, too. How she was going to make the party so much cooler."

"Sounds like they mean to kill her. Have they ever done anything like that before?"

"No . . . no . . . You don't understand. I've only been here a little over a year myself. I'm not saying I wasn't involved but there's a lot of levels to what's going on. I was just at level one. So I don't know anything. At least that's what they think. They made me a gofer."

Tommy began to laugh wildly, as though this was the funniest joke in the world. "It's funny? Doncha see that?"

"Sure," Jack said. "I see. They think you're stupid, but they don't know shit, right?"

"Exactly," Tommy said. He looked up at the sky and opened his arms. "A whole world of possibilities, Mr. Harper. You see that? A whole world of them. That's how it looks at first. Then you end up a guy with a bad memory, a delivery boy . . . And your skin looks like a dying dingo dog somewhere in the outback. You see how it goes?"

"What went wrong?" Jack asked. "What did Lucky promise you?"

Tommy began to giggle like a kid on glue.

"Lucky? Lucky? He promised me the fucking world, man. But he didn't tell me what I had to do to get it."

Tommy looked fractured. He began to shake his head and stared at Jack as though he had never seen him before.

"The Nombees," he said. "They're part of it, man."

"Nombees?" Jack asked.

"Yeah, and the Sazis, or something like that. A tribe."

"The Anasazi? That's an ancient New Mexican tribe," Jack said. "That it?"

But Tommy suddenly looked far away. There was a skewed geometry to his jaw as he bit his lip.

"What's going to happen tomorrow night, Tom?" Jack asked.

"Things, dude," Tommy said. "Things that only a cartoon could understand."

"And where?" Jack continued. "Tell me the place."

Tommy smiled and stumbled near the edge of the cave.

"Where is not known at this juncture," he said. "They think that Dumb Tomcat doesn't understand. But that's where they are so wrong. Though all the connections are misfiring I can still find a thread now and again."

"I know you can," Jack said. "Tell me."

Tommy smiled a cunning grin.

"Under," Tommy said. "Way down in the deep under. I need assurances, Jack. And I need a new name, a new face, and a new latchkey. 'Cause from this sordid place, I must be gone."

As he got closer to his shooting spot, Oscar saw the flash of gunmetal off to the right, on the ridge. He squinted and looked over the rocks. There it was. A gun and a man holding and aiming it. Oscar scrambled up the trail, tried to stand. He pulled himself up by a half-dead-looking plant, which immediately loosed itself from the ground. Oscar went tumbling down the hill. As he rolled over and over he thought of Jack and Jill. But there wasn't a pail of freaking *agua* in sight.

"We've got to stop this thing." Jack said. "Under where?"

"You made a pun," Tommy said. "Underwear? Hahaha. See, I still have a semblance."

Jack squinted at him. The kid was staring at his arms again, and had begun to pick his scabs. As though whatever drugs they'd been giving him were still scraping along his blood vessels.

"Tommy, I *will* help you. I'm FBI," he said. (And wondered how long he would be, after this debacle.)

"Efrem Zimbalist Jr.," Tommy said. "Once upon a time my favorite show."

"Efrem Zimbalist? How the hell do you remember that?" Jack asked. "It was on forty years ago."

Tommy looked at him and laughed bitterly.

"Maybe I saw it on a DVD," he said. "Maybe not. I can't quite remember anymore."

Jack couldn't waste any more time on it.

"Tom, the place, the time," Jack said. "Focus, kiddo. You want the assurances, you got to help me save Jennifer Wu, you dig?"

"Kiddo?" Tommy said. "He called me kiddo. Isn't that sweet? Okay, fuck it. No way I can let them do that girl."

He looked down at his shoes. Then at Jack's.

"An untied shoe is very worrisome on a hillside," he said.

Jack let his eyes drop and saw that his right lace was untied. To humor Tommy he knelt down.

Tommy looked at him and smiled.

"I recall a couple of places but there's this one, an ancient place that's so amazing. I'm pretty sure it will be the place. The place of all places. The proper and right place for a ceremony to be held."

A shot rang out in the canyon. A single, silver sound. Tommy lurched forward, a look of surprise on his face, a red hole in his shoulder.

"Oh, Jesus," he said. "Oh, dude . . . They're with us, Jack."

Another shot barely missed Jack, who scrambled back into the safety of the cave.

"C'mon, Tom," he yelled. "Back here."

"No way. Bye-bye, Mr. FBI."

"Don't go down there, Tom."

But it was too late. Tommy hurried down the side of the hill and disappeared from Jack's view.

In the distance, Jack heard another shot, but he didn't venture out to see if Tommy had been hit.

Oscar clawed his way back up the hill. He was so filled with adrenaline that he didn't feel any pain at all. The shot? Jack?

He saw the shooter headed down the hill now, off to his left. He was still carrying his rifle. He seemed to be chasing someone.

Oscar found a small level spot, knelt, and aimed his gun at the figure as it fled toward the canyon bottom and a black Hummer.

Oscar aimed, led him just a little, and fired.

The shooter cried out and fell into a patch of blue flowers.

As Oscar moved forward, he saw that the shooter was up again and limping down the path. There was no way Oscar could get a second good shot. The gunman leaped into the Hummer and took off, driving fast toward the highway.

Chapter Twenty

Newly flush and stoned on Vikes, Johnny Z had been playing pool at Manny's basement joint on Francisco Street for two hours and had whipped everyone in the house. He'd knocked off a couple of weirdo St. Johnnie's students in eight ball, and he'd beaten a guy down on vacation from New York who thought he was hot shit. Used a lot of street language, and when he made a shot he said, "Bada bing," which Johnny was certain he'd gotten from reruns of *The Sopranos*. Ultra lame.

His Vikes were running down a little and he was about to leave when he heard a cultivated voice speaking to him from behind.

"Would you care to play a game of eight ball, my boy?"

Johnny turned and saw a skinny, older man with white hair and pale blue veins in his temples. He was dressed in some kind of Western hipster outfit circa 1958, with a black vest and a skinny white tie with a silver bull bolo at the top. His pants were black and tapered and on his feet he wore black patent shoes with Cuban heels at least a half-inch high.

The guy's arms were stick thin but his hands were large and his fingers surprisingly long and elegant.

There was something about him that got your attention, Johnny thought, but hell, it was all superficial. The guy was pushing eighty. How good could he be?

"Sure, I'll play," Johnny said. "Wanna lay fifty on it? You know, just to make it interesting."

"Why, that sounds like a splendid idea," the old man said. "By the way, my name is Marty. Marty Millwood."

"Johnny Z." He snapped off the Z in an ultra cool manner.

"Whoa, a pool player's name if ever I heard one. Wouldn't you say so, Millie?"

Marty had turned and spoken to an older, heart-shaped-sunglass-wearing, red-headed woman who stood by his side.

"Oh, yes, I would," she laughed. A deep, throaty, actressy laugh. Yeah, Johnny thought, probably played some rep company somewhere once, dreamed of being a star but didn't have the talent to pull it off. He looked her up and down. In her seventies he bet, but still quite slim and had a nice pair of breasts and a kind of sexy wide mouth. She must have been a looker in her day, back in the 1800s, Johnny thought.

"This is my wife, Millie," Marty said.

"The Millie and Marty Show," Millie introduced them, doing a Betty Boop bow.

They both laughed as though they were pleased by their own ineffable wit. Johnny took fifty dollars from his wallet.

"Lag for break?" he asked.

"Excellent," Marty responded.

This forced, fake, colloquial speech was really annoying the hell out of Johnny. Who the fuck did the guy think he was, anyway? Henry the fucking Eighth?

"Here's my dough," Johnny said, handing the fifty to Millie to show what a trusting guy he was.

"And here's mine," Marty said. He reached into his pants pocket and pulled out a bankroll as thick as a brick. Johnny's eyes opened wide. Why, there must be a couple of grand or even more there. The old geezer was loaded!

Marty handed his fifty to Millie, who smiled and held the bills tight.

Oh, man, Johnny thought, he was going to enjoy beating the hell out of the old dude. And maybe there was a way to get some more of that roll.

Unfortunately for Johnny, the beating had to be postponed. Marty won the lag, and then knocked in two striped balls on the break. He proceeded to knock in two more before he missed.

He wasn't bad, Johnny thought. He had control of the cue ball, and he had a clean, true stroke. But by the fourth ball his stick wavered a little. Probably some old fuck's palsy or something. Millie watched silently, sucking in her breath once or twice when her husband made a shot.

But now it was Johnny's turn, He had a clear run in front of him. In fact, Marty had done him a favor, clearing away all the blocking balls. It would be a snap to hit the four, roll a little way to the left of the five, then put a little topspin on the cue ball and head down the rail for the three.

It would be easy as hell.

But then Johnny got a notion. The old man was here to bet, but if he lost . . . he might walk away. Now was the time to play the hustle. Johnny was certain of it. And he knew exactly how he'd do it.

He'd be the wiseass kid who talks a better game than he shoots. He'd play Mr. Overconfidence, and watch old Marty swell up when he beat the young gun.

Johnny laughed and pointed at the table.

"Shouldn't have missed, Marty," he said. "You left me a clear run. And you know I ain't about to blow it."

He gave a blowhard's smile and leaned over for his first shot. Bang, the four went right in the corner pocket. He watched as his cue ball settled in front of the five, an easy duck. He stroked it beautifully, ran the cue ball down the rail and was nicely set up for the three. He looked at Marty with a supercocky grimace, then sized up the angle, picked up the stick, and shot. Too hard. Just barely too hard, but too hard, nonetheless. Not only did he miss but he'd set Marty up for his run. Three balls in a row and an easy shot on the eight ball, which Marty hit gently into the side pocket.

Johnny made a point of being a bad sport.

"Nice game but you know you were damned lucky, old man. Why, if I hadn't missed that duck, you know I was going to run right out."

"Yes," Marty Millwood said, picking up his cash. "There is no doubt whatsoever about that. Wouldn't you say so, Millie?"

"Absolutely, I would," Millie said. "If he hadn't missed that one he had a clear table. The only thing is . . . he did miss. That's the difference sometimes."

Johnny looked at her with a hostile sneer.

"The difference between what?"

"Between those who talk it, and those who walk it," Millie said.

Now Johnny didn't have to act. A violent sensation shot through his brain. How he was going to enjoy this . . . the old hag!

"Well," he said, "if you guys think Marty is so hot, maybe you'd like to play again?"

"I don't see why not, young man," Marty agreed. "Do you have objections, my dear?"

"None at all," Millie said. "In fact, I look forward to another contest between the young and the . . . how shall we say it?"

"The seasoned, Mill," Marty said. "The young and the seasoned."

Johnny felt like wrapping his cue around Marty's veiny neck. The young and the seasoned. He couldn't wait to whip up on this old son of a bitch. Reminded him of his old man, Woody, the hippie car thief and junkie. Always ragging on the kids, always putting him down. Well, he'd shown him, put his hands right around his neck and squeeeeeeezed.

Like he would with Millwood, the pretentious old fart.

But not just yet.

They played the next game for a hundred bucks, "just to make it interesting," Millwood said, using Johnny's own words against him. Johnny played like an overeager lunatic, as though rage had taken over his mind and he couldn't tell one shot from the next.

He really *was* angry, furious even, but he easily could have reined it in and beaten Millwood.

It was too soon, though. There was big money here; he just knew it. A good hustler always knows precisely when to strike, and Johnny Z had always been one of the best.

He was the man, wasn't he? You know he was, and he was going to bring down this old white-haired asshole and his goofy wannabe Lolita bitch, once and for all.

But not yet. Not in game two, and not in game three, which they played for another yard, and which Johnny lost again.

"Okay," he said. "You got me for two fifty. That's a lot of cabbage. I want a shot at winning it back. I'll play you one game for a grand. I'll show you. You'll see."

He slammed his hand down on the table in a parody of barely controlled rage.

The older man watched and rubbed his jaw.

"A thousand," he said. "Why, that's quite a hefty sum, John."

"Hey, you've already beaten me twice. It's not much of a man who doesn't give his opponent a shot to win it back."

"I don't know," Marty said. "What do you think, Mill?"

Millie looked at Marty and took a sip of her Negro Modelo.

"That is a real head of lettuce," she said. "But I think you should give Johnny Z here a shot, Mart. The only thing is we can't do it today. You have to lead the council at five and it's four twenty now."

"Oh, my goodness," Marty said. "I'm afraid we have to go, Mr. Z."

"Hey," Johnny said, feeling a little panicky, "you some kinda hustler or something?"

"Me?" Marty admonished. "Heck, no. Tell you what, give me your number and I'll call you soon and then we can play again. At my place."

"Your place?" Johnny asked, suspicious.

"Why not?" Marty countered. "I have one of the best rooms around, and a table like you've never seen. I think you'll find it a unique experience."

He smiled at Johnny in such an affable way that he couldn't be denied.

"Okay, then," Johnny said. "Where do you live?"

"The Blue Wolf," Marty said. "Bungalow five. You know the place?"

"Sure I do," Johnny said. "No problem." He looked at Marty suspiciously, but finally gave him his cell phone number.

"Perfect," Millie said, blowing Johnny a kiss. "I'll make us a nice dinner. You're gonna love it, Johnny. Trust me."

Johnny nodded but felt funny inside. What the fuck was going on? Were they blowing him off, hustling his ass? These two old creeps?

He'd like to follow them outside and grab that bankroll. But maybe . . . maybe this way would be better. He'd get inside their home. No telling what kind of valuable stuff they'd have in there. Artwork and rugs, all kinds of stuff he could boost. Yeah, this could be just the beginning.

It was going to work out fine.

"I trust you both," he said. "Just make sure you call me."

"Fine, John," Marty said. "We both look forward to it. Bye now."

The two oldsters smiled and headed out of the pool room. Johnny smiled, then hit the cue ball into the eight and drove it deep into the corner pocket.

Just like the ace he was.

Chapter Twenty-one

Phil was hanging out at the bar looking for trim when it occurred to him that this Blue Wolf joint wasn't a hangout type of place. What he needed was to take a class, like yoga, or meditation. That's where all the broads would be. Of course.

(Meanwhile he kept thinking of Dee Dee, out again with Ziko, probably doing some kind of Kama Sutra thing with him. God, it made him want to break the little fuck's head like a melon.)

He picked a schedule up at the front desk. There was Pilates in an hour. He knew all about that. He'd been doing it for the last five years, before he sold out and retired. Supposed to improve your core strength. But he noticed that a lot of the women who did it weren't very feminine. They were superaggressive business execs, probably ate men for lunch. So Pilates was out. What else did they offer? Oh, here's one. Kundalini Expression: The Art of Zen Sitting.

That should be easy, and maybe there would be some cute chicks in the class.

Phil headed into the Crystal Desert Room. That was clever, the way they turned the desert idea—a bunch of cactus and fucking sand—into a crystal desert, like it was the magical seat of all learning. Sort of what he used to do in his old business days. Give a shithole a good name and watch the folks come running.

His place was called the Evergreen Retirement Community. He'd hired a local hack artist who had painted pictures of big strong evergreen trees with some attractive old people wearing sweaters tied around their waists, holding golf clubs and tennis racquets. He had insisted that they have stunning white teeth and attractive, muscular builds—unlike the real old folks who lived in the snake pit of a building. Most of the denizens of Evergreen were hugely obese old slobs who spent all day eating Twinkies and pounding down the swill he served at dinner. That was another of his gimmicks. "All you can eat" at dinner hour. He got the food cut-rate from a wholesale "meal maker" in Hamilton, Ohio. Third-rate hams, second-rate chickens, and half-dead veggies, and since he bought these "gourmet delights" in bulk he was able to practically give away the food. Of course, he made it up on the exorbitant prices he charged for the condos and the two-bedroom "villas" he sold to the old folks. Between that and the money he soaked them for on their private insurance, he was raking in the dough. The old-folks business was really terrific back in Ohio, but he had to admit it was even slicker down here in the Southwest. Here they not only soaked you for the rooms and booze but they had the phony spiritual thing going as well. What's more, the people who worked here almost seemed to believe it.

Once in the classroom, Phil soon found what he was looking for, a really cute blonde from Sacramento. Her name was Annie. She was in her forties, had the most adorable Doris Day nose, and a really nice figure. She seemed like a real nice girl, too. She told him all about her husband who had died suddenly last winter of a heart attack while snowmobiling up in Seattle. Perfect.

They sat next to each other in the lotus position—well, Phil was *sort of* in the lotus position—and he thought they had a real vibe going.

The Zen master was a Japanese guy. There seemed to be as many Japs here as Mexes. Guess the crystal desert just lent itself to any fantasy you wanted to lay on it. American Indians, Mexicans, Japs. Ain't it funny that in America all the losers are mystics? After you kill about a million of them you sentimentalize the rest.

Anyway, the guy's name was Sensei Larry. Come to think of it, he might have been Japanese-Indian; they had all kinds of mutts down here.

He was very serious and spoke in a flower-soft voice about getting to the core of oneself by breathing in and out and getting the chakras, which were in your back, to rise up.

During the whole "sit," Phil kept stealing little peeks at Annie, who was breathing in deeply. Oh, what nice breasts she had!

She smiled at him once and whispered, "Take this seriously, Phil. You'll learn a lot about yourself."

Well, why the hell not, Phil thought. He'd get into the breathing and holding his back erect and maybe he would have some kind of mystical vision. He could be as spiritual as the next asshole.

He breathed in deeply seven times as instructed, and let it out slowly. Waiting, waiting for a vision. What would it be? A flower? A many-petaled flower that showed the, uh . . . many-petaled layers of existence? Or some kind of mystical animal? A jaguar? A peacock? A prancing caterpillar?

Phil listened to Sensei Larry's voice, low and reassuring. He knew for sure he was going to see something, something he could share with Annie to show her he was a sensitive guy, and pretty soon she'd be sucking his cock like a cheerleader under the stands at halftime.

The thing to do is keep the eyes closed and concentrate on seeing the void. No, not seeing it, *becoming* it. He'd read enough Zen books back in college to get it. You had to not see it, because then you were, like, not *in it*. The way to be *in it* was to *be it*.

You were not a viewer, you were the view, or some bullshit like that.

Phil scrunched up his eyes and tried, really tried (knowing that he shouldn't be trying but come on!) to become the void, or whatever, and see (no, not see, *be*) the many-petaled rose.

He felt his knee killing him from back when he played football. He felt his heart beating way too fast and wondered if anyone had ever dropped dead trying too hard to relax.

He just bet they had. (Or, even worse, maybe he would be the first!)

He shut his eyes harder, practically squashing his eyeballs.

He had to get it right.

Had to see, be nothing.

He rocked back and forth a little now, chanting a makeshift mantra (Go, Buckeyes, Go!), and trying to lose all self-consciousness, and lo and behold he began to have a vision in his third eye. At least he thought it was his third eye. That was what the other meditators were always talking about around Blue Wolf. How do you stimulate the third eye? How do you make it see, really see? How did the ancient Babylonians do it? How did they get the old third eye going, flashing amazing visions of a world past ours, the third eye that Hitler had sought as well, the third eye that could show you . . . show you . . . well, Phil wasn't quite sure what it could show you, but something really great and way beyond having biscuits and gravy at Bob Evans in Ohio.

And now, yes, there it was. A vision taking shape right in the middle of his head, exactly where the third eye was supposed to be.

He could see it forming but it was still kind of misty and ill-shaped. Try harder to try less, Phil thought.

Or is it try less to try harder?

Whatever, he could see it now . . . a vision, starting to really shape up. He kind of half expected the vision to be something like Sensei Lar was talking about: the big open flower of reality! It had to be that!

Only now the mist was clearing and he could really see the thing . . . oh, yeah, now he could *really* see it, and it wasn't a rose or any kind of flower. It was . . . oh, shit . . . fucking Thelma Jackson.

It was her, in all her tattered glory. The sixty-eight-year-old woman who had started a movement against Phil and the entire Evergreen community. Yes, the woman who had signed up fifty, then sixty, then over a hundred and fifty old people who lived at Evergreen. People who followed her into battle against Phil and the Evergreen lifestyle. Yes, Thelma, the evil bitch, who had attacked Phil for not taking care of the rooms, for not maintaining the light fixtures, for hiring sadistic ex-criminals to be on staff at the cheesy dump. (Ex-criminals were so much cheaper.)

Thelma, who said the food was shitty, that the doctors were tenth-rate, and that the on-site grocery store was the biggest rip-off of all time. Thelma Jackson who went to the papers and television and made the goddamned state inspectors come down on Evergreen like killer mosquitoes, probing and prodding and asking questions that Phil couldn't answer.

That bitch cost him millions of dollars in fixes, not to mention the deep embarrassment of being known as a slumlord, the sworn enemy of old folks not only in Ohio but all over the United States of America.

And Thelma Jackson had received some kind of good citizen's medal, while Phil got loads of shit dumped on his head.

And now he had to see her in his supposedly crystal, mystic vision.

His head reeled and he felt his breath come hard as he opened his eyes.

Next to him Annie, of the cute nose and double-pert breasts, smiled, opened her eyes, and said, "I saw myself a thousand years ago. I was an Indian princess in Bombay!"

"That's great," Phil said. "That's just fucking great."

"What did you see, Phil?" Annie asked, smiling in her innocent way.

"I saw . . . I saw a great desert," Phil said. "And coming across it was this . . . this woman in a white caftan, and she beckoned to me. She really did. At first I couldn't see her face at all, but then she got closer and closer and I saw her. And she was . . . she was you, Annie. She really was. It was as though you had something wonderful to teach me."

Christ, Phil thought, what total, weak bullshit. She'd see right through that. For sure.

But no, Annie was smiling. A three-hundred-watt smile now. Man, she ate it right up.

"Did you really see me, Phil?" she asked, beaming.

"I sure did," Phil said. "I felt it when I walked in here today, but I wasn't really one-hundred percent sure until I had my vision. What is it you want to teach me, sweetheart?"

She reached over and touched his hand. Her skin was warm, nurturing.

"I can't tell you now, Phil. But I want to see you, so much. I felt the same kind of thing when you walked in. Can I call you a little later? I have a surprise for you!"

"You bet you can," Phil said. He quickly gave her his cell phone number.

Phil was so excited he was nearly out of his skin.

"Don't worry, sweetheart," he said. "I'll be waiting for your call."

Chapter Twenty-two

Jack and Oscar took a walk on the square and sat on a bench in the park. The shooter had escaped and they had looked for Tommy for an hour but found only his cycle tracks. Tracks that disappeared into the desert.

"He's probably out of the state by now."

"Yeah," Jack said, "but we really need to find out what he was talking about. He told me about this ceremony tomorrow night. The winter solstice. I think he was talking about somebody using Jennifer as a human sacrifice."

"Jesus. He never gave any clue where it was going to be held?"

"Yeah, he did. 'Under,' he said. Underground, somewhere."

"What else?"

"Well, he mentioned the Anasazi Indians. The ancient tribe from New Mexico. And something else. The Nombee?"

"Jesus," Oscar said. "It's not Nombee . . . it's gotta be the Namba . . . the Tupinamba."

Jack looked at him in shock.

"How the hell do you know that?"

"I studied Latin American culture at UCLA, partner. I was thinking about being a diplomat at one time. I was hoping I might get a post in Brazil. I even went down there on a student exchange deal one semester. I found out all about the Tupinamba. They were a very well-organized tribe in the rain forest. Mostly were naked and self-sufficient. But there were a lot of wars with other tribes. Eventually most of them were wiped out."

"That's fascinating, but what the hell does it have to do with Jennifer's kidnapping?"

Oscar stood up and began to pace.

"I don't know. I wish I hadn't spent so much of my time in college comparing brews. I know more about freaking beer than what I studied. But there was something . . . I know it. C'mon, amigo. We got to do some research."

In Oscar's room they did a Google search on "Tupinamba." Within seconds they had thousands of sites. The first few said basically the same things that Oscar had remembered.

Then they came to another site. Oscar pounded the desk.

"Look at this."

The link said: "Tupinamba prisoners."

Oscar began to read aloud.

The Tupinamba seemed to be one of the most enlightened tribes. If they took a prisoner, they gave him a house, food, and a woman to sleep with, and, basically, treated him like an honored guest. For years this is all anyone knew of them. They seemed civilized compared to the other tribes. But anthropologist Mark A. Reynolds of the University of California, Berkeley, found evidence that there was one more step in the prisoner's incarceration. After being wined and dined and treated like a prince, he was, on an appointed day, tied to a stake, burned alive, and eaten by the Tupinamba tribal members.

"Holy shit," Jack said. "And the Anasazi?"

"I don't know about them. I always thought they were peaceful. There was something about them that I read once, though. They believed they had discovered the secret to eternal life. Some kind of black magic."

Oscar quickly Googled that, too, and found a connection to the Tupinamba. Within seconds they were reading about how recent scholarship had destroyed the ancient myth of the Anasazi as ancient, peace-loving Indians.

"Listen to this. 'The Anasazi Indians of New Mexico and Arizona believed they had found the secret of eternal life.'" Oscar scrolled down the page. "Jesus, look here! 'By eating the flesh of their victims they took part in what they called sacred cannibalism. They took their enemies' spirit and youth. They believed that through this ritual they could return to their own youth and live forever.'"

The two men looked at each other in shock.

"That's madness," Oscar said. "Who would believe such a thing now?"

Jack shook his head. "I'll tell you who. People who are going to die. Old people looking for the answer to the most terrifying question in the world: Why must I die? And it's been there all along, staring us right in the face. Christ, they even have a department at Blue Wolf called Ancient Ways, run by that woman Sally Amoros."

"But you said that no one would care that they didn't have the answer to aging."

"Exactly," Jack said. "No one would. Everyone knows it's a sham, a mere cosmetic procedure, a kind of make-believe weekend in which older people pretend they can become young again. No one would kill anyone for telling people that it was all bullshit. But what if they really could reverse the clock? What if they had found something that worked, or half worked anyway? That's got to be it, Oscar. Think of Tommy, his skin . . . half old, half . . . something else. Maybe he was in the middle of changing. He told me there are many levels. You see?"

"Many levels? So maybe it's like if you pay so much you get to turn the clock back ten years? But if you pay more you get the full treatment? You get to become really young?"

"It must be something like that. They must be using young people's body parts as replacements for older ones. And somehow cannibalism has to be a part of what they do. And now I see something else. Why was Kim Walker so anxious to get me to go back to the Jackalope? To make me think that this whole thing was about girls being sent into prostitution."

"A wild-goose chase?"

"Exactly. And the pig. They must have some kind of animal testing lab somewhere around here, too. They were using Ole Big as a test animal and Zollie was trying to save him, but they had already operated on him. That's why his intestines were gone. It's wild but it all adds up."

"That means it isn't Lucky," Oscar said. "He couldn't come up with any of this."

"That's right," Jack said, "but he could use his bikers to grab the people for somebody who then did the operations."

"Alex Williams and Blue Wolf," Oscar said. "But Lucky and Alex hate one another."

"At least that's what they want us to believe," Jack said. "Maybe that fight they had in the Red Sombrero was staged. And now that I think about it, that woman I saw in the hospital, Mary Jo. She said they promised her she'd be young again. Not *feel* young again but really *be* young. She even showed me a picture of herself as a girl. Said they'd make her look like that again."

Oscar shook his head.

"Okay, I don't say I buy it all, but just theoretically what does all this have to do with them kidnapping Michelle Wu?"

Jack looked hard at Oscar, and smiled.

"What did you just say?"

"Oh, right, I said Michelle Wu but I meant Jennifer. Just a slip of the tongue, amigo."

"No," Jack said. "You just might be a genius, Oscar."

"What do you . . . You mean that they may have kidnapped . . ."

"Yes, whoever did this might have kidnapped Jennifer Wu by mistake. Maybe Michelle found out about their secret, and maybe she tried to deal herself in."

"That sounds like our girl," Oscar said.

"Doesn't it?"

"So maybe Lucky sent his boys out to grab her and they picked up her sister by mistake."

"Then her sister knows nothing at all about any of this."

"Maybe. Or maybe they're both involved. Anyway, once they took Jennifer they couldn't very well give her back. She's got to die. We've got to get to Michelle fast. Find out what she really knows."

"Hell," Oscar said, "they could pick her up, too."

Jack dialed Michelle's cell phone number. The phone rang but there was no answer.

"Come on, Osc. Let's get back to the hotel and see if she's waiting for us there."

As they headed out Jack felt a sinking sensation in his heart. This time he had really risked something of himself with her. This time he had been really convinced that she was going to try and change her ways.

Instead, if their speculations were right, she had played him for a bigger sucker than ever.

It was probably her own machinations that had got her sister kidnapped. And the reason that she had gotten Jack involved instead of calling the local cops? Easy. She knew she could manipulate his feelings for her so that she could stay out of jail.

And if there *was* a formula for turning back the clock, and somehow Alex Williams had stumbled upon it, it was a sure bet that Michelle wanted it for herself.

That was how she really was, Jack had to remind himself. In spite of their lovemaking up in his room, in spite of the way she looked at him and her lost little girl routine . . . in spite of all that, Michelle was a predator.

And anyone, even those she loved, who got in her way became her prey.

Chapter Twenty-three

Things were going downhill for Kevin. First he got a D on a quiz about George Orwell's *1984*. Then he got reamed out by his coach for not scooping loose balls at practice.

He knew he was falling apart but he just didn't care. All he could think about was Vicki Hastings. He was already thinking of getting into her car with her and touching her soft white panties and sticking his finger inside of her, the way she moaned and moved . . .

God, it was so fantastic. There was nothing else like it. Who could study, or read about how the world was going to be taken over by "doublethink," when soon he would be in her house, fucking her in the bed, on the floor, and on the dining room table.

He was obsessed. He was completely obsessed and wanted her all the time.

But tonight was the worst. She had told him that her husband was bored with her and, worse, that he had smacked her in the face with the back of his hand and called her a "dumb cunt."

Kevin couldn't believe it. He held Vicki close to him in bed as she cried and said, "You're all I have. I'm so afraid of him."

Kevin was deeply shocked. James was beating down on Vicki? That was totally insane.

Kevin propped himself up in bed and said, dead serious, "If he ever hits you again, you tell me and I'll kick his ass all the way down the block and then light him on fire." He'd heard an actor say that line in a gangster movie once. Robert Mitchum maybe. He thought it was cool. Very cool.

But now he wasn't trying to be cool. He really meant it.

She reached down, held his cock, and kissed his mouth.

"My hero," she said.

"I mean it," Kevin said. "I mean it. If he ever hurts you I will kill him."

"Oh, Kevin," she said, and went down on him.

Kevin fondled her breasts as she sucked him, and he felt his mind slip away.

He really would, he thought just then. If fucking James ever hit her again, he would definitely kill the son of a bitch.

Chapter Twenty-four

The blue lights in the hall made everything look surreal. Jennifer didn't know what to think. How long had she been locked away here?

She had no idea.

Was it night or day? She had no idea about that, either. Panic shot through her and she tried her best to breathe in deeply seven times and then let the air out slowly seven times. Something she'd learned long ago when she had first studied meditation.

You could actually lower your heart rate and your blood pressure if you breathed in deeply and slowly let it out, seven and seven.

But it was a hell of a lot harder to do now. God, where was she? Hadn't Michelle told anyone yet?

And then she had a terrible thought. The answer to the Michelle question might well be, "No, she hadn't told anyone. No one." Why? Because maybe she had been snatched by that freak Lucky Avila because of some hustle her sister had tried to run on him. God help her if that was true.

Because if it was, then who could Michelle go to? Not the cops. What would she say? "Oh, officer, could you please help me? My sis was kidnapped by motorcycle gang members because I tried to rip them off in this deal with, uh, stolen bike engines."

The cops would arrest her, and if some of the people she worked with found out she had squealed . . .

But Michelle would surely do something. She'd call someone to help her. Korean pals in Los Angeles, or maybe some of the Chinese gang members she had partnered with at one time or another.

But what could those guys do out here?

Jen felt it building in her again. The freaking fear. She wanted to scream, to rip the bars down with her bare hands.

Simultaneously, she began to recall something, something she had barely heard, and had paid no attention to at the time.

Michelle had been on the phone to Lucky and she had been kind of teasing him, saying, "I know you're up to something. I saw you the other night and I know you're up to something big. What's it called?"

And though she hadn't heard Lucky's end of the conversation Jennifer knew this must have been it. Whatever *it* was.

Now Jennifer recalled the scene even more clearly.

She had been exhausted from work and had had a few drinks when Michelle had made that call. She had been barely able to stay awake but she was sure there was something Michelle said, just before she went to sleep. Something about letters and numbers. Like a code of some kind. B-25? No, that wasn't it. D-32? No, but something like that. And when she had said it, whatever it was, even across the room she could hear Lucky's voice screaming at her.

"You stay away from all that, Michelle. I'm warning you!"

If only she knew what it was. Maybe it was some kind of bargaining chip she could use.

From the next cell she heard Gerri's voice, a mere whisper. "Hey, Jennifer?"

Jennifer went to the corner of the cell. Leaned her face against the cold bars. "I'm here."

"Good. I fell asleep and when I didn't hear you I thought maybe they'd, uh . . ."

"Taken me away?"

"No, let you out."

"'Fraid not. We have to face it, Gerri. They aren't going to let us out. They just can't. There has to be some reason we're in here."

"Thought you said we were gonna become sex slaves?"

"I did, but I don't really believe that. We're too old for that, and too educated."

"Maybe *you* are," Gerri said, "but I got my education at the University of Good Times."

"What do you mean?" Jennifer asked her.

"Hey, I mean like I quit school in the ninth grade and left home the same year. Got my education in the Bronx, working the street."

Jennifer felt a blush come to her face, which, given their dilemma, seemed absurd. But there it was. She was still the good girl.

"You mean you were a—" It was just so hard to say it!

"A hooker? It's okay, you can say it. Yeah, I was for a couple of years, but after I got the hell beat out of me by my pimp I decided to make a career transition."

She gave a rueful laugh and Jennifer found herself laughing with her.

"What did you do next?"

"Became a nuclear scientist," Gerri said.

They both laughed again.

"See, that was when I discovered that once you quit school there aren't too many things you can do. Had a girlfriend wanted to be a lawyer, she had to go all the way back to ninth grade and start over. Found out everyone else was like seven years ahead of her. But you know what? She did it. Me, I didn't have the patience. I just traded hustling my body for hustling drugs and doing some robberies."

Jennifer was really shocked now. Somehow she hadn't expected Gerri to be that much different from her. An innocent, decent person who had been taken off the street. But now it sounded like Gerri was maybe as bad as the people who had snatched them.

And then she had another thought. Maybe Gerri was as bad as her sister.

"You robbed people?"

"Yeah, I did. Home break-ins and stuff. It was real exciting at first. I mean like so exciting that I sort of forgot that it was wrong. I had to climb up ladders and learn how to turn off alarm systems. Lot of stuff like that. And if someone happened to be home I had to—you know—shut 'em up."

Jennifer could hear the degenerate excitement in Gerri's voice, even now.

"How did you do that?"

"Threatened them with a knife or a gun."

Jennifer felt her stomach turn over.

"Did you ever use the knife or the gun?"

There was a long silence and Jen wished she hadn't asked the question.

"Nah," Gerri finally said. "I never had to cap nobody or cut 'em neither."

But there was something in her voice that made Jennifer doubt that was true.

"So how'd you get to Santa Fe?" Jennifer asked.

"Things was getting hot in New York, so I decided to take off. Some people I met tole me that this was a good town for, you know, the stuff I do, 'cause there's a lot of rich, old people here from Hollywood and other places. People with a lot of a disposable income, if you know what I mean."

Jennifer laughed but not in a joyous way. All through Gerri's story Jen had assumed there was going to be a turning point, some place where Gerri admitted that she had done wrong and had seen the light. Somehow, Jen had thought Santa Fe itself would become part of that happy moral. She was just waiting for Gerri to say something about how the spiritual nature of the town had made her turn to the path to goodness. But clearly that wasn't going to be the end of this tale.

Her jail mate was an unrepentant hustler and criminal. Which made her own kidnapping seem all the worse.

What could they possibly have in common? Nothing. She wasn't an evil person . . . but Michelle . . . it kept coming back to Michelle. She had to ask. "Gerri, did you ever know a guy named Lucky Avila?"

There was a pause and Jen thought she could hear a sharp intake of breath.

"You kidding me? You know him, too?"

"So you *did* know him?" Jennifer confirmed.

"Yeah," Gerri said. "He was the guy who got me to come down here to Santa Fe inna first place."

"You're kidding. Lucky Avila, the motorcycle gang leader?"

"That's what he used to be," Gerri said. "He doing a lot more than that now."

"What do you mean?"

"I can't tell you 'bout that."

"Why not?"

"'Cause he tell me not to. See, I'm still hoping he might talk to whoever has put me in here and they'll let me out."

Jesus, Jennifer thought. She's in with Lucky Avila.

"Let me ask you another question," Jennifer said.

"I ain't talking 'bout his new thang, okay?"

"No, fine. I just want to ask you a question. Did you hear about some of the other people who went missing in Santa Fe?"

"Yeah. I even knew one of them. Girl name of Darlene. She was a real crack ho. She disappear about two weeks ago. And a guy too. Darrell."

"And what did Darrell do?"

"Whatchu mean? For a job?"

"Yeah. For a job."

"Darrell was, like, into taking cars."

Jennifer felt a chill shoot up her left arm.

"And this Darrell, did he happen to know Lucky Avila?"

There was a long pause.

"Well, did he?"

"Yeah, he know Lucky, too."

Then Jennifer was certain she heard a gasp.

"Oh, my God," Gerri said. "You think that Lucky had us all put in here?"

"I don't see him getting anyone out," Jen said.

Then she slumped down on her bunk.

"But he was my partner out West for a while. Why would he get me to come down here jest to put me in a jail? That don't make no sense. See, I was making the man money. He would steer me to the houses and me and two other guys inna crew would break in and steal shit. Lucky got his cut."

"You're right," Jen said. "It doesn't make any sense, unless somehow you were more valuable in here than making money out there."

"Shit, girl," Gerri said. "Oh, shit."

"Maybe you better tell me about that new business Lucky's running."

"I can't."

"You can't afford not to. It may be the only thing we can use to keep ourselves alive. You've got to trust me, Gerri."

There was a long silence.

"I'm not sure. Something about a magic formula. Something about making old people young. Crazy stuff like that."

"It had a name, right?"

"I think I heard him say D-35. Something like that. But what's any of that got to do with us in here?"

Jennifer felt a terrible fear invade her like a cancer. She could barely sit up.

"How old were all these people who disappeared?"

"In their twenties. Like me."

Then there was a long silence.

"God," Jennifer said. "They're making this formula, this D-35, out of us?"

There was another long silence, then Gerri said, "Girl, I think you just hit the jackpot."

"Yeah."

Neither of them said anything after that. Jennifer was shaking so hard she couldn't keep her thoughts formulated.

Finally, Gerri broke the silence.

"We gotta get out of here, girl."

In a panicky voice she began to slam her fist into the bars, screaming.

"No," Jennifer said. "We need to be quiet. Think."

Gerri, however, was way beyond the thinking stage. She screamed, cried, and raged.

But not for long.

From the far end of the hallway they both heard the steel door being opened with a key. After the lock clicked, they heard the hinges on the door squeal and both women pressed their heads against the bars to see who was walking in their direction.

But once Jennifer saw who was coming, she wished she hadn't looked. If all the rest of this had been like a bad dream, this was the part where you could no longer keep the panic down by breathing in and out seven times. The part where the panic and adrenaline ran through her arms and chest into her brain like electric voltage.

Jennifer looked at the man walking down the hall toward them—the man in the black leather shirt and pants, wearing high black boots and a terrifying leather mask on his face with zippers over the mouth and eyes—and she began to scream. It was a purely animal scream, the kind any living thing might let out when it realizes that it's headed for a painful and terrible death.

Then Gerri began to cry and scream. "No, no, no, no . . . please. No, no . . ." over and over again.

But the words did no good at all.

The tall, wiry man with the black leather mask and the unzipped eyeholes took a ring of keys from his black leather belt and opened Gerri's cell.

Jennifer suddenly found her voice and screamed at him, "Leave her alone. Leave her alone."

But that did no good, either.

She saw him go into the cell, and she heard Gerri let out a terrible scream.

She heard what sounded like an electric *zaaaaap*.

Then he was out of the cell again, carrying Gerri over his shoulder. In his right hand was a Taser stun gun.

Jennifer stood as close to the bars as she could, not out of bravery but because she was too terrified to move. Neither her feet nor her arms nor anything else on her body was capable of motion. It was almost as though she had been hit with the Taser, too.

The leather man turned and looked directly at her.

He grunted, a terrible noise that sounded as though the beast was laughing at her.

Then he turned and carried Gerri down the hallway and through the steel door, which closed with a terrible clang.

Jennifer began to scream again, screamed from a fear she hadn't known even existed.

Now she was utterly alone. And the very next in line.

Chapter Twenty-five

Phil heard from Annie. She was so cool, and she called him Philip, which was oddly thrilling.

"Tonight, Philip," she said. "Eight o'clock in Room 101, downstairs in the residence building."

He had asked her what was happening there, but she just teased him.

"Can't tell you. It wouldn't be a surprise then, would it?"

Phil felt just like a kid going on a first date. Excited, scared, jittery, and barely able to wait.

Now he paced on his small balcony, looking out at the stars and the mountains. The rest of this trip was going to be so far removed from the first part. He could hardly believe how much things had changed.

Annie made him feel so young. So virile.

Great. It was going to be just great!

He started imagining taking Annie's blouse off as he kissed her shoulders. The fantasy was so intense he barely noticed Dee Dee come in the front door. She shut it ever so gently, and Phil thought about how when you knew someone like he knew Dee Dee you could tell when they did the "guilty shut." Yeah, that was it. Just a little more finesse than she ordinarily would use to show her husband that she was still a caring and decent person, but a little too decent and a little too caring for Dee Dee, the bitch!

"Philly?" she called, her voice in the "guilty sweet," too high register.

"Out here, baby," Phil said, going for the mocking but not too mocking voice so she couldn't tell if he was psychotically angry or not.

She pranced out onto the balcony, looking kind of too fresh. He knew the look. It was the fresh-makeup-and-combed-hair look, the identity a guilty woman assumed after fucking her brains out for the last five hours.

He took a deep breath and smiled at her.

"Did you and Kiki have fun?"

"His name is Ziko, as you well know, Phil," she said, plopping down in the recliner and looking out at the lovely mountains.

"Yes, of course," he said. "Did you have a good time?"

"You bet," she said. "What did you do, nap?"

The way she snapped out "nap" was unbearable. It sounded all hard-edged and metallic, like two pieces of chrome banging together. "Nap," as in "you old piece of shit who can't get it up anymore, Flaccid Guy!"

Phil felt his temperature rise. The way she had pushed and pushed him to make the business successful. The way she had made him cut corners. Why, he would have been happy with half the money they sold it for, but Ms. Greedy had to have it all, every goddamned last dime, no matter who they hurt.

And, he thought, looking at her with fresh eyes, they had hurt plenty of people. Hundreds of them—no, be honest, probably thousands of them—over the years.

But it wasn't him. No, it was Ms. Nickel and Dime, gotta have it all. It wasn't him who was greedy.

Was it?

He looked at her sitting there on the patio with her legs propped up on the drinks table. He thought about how he used to live to see those thighs. How important it had been, how impossibly wonderful her breasts had seemed.

But now, now her legs, her breasts, her ass—none of it did a thing for him. Nothing at all.

He thought of Annie, impossibly cute Annie, with whom he would soon be bopping in the boudoir, and he felt such happiness and freedom.

He was still almost young and cool, and he didn't have to listen to this skank ever again.

He started to ease into a wild sexual fantasy about Annie, but Dee Dee's chrome-clank voice cut through his reverie.

"I'm not going to be around tonight," she said. "Ziko and I are dining together at a special party with his friends."

"That's wonderful," Phil said. "May you have a wonderful time together, Dee Dee. And don't worry about me because I've run into someone and I'm also dining out. And I might add she's way hotter than you."

Dee Dee looked horrified. Her lips curled up and her eyes turned into rattlesnake slits.

"You son of a bitch. What is she, some kind of nurse/whore you paid to change your bedpan?"

She threw her cocktail in his face and headed back across the room.

"Have a great night, loser!" she screamed, opening the door.

Phil threw his own glass after her.

His head was splitting, so he popped an Advil. It was all over. This relationship was history. He had a new thing going with lovely, youthful Annie. In a mere two hours!

Better pop a Viagra, too, and get ready to rock and roll!

Chapter Twenty-six

Michelle was furious with Jack. He hadn't called her, and he and Oscar seemed to be running around in circles.

She should have handled this herself all along.

What she needed to do, she had decided, was to stake out Lucky's place until he led her to wherever he was holding Jen. She should have done that in the beginning, really. But she still had a hard time believing that Lucky would take her sister. There was no need for it. She had found out that he was pulling some kind of deal with drugs for the old people at Blue Wolf, some concoction that was supposed to make them feel younger for a while. She had been half kidding when she had mentioned to him that she wanted in on it. It had to be bullshit anyway, right?

But Lucky had become furious, told her that she had no idea what she was getting into. That made her all the more curious, so she had followed him around for a couple of days until she saw him meeting with his supposed enemy, Alex Williams.

She didn't really know what they were up to but she had tortured him a little while they were having sex, telling him again that she wanted in on whatever it was they were doing. That was when he warned her again.

And so she had backed off, had the lunch with him and her sister. But Lucky had gotten furious at her. She had thought it was because they didn't want a threesome but now she understood.

He had gotten angry because he felt the pressure from his boss, Williams.

They had decided to kidnap Jen in order to shut her up.

She had known she could never get Jen back on her own, so she had sent for the most capable man she knew, Jack Harper.

She had believed that Jack would find Jen, bring her back, and the villains would lose their bargaining chip. Then they would have to pay her.

Only Jack hadn't gotten anywhere. And now she had started to really worry. Maybe she had it wrong. Maybe they had no intention of giving Jen back.

It came down to one thing: she would have to get Jen back herself. She would follow the bastard until he went to her sister's prison and she would kill him and they would get away.

Which was what she was doing right now.

She sat on her motorcycle and used her Leupold Wind River binoculars to keep tabs on the entrance of Lucky's hangout, El Coyote. Anywhere Lucky Avila went she was going as well. Maybe it was a lame idea, but at least she was doing something.

And now, after sitting there for two and a half hours, it looked as though her patience was about to pay off. Lucky had just left El Coyote in his black Hummer, with that giant idiot who worked for him at the wheel of the car.

She waited until they were a little way down the highway, then quickly went after them. Thank God it was getting dark. She could stay far enough behind them on the twisting road so they couldn't see her.

Still, she worried that they might catch sight of her on a straight-away, though with her helmet on Lucky probably wouldn't guess who she was.

They had only gone about nine or ten miles, to just beyond the Red Sombrero, when they turned off the road.

She slowed down, waited for them to get a few hundred feet up the road, and then made the turn herself and cruised after them.

This must be it, Michelle thought. There would be some old mine out here, or one of the hundreds of ancient Indian caves. She'd heard of people living in them for years until the government came and threw them out.

But if you were Lucky Avila you could pay off some government worker and no one would be the wiser.

She felt a twinge of excitement. Yes, this was it . . . she was certain.

She recalled something she'd read on the Internet about New Mexico's underground tunnels. Many of them had started out as caves but then various business groups and apocalyptic doomsayers had connected the caves using giant boring machines, something called the "Subterre." It was like a giant submarine, which some sources said was run by both humans and aliens.

Michelle didn't believe any of this, but she had heard of tunnels under the earth from her own grandmother and from other members of the crew she'd been in. After all, there were drug tunnels from Tijuana to San Diego, tunnels with air conditioning.

She knew *that* was true because she'd been in them.

And the Indians of the Taos Pueblo were said to have built an underground system in case the white men who had tried for years to wipe them out should ever come after them again. Just like the tunnels in Vietnam, which saved the villagers from napalm bombs.

It was wild stuff, all of it, but Michelle had been coming to Santa Fe long enough to know that things that sounded like sci-fi or the ravings of a lunatic could often be reality here.

She parked her bike, took out her Glock, and moved through a small passage in the rocks. She was terrified that she would make a telltale noise and that Lucky would pounce on her.

She moved forward through a wash and came to two giant boulders. There was a slender crack between them and she could see out into the endless desert.

There, the moonlight streaming down, she saw Lucky standing above a kneeling, whimpering Zollie.

With his right hand, Lucky stuck his .38 in Zollie's face. In Lucky's left hand was a plastic bag with something in it.

"You took the hog, didn't you?"

Zollie shook his head.

"No, I didn't."

"I told you we needed Biggie. I told you and you just ignored what I said, right?"

"No, honest I didn't," Zollie said. He was crying now and shaking his head back and forth.

"Tell me the truth," Lucky said. "I need to know for sure. If you tell me the truth everything will be all right. I can still protect you."

Zollie wept harder and Michelle felt panic sweep through her. What should she do?

"Tell me now, Zol," Lucky said. "You know you want to."

"All right," Zollie said. "But you promise you'll let me go?"

"Of course I will," Lucky said.

"All right then. I thought if you guys were going to do some experiments on Biggie that you would bring him back afterward. I thought I could nurse him back to health. But when I got him in the car, I saw how cut up he was. So I just drove out of there with him. You understand that, doncha?"

"Of course, I do," Lucky said. "See, that wasn't so bad. So where did you take Biggie?"

"I took him home to bury him."

Without a word, Lucky smashed the gun into Zollie's face, breaking his nose, causing blood to gush down his shirt.

The big man fell over on his side, screaming in a high-pitched wail.

"Liar," Lucky said. "You know you can't lie to me like that. Get up. Back on your knees."

Lucky crawled slowly up to his knees, crying and bleeding.

"Now tell me where you took him," Lucky said.

"I took him to the Jackalope. It was my shift there. I carried him to this place in their old storehouse so nobody would see him in my truck. I looked him over and realized you guys had operated on him. I was going to take him home after my shift and bury him. It was very upsetting. He was like family to me."

"I thought *I* was like family to you, Zollie."

"You were. I mean you are. But he was like a little brother or something. I was gonna give him a nice home-style burial but that guy, Harper, he got in the way."

"Yes, he did," Lucky said. "And if he saw the surgical cuts on the hog, he'll be able to put two and two together."

"No. Wait. I'm almost sure he didn't see anything like that."

"Really?" Lucky prompted.

"Yeah, for sure," Zollie said. "See, it was real dark in there. And I came right in after he got there. I kicked his ass, too."

"I'm sure you did, Zol," Lucky said. "'Cause you are one badass mother. Well, I must say, Zol, this has been very disappointing."

"I'm so sorry, Lucky," Zollie said, weeping.

"I'm sure you are, big guy," Lucky responded.

He put the pistol in his belt and quickly took something out of the bag. Michelle couldn't make out what it was.

"What's that?" Zollie asked, his voice high-pitched again.

"It's a toy," Lucky said. "I believe there just isn't enough play in the world. Everyone is so darn serious."

"That a Super Soaker?" Zollie asked.

"Yep," Lucky said. "You got it, hoss. 'Cept I had it retrofitted by one of the boys to make it a real, honest-to-God grown-up toy!"

"What 'chu going to do?" Zollie asked, shaking and crying.

"Just gonna give you a good soaking," Lucky responded.

"What 'chu got in that thing?"

"Well, I'll give you three guesses," Lucky said. "And to make it easy for you I'll tell you up front that it ain't water."

He pumped the gun forward and back. A stream of gasoline shot out and ignited as it hit the cigarette lighter that was now embedded in the barrel. The lighter was attached to the gun's trigger and activated as the gasoline shot through the barrel. The gas ignited and a flame engulfed Zollie's surprised face. The big man screamed and rolled over, trying to put his face out in the dirt, but Lucky, laughing wildly, shot him with the Super Soaker again, this time on the back and legs.

Zollie screamed and tried to roll again but then a third flame finished him off.

Michelle gasped and turned away. And found herself looking directly at two men with shotguns. One of them hit her in the face, knocking her to the ground, unconscious.

"Well, well," Lucky said, as he walked around the boulders and looked down at her. "At last the chicken has come home to roost. Pick her up, fellas. I know just where she needs to go."

Chapter Twenty-seven

Jack and Oscar were in Jack's room at La Fonda looking at Blue Wolf's building plans, which had been filed with the city. It had been easy to get them: a simple request from the FBI to city hall and within minutes they were looking at the old drawings.

The problem is they had been over and over them for hours and there seemed to be no way there could be a secret underground lab set up beneath the hospital.

Jack nodded and felt an intense frustration rising. Then he spotted something.

"What the hell? Look at this."

"Look at what?"

"Look at the name of the engineer on the plans."

Oscar looked down.

"Says approved by city engineer Gerald Hoffman."

"Right," Jack said, "and when I first met the Blue Wolf council I was introduced to a guy named Jerry Hoffman. He was Blue Wolf's architect."

"Very interesting."

"Isn't it? Let's say you're a young guy in Santa Fe and you have this cozy job as a city engineer. Not bad, as city jobs go, but maybe it's as high as you can get in city government. Then you meet a guy like Alex Williams who says Blue Wolf is going to be building for years and years."

"Yeah, so you maybe don't worry about a basement they put in the building."

"Or wherever it is. What we need is something that tells us more about the surrounding landscape."

"I know exactly what we need."

Jack typed into his laptop: "Geological Surveys, Santa Fe, New Mexico."

A few minutes later they had found what they were looking for: geological surveys of Santa Fe from the 1800s to the present.

They quickly went through the first few, then found something interesting. It was a survey that had been done by an architect named Gerald Hoffman and a geologist named Gary Wohl.

Jack was stunned.

"Look at this. Wohl says in this survey that they were looking for one of the lost Tewa Pueblo Indian tunnels that the Indians had built to hide from the Spanish conquistadores. The caves were never found but are said to still exist. Wohl claims to have found remnants of the old cave and tunnel system."

Jack looked at it and shook his head in amazement.

"It's odd, though. The rest of the report gives the soil and rock composition but never says whether or not they found the actual cave."

"Come on," Oscar said, "that's because there is no cave. Even if it *had* been there it would be gone by now. The sands out there are shifting constantly. Whatever existed probably would have caved in by now."

"Maybe not," Jack said. "They built those burial caves to last. They might have thought they would have to be underground for long periods of time. Let's say Blue Wolf found the remnants of a cave and then, if they had a need for secrecy, maybe they rebuilt it deep in the ground. Maybe no one but a few of the elect on the staff even knows about it. Then they could take people from Blue Wolf to the cave for the ceremony."

Oscar shook his head. "But these are all just old legends," he said.

"But remember that Tommy said something about 'under.' Underground. That's got to be it. Whatever is happening is happening out there. And I just thought of someone who might know a lot more about it than she let on."

He turned off the computer and grabbed his shoulder holster.

"C'mon, Oscar, we got a party to crash."

They roared out on the highway toward the mountains of the moon.

They were stopped by the guard at Blue Wolf, but Jack showed him his FBI card and they were quickly buzzed through.

They drove to the residence buildings, parked in the lot, and walked into the lobby.

Jack hit the buzzer and Kim Walker answered.

"Hi, Kim. It's Jack Harper."

"Jack, what a surprise. But do you always just show up without calling? I'm afraid I'm rather busy just now."

"This won't take long, Kim," Jack said. "I think I've found Jennifer and I really need your help."

"Jack, I'm happy for you," she said in a hesitant voice, "but I'm not at all sure what I can do. And I'm afraid I'm going out tonight."

"This is a matter of life and death," Jack said.

"Well, all right then, though I can't imagine what help I'll be."

She buzzed the door and Jack and Oscar were inside, headed up to the fourth floor.

Kim Walker was dressed in a bathrobe, her wet hair combed back.

"Kim, this is my partner," Jack said. "Oscar Hidalgo. I haven't been frank with you, I'm afraid. We're both FBI agents."

She turned away and walked toward the bar.

"Is that right?" she said. "Well, that's very interesting. But as I said before, I'm not sure how I—"

"I'll tell you what's interesting," Jack said. "Kidnapping. Kidnapping is a major crime. Especially if there's violence and guns involved. Don't you agree, Oscar?"

"*Si, es muy malo.* You could go to prison for eight or nine years for just holding the person. Then, when firearms and violence are involved, well, that could make things much more interesting. Like eighteen years. And, of course, if the person kidnapped is a woman, well, many judges are very unforgiving. Could be maybe twenty-five years."

Kim Walker's hand began to shake a little. She poured a glass of white wine and sipped it.

"Now those are tough sentences," Jack said, "but what is really tough is if the kidnapping victim is killed. Then the miscreants become candidates for a first-degree murder charge."

"Murder?" Kim asked.

"I know what you're going to say," Jack said. "That you wouldn't have anything to do with murder. But see, if you're an accomplice to murder, meaning if you don't tell us what you know about Jennifer Wu and if, tragically, she happened to be killed, then you would be a

full accomplice to murder and suffer the same fate as the actual kill-
ers. Which would be life in prison. Many people think that might
actually be worse than the death penalty."

Kim Walker's face looked pale as she quickly drank her wine. She
pulled her robe up to her neck, as though she were trying to disappear.

"Well," she said, "I don't think this has anything to do with me."

"That's a good thing," Jack said. "I'd hate to see you in jail as a
lifer. They don't have many massages in prison, unless you count
the ones you get from the two-hundred-and-fifty-pound dykes who
share your cell."

"And to think I really liked you," Kim said.

"Did you?" Jack responded.

He walked toward her and stared down at her.

"I liked you, too, until I started wondering why you were so anxious to meet me. Listen, Kim, we know something is going down
tomorrow night. You tell us what it is and we'll talk to the district
attorney for you."

"You have no idea what you're getting into," Kim said. "This isn't
a criminal gang you're breaking up. It's the most important discovery
since . . ."

"Go ahead and say it," a voice said from behind them. "Why be
falsely modest? It's the most important discovery since the beginning
of human history."

Jack and Oscar turned and saw Lucky Avila and two of his goons
walk into the room. They held pistols in their hands.

"Drop your gun, Jack. I'd hate to have to kill you before you had
a peek at what we're talking about."

Jack gave Oscar a quick look but neither of them had a real chance.
They did as Lucky demanded.

Lucky smiled and went over to Oscar.

"I don't know you, friend, but you've chosen the wrong side in this battle. Turn around."

Oscar was slow to do it, so Lucky cracked him on the side of the head with his gun butt. Oscar went down hard on the condo floor.

Jack stepped forward to help him but was bludgeoned by one of the other boys and fell on top of his partner.

"Don't they look peaceful there?" Lucky commented. "Well, they wanted to know what was really going on and now they're going to find out. Roll them up in that rug and get their asses down the stairs to the car."

Kim shook her head. "They're FBI," she said.

"Yeah, I know," Lucky said. "If they weren't, they would *already* be dead. This has to be handled with some tact and discretion."

"Not your strong suit," Kim said.

"Shut the fuck up before I decide to make you the star of the show."

Kim didn't need to be told again.

Chapter Twenty-eight

Even Wade had noticed how much Kevin was dragging. He asked him how he was doing and Kevin said he was just tired from studying for finals, but the look Pop gave him said it all. He flat out knew Kevin was holding something back.

Which made Kevin think he should just break up with Vicki and go back to being a kid again.

But he just couldn't do it. Not yet. Every time he thought of not seeing her again it drove him crazy.

Leaving her there with her creepy husband, James. He'd learned a lot about him. James was a crazy man, wildly impulsive. Sometimes he beat Vicki up when he came home loaded and she'd said that once he'd even tied her up and threatened her with a gun!

When he thought of that, how weird James was, Kevin would forget all about leaving her. Instead, he would go the other way, and start thinking about leaving *with* her. Maybe they could just get the hell out of Los Angeles, go to New York or someplace where they would never be found. Why the hell not? She could work and maybe he could still go to school. The thoughts floated through his overheated brain like pieces of scrap paper.

He cradled his lacrosse stick and looked down the road.

And there she was, coming toward him in her car. Waving to him from behind the wheel. Even a half block away he could see her smile and thought he could already smell her perfume.

She stopped the car next to him with a screech, then rolled down the passenger window and leaned across the seat toward him.

"Hey, buddy, you're looking kind of lonely standing there in the dark."

"Maybe I am," he said.

"Well, maybe you should get in with me, then."

"You think so, miss?"

"I do," she said. "I just can't resist a man with a big stick."

Kevin laughed and felt the wonderful sensation of illicit joy. Within two seconds he was in the car, putting his hand on her white thigh as they drove toward a golden moon.

In bed she was wilder than ever. Long ago he had seen some old Western with his dad and one character had called a woman—Jane Russell or someone like that—a "regular wildcat," and Kevin had laughed at how lame the metaphor was. But not anymore. Because that was exactly what Vicki was: a regular wildcat, a mountain lioness. The way she arched her back when she was coming, the way she scratched at him . . .

Never let this end, he thought. Never, ever let this end.

Then, just as he was shooting off in her mouth, the bedroom door opened.

"Well," James Hastings said, "isn't this cozy?"

He was wearing a herring-bone overcoat, which gave him a very East Coast, preppie look. He also had stylish glasses, and his haircut looked like it had cost five hundred bucks. When he smiled the whiteness of his teeth practically blinded Kevin.

On the bed Vicki scrambled under the covers, peeking out like she was a little child terrified of a whipping from her father.

Kevin reached for his shorts and quickly put them on.

"James," Vicki said, "I can explain."

"Of course you can," James said. "How about you, kiddo? Can you explain?"

Kevin felt as though someone had lit a Bunsen burner under his head. His cheeks and ears were flaming hot.

"I'm sorry," Kevin said. "No, wait. That's not true. I love Vicki."

James Hastings unzipped the briefcase he had with him and took out a gun.

"Oh, God," Vicki said.

James laughed and aimed the gun at Kevin's crotch.

"I can shoot you right in the balls and no one would ever blame me."

Kevin felt himself shaking but he reached over and took Vicki's hand.

"You couldn't get away with it."

"Yes, I could," James said. "I'm the CEO of my company. I'm the head of three notable charities. I play golf with the mayor at the Brentwood Country Club. There's no jury in this town that would convict me. But I'm not going to touch you."

Kevin heard the words but noticed a cruel smile on James Hastings' face.

"Vicki is going to do it."

Kevin was so astonished by what James had said that for a second he couldn't quite believe he'd heard it.

"You're crazy," he finally said.

"Am I? Get out from under the covers, Vick."

She was whimpering now, but crawled out from under the quilt like a slave.

James handed her her short, sexy, silk robe, the one she'd used to drive Kevin crazy during their first few liaisons.

Funny, he thought, she doesn't look sexy in it now.

James handed her the gun.

"Shoot him," he said.

She was crying. "I can't, Jim. I can't."

Kevin was shaking with fear but he also wanted to laugh. This was so absurd. James Hastings had no idea of what his wife was like. The very idea that she would even consider shooting him was so ridiculous. They were in love, for Chrissakes.

"You *can* shoot him, and you will," James said.

She shook her head violently back and forth.

"No, no, no," she said. "I can't. I don't want to."

James smiled and shook his head as if to say, "These darn kids. No discipline anymore."

"Well then, what *do* you want to do?" James asked, in a sugary voice.

She looked up at Kevin then, and there was something so achingly beautiful in her eyes that Kevin wanted to put his arms around her and take care of her. Now and for always.

"Did you hear me, Vick?" James asked. "What do you want to do?"

"I can't use the gun," she said.

"No?" James asked.

"No," Vicki said, "I want to use the knife."

"Ohhh," James said. "Like the one in Chicago. What was his name?"

"Simon," she said lightly. "His name was Simon. Now will you please tie him up, James?"

"What are you saying?" Kevin asked, incredulous. "Vicki, I love you."

ROBERT WARD

She looked at him and shook her head in a sad, reluctant way.

"No, you don't. You're just like all the other ones. So young. Never had an older woman. Oh, it's all so exciting at first but soon you'll start seeing how deep the wrinkles are on my face and you'll start comparing them to the girls at school. Their flawless faces. Their perfect, nonsagging breasts. Their legs with no ugly broken veins, and you'll ditch me just like all the other boys did. And what will happen to me then? I'll be left alone, weeping, broken-hearted."

"I won't do that. Not ever," Kevin cried.

Vicki's face was all exposed teeth as she screamed into his face.

"Yes, you will. All that matters in this world is youth and beauty. Once it's gone you're nothing. Less than nothing. You'll laugh at me!"

"I won't!"

"Yes, you will!" Vicki screamed. "You all do. And you'll tell other people about this old freak who fucked you for a while. And you'll laugh at the weirdness of it all."

"But I won't," Kevin said.

"That's right," Vicki said. "You won't. None of my lovers will ever laugh at me again!"

"It's time, Vick," James said.

Kevin felt as through an electric shock was passing through his body.

God help me, he thought.

He saw James reach into the briefcase and take out a tightly wrapped coil of nylon rope.

"Oh, Dad. Dad . . ."

But then he thought of his dad. And somehow just seeing him in his mind's eye made him just a little less afraid. He remembered something his father had told him about the Clutter family, the ones that Hickock and Smith had murdered in their own home. They had been watching *In Cold Blood,* with Robert Blake, and after the killings Kevin had been badly upset and said, "All along I thought they were going to let them go." But his father had shaken his head and said, "No, son. If you learn one lesson from this movie it should be this: if you're ever facing someone with a gun, never, ever let them tie you up. Once they do that you're already dead. Clutter thought that by cooperating with them he would save his and his family's lives. But he was dead wrong. Once they tie you up, they feel contempt for you. You're no longer a person to them but a *thing,* like a rabid dog or a sick animal that has to be put out of its misery. That's how the mind of a murderer works. They like to see you sitting there waiting for them to gut you."

Holy shit, Kevin thought. Time to make a move.

He lashed out at Vicki, knocking the gun to one side. The gun went off and he heard James Hastings scream.

There was a brief second when they both looked at James to see what had happened. The bullet had passed though his left forearm. Blood streamed down his overcoat.

"You little bastard," James said, and reached down to grab the gun but Kevin kicked it away, knocked him over, and ran out the bedroom door.

He ran down the steps toward the front door but it was locked from the inside. With a key.

He heard James screaming at him from upstairs and he headed to the back of the house. His lacrosse stick was in the kitchen and he picked it up as he went by and out the back door.

He was running through the yard for the gate when he heard James come outside.

Kevin dove behind a tangle of bushes and watched as James came toward him, the gun in his hand.

"C'mon, kiddo," he said. "C'mon. It was just a little joke we were playing on you."

Kevin held his breath. A little joke. Yeah, real funny, motherfucker.

He reached down and felt a rock in the dirt. He dug it out with his hands.

James was getting closer, looking around in the moonlit garden. Kevin could see the blood dripping down his left arm and hand. The gun was in his right hand.

"C'mon," James said again. "Come back in and we'll all have a little drink and a few laughs. Really."

Kevin picked up a handful of pebbles, said a small prayer, and threw them to the left, near the garage.

James turned, aimed his gun there, and as he did Kevin got up with the rock in his lacrosse stick.

He aimed it at James's head and flung it exactly as he would a lacrosse ball. The rock sailed through the air and crashed into the back of James's skull.

There was a crunching sound and James fell down in his garden, his eyes still open.

Kevin ran to him and grabbed the gun. He felt for James's pulse. It was beating steadily, but James wasn't going anywhere for quite a while.

He found her in the house, lying under the quilt with the steak knife sitting on the table next to her.

She looked up at him and smiled.

"It was going to be so beautiful," she said. "If you were a little more objective, even you could see that. Besides, no matter what you say now, I know you would have laughed at me. The young hate the old."

Kevin reached down and picked up the cell phone. He dialed 911.

She started to get up but he shook his head.

"You leave that bed, you fucking die," he said.

It wasn't his voice that said it, it was his dad's. She didn't move a muscle until the LAPD showed up at the front door.

Chapter Twenty-nine

Johnny stood by the bright blue door of Marty's condo. Looks as though it was hand painted, probably by the old broad Millie Millwood, he thought. Yeah, Johnny had seen those hand-painted doors before, in Provence. These old boho types always liked to think of themselves not just as Americans but as "citizens of the world." Boy, that just pissed Johnny off. What the hell was wrong with America? Not a goddamned thing. Where else could a guy like him flourish like he did? He loved his country and he hated those old boho assholes who ran around talking about cheese and wine and fucking baguettes! Oh, no, a loaf of Wonder Bread wasn't good enough for them. They had to eat a freaking baguette. Fags! And what was wrong with French's mustard? Not a goddamned thing, but the Martys and Millies of the world had to eat Grey Poupon, and special mustards made with some kind of rare fucking mustard seed that probably came from Arle and was pissed on by van Gogh or something. Well, fuck them. Fuck all of them.

Asswipes.

He rang the doorbell, waited, and seconds later Marty let him in.

"Hello, John," Marty said, smiling. "You look particularly well tonight."

"Thanks, Martster," Johnny said, turning on the charm. "You're looking very sharp yourself, man."

Actually, John thought, Marty did look pretty good, considering he was ripe for a permanent rest in a coffin. The old man had some color in his cheeks and his blue eyes were clear and focused.

Of course, the fact that he wore an absurd boho-type ascot, circa 1925 Paris, made him seem more than faintly ridiculous. And what was with the maroon velvet smoking jacket? He looked like some character out of an old detective novel Johnny's mother used to pretend to read while covering her face with Noxzema and smoking Camels in the hundred-degree D.C. backyard heat.

From behind Marty emerged Millie, dressed in her vintage Victorian black lace number with a real blood rose corsage. Christ, Johnny thought as he stepped inside, they were doing the Addams Family. Where the fuck were Lurch and Cousin Itt?

The condo was something right out of the Gilded Age. The chairs were all ancient, cane-backed babies, and the walls seemed to be papered in some kind of crushed velvet. It was so absurd. They had come all this way to Santa Fe only to re-create a lame version of nineteenth-century fucking Paris.

Johnny didn't know enough about history or interior decoration (a fag hobby) to be able to tell the difference, but the important thing as far as he was concerned was it wasn't now, and it wasn't American.

They were a couple of phony old assholes and deserved what he was going to give them.

But this gig might be a tad more complicated than he had figured. They had invited a bunch of their friends, lamesters of all kinds. People who looked seven-eighths dead.

"Johnny, we'd like to introduce you to the people who are known as the council. All of these people have been civic leaders in Santa Fe for many years. This is Alex Williams, the president of the Blue Wolf council. Alex has been one of the great patrons of the local O'Keeffe Museum."

"Pleased to meet you," Johnny said, looking at the old stick figure who thrust out an awkward, veiny hand.

"The pleasure is all mine," Williams said in a friendly baritone.

Johnny took the man's hand and pressed it tightly. And he was more than a little surprised when the old man squeezed his hand back. Really squeezed it. God, the old bastard was strong as hell.

"Over here," Millie said, "we want you to meet Don Dietz."

Johnny turned around to meet the next guest and was shocked to see an amazingly overweight man with an oxygen mask strapped over his nose and mouth. He gave Johnny a thumbs-up as Millie listed his many contributions to the city's well-being.

"He kept the powers that be—the others powers that be, that is— from turning the city into one giant strip mall," Millie said.

"Way to go, dude," Johnny said, backing away from the grotesque figure as fast as possible.

The rest of the guests were equally distinguished and equally worn-out looking.

There was a guy named Russell who was trussed up in a back brace. And there was Sally Amoros, a once beautiful blonde opera singer who was all hunched over due to osteoporosis. And there was some guy named Desmond, who was apparently a comptroller but who made sure to tell Johnny that he only had one real leg, having lost the other one to diabetes. And there were more: a woman named Helena who had a crushed hand, a guy with an eye patch, and another woman named Suzanne Lutz, who had a tumor sticking out of her neck. Some of these people were on the council and others were on some fund-raising committee called "the choosers," whatever that was.

God, what a group of freaks. Johnny looked around and it was all he could do not to break into hysterical laughter. (Or was it a scream? He wasn't quite sure.)

Being in a room of old, totally beat-to-shit people set his heart beating and his mind racing.

Wouldn't it be fun to get a flamethrower and incinerate the whole lot of them?

Finally, he could stand the tension building inside him no longer.

"Hey, Marty," he called out. "We ready to play?"

"Of course we are," Marty responded in his most affable voice.

"What're the stakes?" Johnny asked, taking out his newly stolen cue.

"That's strictly up to you," Marty said, smiling.

"All right, dude," Johnny said. "How about three hundred a game? For starters."

"Fine," Marty said. "Three hundred it is. Follow me."

Chapter Thirty

Phil headed down the hallway to Annie's condo door. He had already forgotten all about Dee Dee. It was kind of amazing. Soon he'd get his hip operation and he'd be a new man. Hell, he was still young, and he could hire lawyers that would keep her from getting one red cent.

He'd keep all the money from the business, and he'd be available for women who appreciated him, great-looking pert-breasted women like Annie.

But not just Annie. Oh, no. He wasn't going to make that mistake again. He was going to have many women, the more the merrier. White women, Indian women, Chinese women, Thai women—oh, man, just the thought of Thai women—every kind of woman he could imagine. Because he was going to travel, seek out all kinds of new sexual adventures.

To hell with one woman. To hell with all that "I thee wed" crap.

He was going to be a swinging dude!

And he was starting right fucking now, baby!

He rang the doorbell to Room 101. Inside he could hear Sinatra singing "Young at Heart." Perfect, 'cause that's what he was going to be from now on.

Young at heart, baby. You bet!

The door opened and there was Annie. Dressed in a tight sweater and skinny jeans, she looked like a million bucks.

"Hey, there, Phil," she said. "Come on in."

He walked inside and saw a bunch of other guests hanging out, talking animatedly. They were eating caviar and drinking champagne from a wet bar that was in the corner across the room.

Annie made eyes at Phil and he felt the delicious sliver of sexual longing throughout his body.

This, he thought, was more like it.

"This is great," Phil said. "Fantastic."

She kissed him on the cheek, a lingering kiss that gave him chills down his neck.

"Have some champagne," she said. "Then there are some guests I want you to meet."

She led him toward the bar. There was a very pretty barmaid, part Mexican, named Sylvia. A barmaid who smiled at him in a way he hadn't experienced in a long time.

Hell, he thought. He was as attractive as ever.

Unlike that guy over in the corner. The old guy with so many rings of flesh hanging off his neck that he looked like one of those redwood trees. Each ring must stand for twenty years, which, from the look of him, would make him at least 150 years old.

And the woman he was with? She looked like a weed in a dress.

Why, the two of them reminded him of so many people he used to, well, best not to think about all that.

The lawsuits, and the anger, and the half-crazed relatives coming to harass him . . .

No, best to have this lovely glass of Perrier-Jouët and think about now . . . now and the future.

All that old-folks unpleasantness was in the past.

As his shrink had told him just last month, before he and Dee Dee had won a prize to come down to Blue Wolf for a week, all expenses paid, he had survived the serious ugliness and was a happy, happy man.

He drank the bubbly and smiled. Yes, sir, this was going to be quite a night.

Now Annie was refilling his glass, and Phil started to protest but then thought better of it. Why not? Why the hell not?

Annie smiled at him. God, she had a bright, white-toothed grin.

Phil hadn't really noticed it before, but her teeth actually glowed with good health.

It was pretty incredible. You couldn't tell just what the hell age she was. She might have had some work done, as they said, but he couldn't be sure.

Not that he was at all against her if she had. Who wanted to look old, like the two ancient geeks in the corner who were still looking over and smiling at him, like they were in love with him or something . . . Or was it more than that? Those smiles seemed almost knowing. Yeah, isn't that what they called it in books? "Knowing smiles."

But that was ridiculous. What could those two old crocks know anyway?

Nada. Nothing. Zero.

He walked into the other room and started meeting people.

Young, attractive people. Annie's friends. Some great-looking women, too.

This was his new scene. No question about it. Youth, vigor, and action.

That was what the new Philly was all about.

Chapter Thirty-one

Johnny had to admit that the game room was awesome, all oak and brass. And the table was terrific, deep green felt that looked like a summer lawn on a great estate.

Johnny could scarcely believe his luck. It was as though the table had been invented expressly for him.

All his fears of losing to the old crock vanished and he played the best games of his life.

Playing straight pool he ran the first ten balls, and when Marty missed on a tough corner shot, he ran fifteen more. Marty stood by sort of clucking to himself like an old rooster. "Well, well, my boy. Quite a good shot. Didn't play quite this way last time, sonny." Et-cetera, etcetera, ad nauseam.

He reduced the old goof to babblemania in no time. The wizened old bird seemed to have lost all his confidence as he missed shot after shot.

Within an hour or so Johnny had won back all he had lost and was pressing on with his bets.

"Let's move it up to five Benjamins," Johnny said.

"That's steep, John," Marty responded.

"Can't handle it, Martman?"

Johnny laughed and downed his fourth Chopin vodka, felt it kick in with the Vicodin he'd just swallowed. A fine mixture. He was a well-tuned Porsche 911, and he was cruising down a twisty road but he couldn't crash if he tried. He was in the groove, baby. He was the man!

"Okay," Marty said. "I'll give her a whirl."

Johnny laughed out loud. The guy sounded like some old prospector now. A Model T? I'll give her a whirl? Yep, by crackie. I mean, who was this dude? Mr. Europe, or some old gulch rat? Johnny laughed as he shot and made another amazing banker.

"How'd you like that one, Martkowski?"

"Loved it, son. Bet you can handle just about anything."

"You got that right," Johnny said.

"'Ceptin' women, I bet," Marty said.

"Women? No problem. I take what I want from 'em, and ditch 'em. End of story!"

"Really?" Marty said. "What about children? You ever have any kids, John?"

"Nah. Well, let me amend that: maybe, but I walked right out on 'em. Bye-bye, baby, bye-bye."

"So you have no children and no wife?"

"I got me," Johnny said. "Me and my wits."

"Must be lonely, John," Marty said, missing an easy shot. "Don't you worry about getting old and being all alone?"

Johnny chalked his cue.

"Tell you the truth, Mart—no offense—but before I'd get as old and fucked up as you and your council in there, man, I'd take a handful of Vikes, drink a half gallon of vodka, and kiss this sad world good-bye."

"You might change your mind, son, when you get up to our ages. People all sound brave when they're young. But when you see that cold hand of death coming for you, most folks will do anything rather than shake it."

Johnny made a nice cushion shot and looked hard at Marty Millwood.

"Let me tell you, Mart. I've seen enough of this world, and when my time comes I'll spit right in death's ugly old face. Now can we lose the inquisition here and play some pool?"

"By all means, John," Marty said. "I meant no offense, son."

"None taken," Johnny said. "Now rack 'em up, Martburger."

They played five more games and though Marty had a good run in the first one, he was no match for Johnny, who was red hot. There was no beating him. He made banks, impossible combinations, and had total control of the cue ball. Every lie he got was better than the last, and most of his shots were easy ones.

By the end of the night he had won over two thousand dollars of Marty's money.

Marty looked ancient, dilapidated, crushed. Which is just how Johnny liked the old goat.

"Time to pay up, Martini," Johnny said.

Marty nodded.

"Yep," he said. "I am plumb tuckered out."

Johnny laughed. Marty was finished. In fact, all of those old farts in the other room were finished, too. He was the king. That was one of the best things about picking on old people. What could they do about it? Nada. He could go right into the other room this second and start smashing their old bones apart and what could they possibly do? Nothing whatsoever.

They were the deadsters and he was their king.

He saw Marty go to the end of the room and move aside a cornball painting of an Indian on a pinto horse looking into the sun. Behind the picture was a safe. How interesting. Johnny cruised down to that end of the room and looked over Marty's shoulder.

The safe was filled with money, tons and tons of money. Big stacks of bills. Why, the money he'd just won from Marty was nothing compared to this. And it was there for the taking!

Marty turned with a few paltry bills in his trembling old hand.

"Here you are, son," he said. "Twenty-five hundred dollars."

"How generous of you," Johnny said. "But I think I'll have a little more, if it's all the same to you?"

"What do you mean, John?" Marty asked, in a shocked falsetto.

"I mean all of it," Johnny said. "I'm taking every cent in the safe. And here's the deal: if you say one word to the cops I'll come back here and strip the skin off you and the fair Millie. You dig?"

Johnny was using his toughest, lowest, most terrifying voice, the one that worked on oldsters all over California and Arizona. It was easy to scare the living shit out of the deadsters, because they were already afraid of everything anyway. Crime, war, terrorism, hurricanes, snakes, spiders, heart attacks, dogs, cats, worms, snails. They were helpless and they knew it. A guy like Marty Millwood had no shot against a jungle cat like the cooking Johnny Z.

So how come the old dude wasn't shaking in fear, wetting himself, crapping his pants?

Instead, Marty did something that sent a chill through what was left of Johnny's immortal soul.

He smiled. A small, subtle grin.

What the hell? Why?

"What's so fucking funny, Marty?"

"Nothing. It's more ironic than funny."

"Yeah, well, fuck your irony. You take off that smoking jacket and wrap all the money in it. Then we're going to march right through the front room and I'm outta here. And don't think you can call a cop to hunt me down before I get back to you. Because even if they catch me and lock me up, I have plenty of friends who will finish the job for me. Get it?"

"Oh, yessir," said Marty, in a mocking way. "I get it, all right."

But Johnny *didn't* get it. Why was this old turd laughing at him when he was cleaning him out? Ah, who cared? The old guy was just trying to pretend he wasn't bothered, to save face. That had to be it. In a few minutes Johnny would be gone like a cool breeze.

Marty Millwood turned back around, smiled a little wider, and sprayed something horrible into Johnny's face. God, it burned so bad. His eyeballs were on fire. He groped forward and screamed, "My eyes. You son of a bitch!"

Then he felt a bony old knee crush his testicles and he fell to the floor, screaming.

"You bastard. I'll kill you."

"Good night, John," Marty said. He smashed Johnny on the head with the cue ball. Things got very hazy and he tried to stand up but he couldn't quite pull it off. Behind Marty he could see the door opening and all the guests streaming in to look down at him.

"Help me," he said. "Help . . ."

But from the little he could still see, not one of them had a helpful look on his or her face.

He tried to get up again but this time Millie picked up the eight ball and bashed him in the head. Her shot was even harder than Marty's.

"One for good luck, creep," she said.

Johnny Z felt an explosion in his head, heard some old folks chuckling, and fell back onto the rug into darkness.

Chapter Thirty-two

Phil was feeling really good. Really, really good. The champagne had made him sort of . . . no, not *sort of,* but definitively, hahaha, ecstatic . . .

Hahahaha.

He actually heard the sound in his head like there was a bubble in his brain with the cartoon word "hahahahaha," and what was really far out was that he, Phil (that would be him, Phil, Philly, Philster, his own self), could see the bubble that was attached to his brain by an invisible string and which now floated above his head. Was that amazing or what?

"Happy floating bubble," he said to Annie.

She looked at him and smiled. Such a sweet smile. Of course, she had no idea what he was talking about because he had failed to finish his complete thought.

Suddenly that seemed hysterically funny to him, too. The concept of complete thought seemed highly silly in the extreme.

He thought of a giant professor in the sky who was marking him down, like one of his old teachers in college, for failing to deliver a complete thought.

He wanted somehow to convey this idea to Annie but she had taken him somewhere in the back of the condo, into a third room that seemed much bigger than he had first thought it was.

This was an odd room to be in because the party was happening out in the other rooms . . . haha . . . so, maybe, Phil thought, she was going to give him a little sex right here.

But, now he saw he was wrong. There was another woman here in the new room, and she was standing with a man over in the corner and they were laughing it up. Well, no, that wasn't quite right.

She, the woman, whose back was to him, was laughing it up, giggling in a high-pitched way, and suddenly Philly got a terrible case of the horrors.

Shit! No way! It couldn't be! But as he walked (stumbled, actually) forward, he realized that yes, sirree-bob-a-rootie there was no doubt that the giggling, hysterical woman whose back was to him was none other than his wife, Dee Dee. He knew that back, and he knew that dyed blonde hair, and he especially knew that high-pitched giggle.

And it occurred to him that she was drinking from a fluted glass the same as he was.

Wasn't that odd?

Champagne. Cold, bubbling, sparkly champagne.

And she was just as ecstatically loaded as he was.

And she was just as unsteady on her feet.

And now she was turning to see who was approaching her here in the back room.

This back room with no windows. It seemed more like a storeroom than part of a condo.

Now Dee Dee was looking at him and her mouth was open in some kind of mixture of embarrassment and horror, and she was saying, "Oh, no. How did you get here?"

And he felt the same thing but with a monster dose of shame, too.

"I was just about to say the same . . ." But he couldn't get the rest of the sentence out. He couldn't do the complete thought but somehow that wasn't amusing anymore, nor was cute, button-nosed Annie's witty, youthful grin.

No, it wasn't what you would call an affectionate or amused grin. More like a predatory grin, a "Gotcha" grin.

Definitely a "Gotcha" grin, and he was feeling really dizzy.

Phil wanted to cry out to the other people at the party, but then he had a nearly complete thought, which was, No, the other party-goers weren't going to help. Not at all. Because they weren't really partygoers at all, were they?

Because they were actors somehow, hired by someone, like the old people who had been staring at him with the knowing smile, and none of them were going to help him or Dee Dee one bit.

In short, Phil thought, as he fell into a trancelike sleep, he had been played, and so had Dee Dee, and wasn't it funny that as he fell off the shelf of consciousness, he suddenly felt an old, familiar love for his wife blooming in his very stoned soul.

Chapter Thirty-three

Jack and Oscar awoke in a locked cell, their arms and legs bound by chains. Both of them had massive headaches.

The room was cold and dark but when Jack's eyes finally adjusted he realized they were in a basement cell of some kind. There was a shaft of light coming through a barred window on the door.

"Oscar, you okay?"

"Never better, hombre. You got any idea where we are?"

"Hell, or just down the block from it."

Jack blinked and looked at the wall. He saw a patch of greenish-blue stone. Turquoise. The same color of dust he'd seen on the great hog and on Tommy. An old turquoise mine.

From outside they heard a roar, like men watching a boxing match. "What the hell?"

"I think the show is about to begin, Osc. We need to get out of these chains fast. You happen to bring a skeleton key with you?"

"No," Oscar said. "I left that at home with my decoder ring."

"Shit," Jack said. "We need to check this place out."

Chained together, they shuffled their way across the room, tripping over a couple of cots and the charming open latrine.

"The only weapon we have is the bed. If we could pull it apart we could use the legs to beat the guards' heads in."

They both pulled on the steel legs. They didn't budge.

"Son of a bitch is welded together."

"You gotta give it to the boys," Oscar said. "This is a well-made house of horrors. We could be fucked this time, hombre."

Jack smiled in the dark and to Oscar his shining teeth looked like the keys to an open accordion.

"Before you write your will, I have another idea."

Outside, the huge, black-masked guard, Hans, waited by their door. His orders were not to let anything happen to them until he had word from the higher-ups.

Hans stood with his mouth open and his tongue hanging out.

"Fuckers," he said to himself, over and over again.

He shut his eyes and imagined all sorts of novel ways to kill the two chained-up fuckers inside the cell.

Then he heard a scream, a cry of pain.

And the words, "He's dead! Dead!"

Oh, no. If one of the guys was actually dead . . . shit. Lucky would hold him responsible for it and crack his head with a ball-peen hammer!

He got his keys, ran inside, and saw the Mexican guy standing next to the white guy, who was balled up on the floor. His tongue was sticking out of his mouth at a grotesque angle.

"He's dead," the Mexican guy said. "He tried to get away and I told him to stay put. But we fought and he's strangled by my chains."

"What the fuck? You killed your partner?"

"Not on purpose. It was an accident. Look."

"Bullshit. This is some kind of trick."

"I'm telling you, dude. And in case you don't know it, we're FBI. You kill an FBI agent and you end up with the serious lethal inject."

"Okay, I'll check. But stand back," Hans said. He held his nine-millimeter Glock out in front of him as he moved toward Jack.

"We have a problem," Oscar said. "I can't stand back."

"Of course you can stand back," Hans said. "And you better do it, too. Waaaay back."

"Senor, there is nothing I would rather do than stand back," Oscar said. "But since you chained us together and he's lying there dead I can only kneel back a couple of inches. 'Cause if I stand back I drag him with me, and then we are over there but still together."

Hans thought that if the Mexican fucker didn't stop explaining why he couldn't stand back he would kill him right now.

"Of course, if you wanted to unchain me, then I could stand back, anywhere you wanted. I could stand back over there, or over there, or over there. The whole world of "standing back" would have endless possibilities, but since I am chained . . ."

"All right," Hans screamed. "Shut the fuck up. You can stay here, but I don't want you hovering over me. So kneel down."

"I will not hover," Oscar said.

"Fuckin' A you won't. A hovering prisoner will soon be a dead one."

Hans moved forward cautiously and then knelt down next to the prone figure, still aiming his gun at Oscar but now from the side.

He looked down at Jack's bent neck and saw scrape marks on it.

"How the fuck did you do this?" he asked.

"It was most unfortunate. He and I got into a little wrestling match . . . Here, I'll show you."

"Huh?"

Too late. Oscar took the chain that bound Jack and himself together, quickly wrapped it around Hans's neck, and pulled. Hans made serious sounds of agony and managed to shoot off his Glock. The bullet passed through Oscar's right arm and Oscar groaned and fell backward, but suddenly Jack was awake and together they strangled the giant.

Hans lay on the stone floor with his tongue hanging out.

"You hit?" Jack asked.

"Not too bad."

"Just a flesh wound?"

"Fuck you. I always wondered what that meant. A flesh wound. Is that better than, say, a bone wound?"

"I think that's the idea. Nobody says it anymore. They always used it in old cowboy movies. My dad still says it."

Jack took Hans's keys and unlocked their chains, then used Hans's shirt to make a tourniquet for Oscar.

"Why does he say it?" Oscar asked.

"Usually about relationships, like "That last woman thought she had my heart in her teeth but it was only a flesh wound.'"

As he talked, Jack gently helped his partner get his shirt off and looked at the bullet hole. It was high up in Oscar's biceps and there was a good deal of bleeding, but it looked as though it had passed through cleanly. Indeed, only a flesh wound.

Jack tied the tourniquet tight and Oscar got up but had to put his hand on the wall for balance.

"You dizzy?"

"Not as much as you, bro."

"You should get out of here. Get to an ER."

"Bullshit. We got to get in there and break up that meeting."

Then someone knocked on the cell door.

"Who is it?" Jack said, using a low, growling voice, which he hoped would fool whoever it was at the door.

"It's Lucky," a voice responded. "I want to see the Feds."

Oscar put on the giant's leather mask and went to the door while Jack waited behind it.

Oscar opened the door.

"Where are the assholes?" Lucky asked, walking in, one of his boys behind him. They were both wearing shiny metallic gray robes and white masks. They looked ridiculous, but still, somehow, frightening.

Oscar pointed at the cot.

Lucky saw a foot sticking out from beside the cot.

"I hope you didn't ice them for good."

"He didn't," Jack said, smashing his gun into Lucky's shoulder, a glancing blow that knocked him off balance as he reached down into his robe for something. A pistol, Jack thought. But instead, Lucky unzipped his robe and pulled out what looked at first glance to be some kind of gun from an old Buck Rogers movie. Jack recognized the Super Soaker as Lucky slid away from him and started to pump the rifle.

"It's dinnertime," Lucky said. "And tonight we're having fried fuzz!"

He was still pumping the gun when Jack rolled to the right. A slash of fire went by him. Jack didn't wait for Lucky to shoot again. Instead he rushed him and knocked the gun from his hand.

Lucky crawled after it but Jack grabbed him by the neck and slammed his forehead into the floor. Twice.

Meanwhile, Oscar reached out and grabbed Lucky's boy and kicked him in the balls. The man went down with a terrified squeak.

The two FBI agents looked at one another and shook their heads.

"What the fuck is that thing?" Oscar asked. "It looks like a freaking toy."

"Yeah," Jack said, smelling it. "It's a kids' toy turned into a flamethrower. Man, a couple of inches to the left and I'd be a crispy critter."

Jack smiled.

"Nice of them to bring our costumes with them," Jack said as they set to stuffing rags in their prisoners' mouths, taking off their clothes, and chaining their arms behind their backs.

"That gun might come in handy," Jack said.

He looked down at the unconscious biker and saw a clip on his belt. Jack took it off and attached it to his own belt.

"In the twenty-first century, the well-dressed FBI agent is always equipped with a toy flamethrower," he said.

He closed his robe. There was a bulge but not much of one.

"Time to check out the scene," he said as he and Oscar donned their masks and headed out into the hall.

Chapter Thirty-four

Jennifer had screamed until she could scream no more. Then she had fallen down at the foot of the bars, too exhausted to even make it across the tiny cell to her bed.

She woke in the dark and started to whisper to Gerri but then remembered that Gerri wasn't there anymore. The leather-clad man had taken her away. God only knew where.

She took seven deep breaths and tried to focus her mind on the darkness.

It was dark, and dark was terrifying, which is exactly what her tormentors, whoever they were, meant it to be.

They were counting on her fear to paralyze her. She pulled herself up and stumbled to her bed.

Then she nearly jumped three feet into the air.

Something moved in the bed.

Someone was there, sleeping.

She trembled in fear, then breathed in deeply and was finally able to say, "Who the hell is that?"

She heard someone clear her throat, saw the shape move, then heard a voice, a very familiar voice.

"Hi, Sis. You okay?"

Jennifer couldn't believe it.

"Michelle?"

"Yeah, guess we ended up in it this time, huh?"

Jennifer moved toward her.

"*We? We* got in this together?"

"Well . . ."

"No," Jennifer said, moving closer. "Not *we*, Sis. You! You got me into this, and now we are both going to end up being organ donors to some rich bastards!"

Michelle stood up and rubbed her neck.

"It's actually worse than that," she said. "The way I understand it, parts of us may be . . . on the menu."

Jennifer hauled off and smacked her sister in the face. The blow was so hard she knocked Michelle to the floor.

"Goddamn. I didn't know you could hit like that," Michelle said.

"There's plenty you don't know about me, Sis," Jennifer said. "I've spent my whole life cleaning up your messes and now you've gotten us into this. Well, they aren't taking me without a fight. And when we get out of here I'm going to settle up with you!"

Michelle got up and hugged her, and in spite of herself Jennifer hugged her back.

"You know what?" Michelle said. "I'm starting to really like you. We got a lot of living to do before it's all over. Now tell me what the guard is like."

"Shit," Jennifer said. "You don't want to know."

Wearing their ridiculous costumes and armed with three pistols and the makeshift flamethrower, Jack and Oscar made their way down the hall. Jack's mask was too narrow for his face, so the eyeholes didn't quite line up with his eyes. This caused him to stagger behind Oscar, whose mask fit neatly. Jack walked into the wall two or three times, and he thought about how he would excise these failings in his memoirs. If he lived to write them.

They weren't sure if they were going toward the human sacrifice or away from it when they heard a commotion a couple of doors in front of them.

It sounded like . . . but it couldn't be.

Jack and Oscar arrived at the door and were extremely surprised at the sounds of sex.

"Ohhh, I want it. I want your big cock in me."

Jack looked inside and saw what could only be a naked Jennifer Wu writhing on a bed, pleasuring herself.

"Hey there," he said, so stunned that he half forgot that he was wearing his white mask and robe.

"Hey look . . ."

He reached down for Hans's keys and quickly opened the cell door.

Then he and Oscar, still masked, walked inside and tried to sound reassuring.

"Girls, whatever you're trying to pull off here isn't really necessary, 'cause—"

He never finished the sentence, because from behind the bed came a leaping, screaming, and clawing Michelle Wu. Jack was usually able to handle two men at once, but there was no way he could ever have been ready for this howling, maniacal tomcat who scratched at his eyes and aimed a killer karate kick at his knee.

Meanwhile, the woman on the bed had quickly pulled up her Levi's and was attacking Oscar with all she had.

Both Oscar and Jack fell to the cell floor, rolling around in their metallic white robes and pointed masks as the girls rained pain down upon them.

Finally, Jack managed to scream, "Michelle, stop. It's Jack and Oscar! And you're fucking killing us!"

She let loose a banshee howl and hit Jack with about ten thousand more punches.

"Jack and Oscar, here to the rescue," Oscar said.

The punches and war cries stopped. The boys sucked in air.

"It's about fucking time," Michelle said.

Jack felt bruises and bumps appearing all over his body. He was a giant purple plum of a man.

A plum in pain.

A few minutes later the four of them—Jack, Oscar, Michelle, and Jennifer—were out in the hall.

"We heard something coming from that way," Jack said, pointing at two steel doors. "I think that's where they're having their warm-up pot roast. But you two have to wait here until we deal with it."

"We'll be back for you," Oscar said.

"Yeah, right," Michelle said. "You want to go down there to the picnic, that's fine. But I know another way out of here. Down the back way. There are steps there and the exit comes out just across from the Red Sombrero."

"I'll be damned," Jack said. "That's where Tommy met us, Oscar. This place must be the cave right below the ledge. "

Jack looked at the green walls. He should have known that's why Tommy met him there. If he had only seen it then.

"So you guys go ahead and we'll meet you outside," Michelle said.

Jack nodded.

"Thanks for saving me," Jennifer said. "I'm sorry we attacked you."

"No problem," Jack said. "Michelle hits like a girl anyway."

They all looked at the huge lump on his forehead and no one said a word.

"Listen," Jack said. "When you get out call the FBI and the local cops and get them out here. Right away. Okay?"

Michelle looked away and Jack grabbed her arm.

"I should have let them take you. Maybe I would have if your sister wasn't in here with you."

"Jack, I can explain. It's not like you think."

"Stop," Jack said. "Don't say another word. I get it. I see the whole scam. We'll deal with all that after this is over."

"I wish you'd—"

"Shut up, Michelle," Jack said. "I got the picture and I don't want to hear your bullshit ever again."

"Okay, Jack," Michelle said, lowering her eyes as though she were heartbroken. "If you say so, Jackie. But I still love you."

Jack slapped her in the face, hard.

"Now go," he said. "Before I change my mind and arrest you."

She didn't look at him again, but grabbed her sister and the two girls headed down the hall toward the back steps.

Jack and Oscar moved forward toward the two steel doors.

As they got closer they heard another round of wild cheering and applause.

"The party's getting wilder," Jack said. "I think we better move along."

Chapter Thirty-five

Jack used Hans's key ring and he and Oscar passed through two steel doors. He'd half expected to see a mob of people, but what faced them was a darkened room.

Oscar reached out, fumbled with the light switch, and flicked it on.

And heard a bone-chilling, high-pitched chatter and screams he could never have imagined. It was like being in a pit where everyone was yelling at once but not in English. In fact, he realized, not in any human language at all.

He and Oscar looked around and saw them. Hundreds of animals: baby chimpanzees, dogs of all sizes, pigs—huge, ugly, spotted pigs—mice, and rabbits, most of them trussed up in ways beyond imagining. It was like something out of Bosch, Jack thought, but worse, far worse. For all his horror, Bosch was only painting images from his twisted mind.

These nightmares were real.

Rabbits with steel bolts shoved through their heads, dogs with horrible, bloody scabs on their backs where their fur should have been. Pigs covered in running sores and screaming monstrous, agonized squeals.

"*Madre de Dios,*" Oscar said.

Then, as they walked down past the endless row of cages, they saw trays with dead animals on them.

But not *whole* dead animals. More like pieces of dead animals: guts and ears and noses and piles of intestines.

And the smell of the place! At first Jack hadn't noticed how foul the odor was. He'd been so surprised by the hideous visual tableau and maniacal sound level that the smell hadn't quite reached down and strangled him. But it did now. The smell of suffering beyond belief. The smell of rotting corpses and chemicals. There were no words to describe it. A sweet, foul smell that made both men dizzy and nauseous.

"We should let them all out, compadre. Let them be free."

"Yeah," Jack said. "But God knows what they would do to us if they got loose."

"You think an animal wants to take revenge?"

They stared at baboons with electrified caps on their heads looking out of their cages at them with what seemed to be a fury that knew no end.

And the screaming pigs—the ones with their guts exposed from monstrous operations. The pigs with the red eyes glowering at them. Wild javelina pigs, each with some kind of hole in its back into which a green liquid dripped steadily from a catheter.

"We let these animals out," Jack said, "and they are going to make short work of us."

"I wouldn't blame them," Oscar said.

They wandered down the rows of terrifying half-destroyed animals, Jack feeling a terrible rage that anyone could do this to such helpless beasts. They reached another door. It was steel, and locked, but Jack found the right key on Hans's chain and swiftly opened it.

The new room was lit in purple neon.

And it was cold, ice cold. The freezer.

Oscar's teeth chattered and he felt faint.

"What the fuck is this?"

"Where they make ice cream?" Jack asked.

They moved forward slowly, shivering.

Then they both saw it at once. The frozen body of a black woman with her stomach carved away. Two bolts that looked like the same bolts that were in the rabbits' heads, but jumbo-sized, went right through Gerri's head.

"Like a black female Frankenstein," Jack said.

Gerri, or what was left of her, was hanging from a hook in the wall. Her eyes were gone and her mouth lolled open, an old door with broken hinges.

Though frozen solid, she seemed to be still screaming.

"Oh, man," Jack said, somehow moving down the rows of other bodies that hung from the wall. People with eyes pulled out, arms missing, lung cavities exposed.

And then, at the other end of the hall, they heard voices. Crowd murmurings. And mad, wild music, some kind of high, weird, techno shit played by a maniac on goat speed.

Before they got to the door, Jack saw a big metal freezer trunk.

He toyed with the clasp and though he didn't know how he did it, the latch clicked. As Oscar looked over his shoulder, Jack slowly lifted the lid and looked inside.

Inside, there was a familiar boy, or what was left of him. He had a bullet hole in his arm, and another in his head. His lifeless eyes were open and staring up at Jack. His face was icy blue and his mouth was open as if he'd died in disbelief. His skin looked like old crêpe.

"Tommy," Jack said.

"Madness," Oscar said.

But there was no time to grieve.

Just beyond the next door they heard the noise grow louder. Above the insane music and the mad laughter, they heard something completely distinct. People who weren't laughing and chatting away. No, these people were screaming.

"What are you doing to us?"

"Whyyyy?"

"Pleeeease! This must be a mistake. God . . ."

And then another voice. A deep, amused voice.

"Sorry, this is no mistake," a man's voice said. "You and everyone else who came to the cave were chosen for an excellent reason."

There was a brief silence and then Jack and Oscar could hear a high-pitched crying, like a bird that's having its feathers torn out, one by one.

And words, too . . .

"Oooh, God, no no no no no no . . . somebody help us. Please, God, somebody help us."

Jack looked at Oscar as they moved toward the last door.

Chapter Thirty-six

When Johnny Z came to, he was tied to a gurney in the back of a meat truck. In front of him was an aluminum wall, and although he didn't know it, on the other side of it were various cuts of frozen meat—steaks, roasts, pork chops. They were packaged and had been placed on shelves by two men wearing winter jackets and ski gloves. The temperature in the freezer was about ten above zero.

If a cop stopped the truck and asked to look in the back all he would see was frozen meat.

They wouldn't think to look beyond the refrigerator wall, where Johnny was tied up, rags stuffed in his mouth.

Johny's teeth chattered and his eyes darted around the room looking for some way out.

Formerly helpless old Millie, wearing a warm winter coat, looked down at him with snarling contempt.

"Hey there, big guy, how are you?" she asked. "Probably wondering where you're going. Well, I'll tell you. You're going to a party, a party you will never forget. Trust me on that."

Johnny tried to talk but all that came out were idiot mumbles.

* * *

They took him out of the back of the truck and put his gurney down on the desert floor. Then Millie took the gag out of his mouth. Johnny looked up at the moon. He felt a terrifying panic and the moon was so luminous and beautiful that he almost wanted to cry.

Millie stood next to him. In her hand was some kind of remote-control device.

"Look up there, Johnny-boy," she said in an almost motherly tone.

She pointed at a mountain in front of them. Rocky, sandy, not all that steep. As mountains go, you wouldn't stop to take a picture of it.

"So?" he said. "A fucking hill. Who cares?"

"But watch this."

She then aimed the remote at the hill and pushed the button.

Johnny's mouth dropped open.

There was a whirring sound and the earth on the hillside parted. Two boulders slid open, just like elevator doors.

"What the fuck?" Johnny cried.

"This is the party we told you about," Marty said.

"Party?"

"You're probably wondering where all the guests are. Well, they enter on the other side," Millie said. "You're one of the star attractions. You wouldn't expect the star to come in the same entrance as the audience, would you?"

"Star attraction? What the fuck are you talking about?" Johnny screamed.

Marty smiled and stuffed the gag back in his mouth.

Two men picked up Johnny's gurney and began to carry him up the hill.

Johnny tried to talk but the words just sounded like, "Waitaman-fuckers basflerds."

Marty and Millie and the two bearers found him hilarious and began mimicking his pronunciation.

Before he could object any more, they had already walked up the pathway, gone through the doors, and were inside.

The doors in the hillside closed behind them.

They took him into a great underground room lit by wall torches. He felt such fear that he was sure he would lose control of his bowels. How Marty and Millie would love that.

Marty and Millie. He still couldn't get over it!

The two old fuckers had somehow tricked him, the fabulous Johnny Zaprado, by playing on his greed. The whole match had been a setup. He should have seen it coming a mile away.

But who would think them capable of it?

Old people had been his criminal specialty *because* they were so helpless and such goofs. Really, until now he had never had one iota of trouble bashing them around, stealing their money, and screaming into their fragile, tissue-paper-thin-skinned faces.

Until now, until this very moment . . . and where the hell was he?

Inside a freaking mountain! Moving through some long tunnel, with torches flickering on ancient walls.

They passed through some doors and took him into a big meeting room. The kiva.

He squinted and moved his head slightly so he could see who was there. From the sound of it, there was a pretty large gathering of people, maybe a hundred or so.

But there was no way he could prepare for what he saw next.

All the guests wore metallic shimmering gray capes and really bizarre white masks with strange little eye slits and oversized mouths. Very grotesque-chic.

It was some kind of weird masquerade party. Maybe they were going to teach him a lesson. Old creeps were good at that kind of thing, teaching young people a lesson. That had to be it. They were going to scare him a little bit and maybe give him a few memorable bruises and then dump him a few miles from town and let him think about taking on old folks again.

He could almost hear them hanging around, saying, "Well, we'll teach that young hustler a thing or two, by crackie."

So let them scare him if they wanted. Let them do whatever they had in mind. He could hack it. But when he healed up afterward, oh, baby, were they going to get a rude surprise! Yeah, he was going to track all of them down and crush their ancient asses.

To think that they had tricked him, Johnny Z, like this. They were going to pay and pay and pay and . . .

But wait now. What was this? Something weird was happening. His two new bearers—two people dressed in the same silver tunics and weirdo almost-alien masks. As they carried him through the great, torch-lit hall, the place became utterly silent.

And where were Marty and Millie?

As he managed to raise his head a little and look around the cave, he realized every masked eye was staring down at him.

What the hell was going on?

He watched as the crowd moved in on him. They crowded so close to him that his bearers could barely carry him through the curious, masked mob to the front of the room.

But get him there they did.

Then Johnny looked up and saw something that he could no longer pass off with a laugh or with his usual psychotic revenge fantasies.

He saw something so horrifying that for a good three or four seconds he didn't really recognize it, even though he was staring right at it and could see it plainly.

It was . . . but it couldn't be . . . no way.

But it was!

What Johnny Z saw was two other people in front of him. A middle-aged man and an attractive woman Johnny assumed was his wife, and they were naked.

But being naked was the least of their worries because they were also on a makeshift stage at the front of the room, and they were . . . oh, God, was he actually seeing this?

Yes, he was. Oh, God help me, he screamed in silence.

The two of them were each nailed to a cross.

The older man and the younger woman were totally nude and were being freaking crucified.

Crucified! With real nails in their palms and their ankles.

And look at the size of those nails. Fucking huge. The kind of nails you might use in building a bridge.

And all the people in their shimmering gray capes and their weird white masks were looking at the poor crucified bastards and ooohing and aahing. Then Johnny noticed something odd. The two crucified people should have been screaming their lungs out but they weren't. They were utterly quiet. He looked at their mouths and realized why. There were gags stuffed in their mouths.

But their eyes . . . ah, their eyes told the story without words.

Their eyes were wide open and filled with nameless, unspeakable terror. Their eyes were doing all the screaming for them.

And now they were prying open his mouth and sticking in rags soaked in chemicals that scorched his tongue and the roof of his mouth, and there was a gag being tied tightly all the way around his neck, and he was trying to beg and scream but could do neither.

They were pulling him off the gurney and moving him to his very own cross and they were starting to rip off his clothes. He was stunned that he could feel shame as well as terror.

But he did. He wanted to apologize to everyone for the roll of fat on his stomach. And he wanted to say he had intended to go on a diet because when you get . . . when you get *fucking crucified you really want to look your best*!

But that line of thought was soon cut off because there was a man walking toward him with a big hammer in his hand, and sticking out of the mouth hole of his mask were four huge motherfucking nails.

Johnny Z began to scream and scream and scream some more.

But all that came out was a muffled torrent of animal sounds, like the bleating of a screaming pig, with no hope of mercy from his torturer.

All the masked people in the crowd began to laugh. Wild, crazed, lunatic laughter that echoed around the green-gray walls and shook the very foundations of the room.

Chapter Thirty-seven

"Can you fucking believe this?" Jack asked.

He glanced at Oscar, whose mouth was hanging open.

Three people being . . . Jack could hardly say it in his mind . . . *crucified right in front of him and his partner.*

But what could they do about it? If they pulled their guns they'd be outnumbered by a hundred to two.

There were two robed and masked guys standing by the crosses. Obviously guards, with their guns under their robes, Jack thought.

"What do we do?" Oscar whispered.

"Wait for our chance. See what the big guy is going to say."

"Jesus! This is *muy malo.*"

From in front of them one of the other audience members turned and hissed, "Would you two stop arguing? Some of us are trying to assume a meditative mood."

"Sorry," Jack said, turning slightly. "I was having a little trouble seeing the crucifixion."

"Well, try to have some consideration, young man," the old voice beside them chastened. "You two aren't the only people in this room!"

Jack looked at Oscar and shook his head.

* * *

Up on his cross Johnny Z was learning a new, active definition of the word "pain." The pain in his palms radiated to his arms, then twisted into his shoulders, back, and neck.

He turned his head slightly and looked at the middle-aged guy next to him.

Who was he? What had he done?

What had the girl done?

What could *any* of them have done to deserve this?

As Alex Williams took his position in front of the audience, just in front of the three people on trial, he thought of the high seriousness of what was transpiring here tonight.

It was funny how things had started long ago, started as merely an act of revenge against a young man who had killed an older man but that had now grown into so much more.

Out of that first primal instinct for revenge a flower had grown. Hell, more than a flower, a whole garden of flowers.

Here it was in front of him, a visionary company of geniuses, people who enriched the world: a collective, as it were, unlike any other collective that had ever existed.

Alex looked out at them as the last few took the seats in the back of the audience.

A hundred and five of them now and soon to be more. But not too soon. No, they couldn't simply add people. Every single member had to be vetted, carefully considered, and voted on by the inner council.

That was crucial.

Questions had to be asked. Serious questions.

How much had they helped humanity?

If they were accepted, what future good could they do for mankind?

Why should one person be chosen over another person with similar credentials?

What is their concept of "the good"?

And the most important question of all: how much money would they pay?

Not that he was in any way a cheap materialist, but one had to be realistic. What he had to offer them was the most remarkable breakthrough in man's history. The dream of every man and woman who ever lived.

Immortality.

Once the formula was perfected, price would be no object.

He could ask any price he wished. He really would be (and the thought made him blush) the most powerful man in the world.

It was a great day, Alex thought, his mind whirling as he heard the crowd settle down and look up at him. At *him,* their leader, *the* visionary among other lesser visionaries. The man who had discovered the secret, the secret that Western science had glossed over.

He who had started long ago and taken a path that revealed the true secrets of life.

As the great folk singer Bob Dylan had once sung (before he sold out), "He who is not busy being born is busy dying."

How true that was, Alex thought, how true.

There had been a time, long ago, when Alex had thought that his entire generation was busy being born, but it had not been so. They were like all the other generations before them: sellouts. Busy all right. Busy making millions.

Only he and his band of brothers understood the true nature of the magical mystery tour called "Life and Death." (Such inadequate words.)

Only the chosen few.

But wasn't that the way it had always been?

Jesus, Muhammad, Einstein, and some day soon, Williams.

Just a few, but those were enough. Enough to see that humanity went on to its great destiny.

He turned now and looked at the suffering, twitching, eyeball-popping threesome on their crosses.

He saw the girl look at him with an expression that said, "Please, please, have pity on me and I will suck your cock for all eternity!"

Alex Williams only smiled up at her.

He felt many things toward her—hatred, fury, even gratitude—but sorry, missy, pity didn't make the list.

He looked back at his audience, ready now. Ready for the beginning of the trial.

The trial at which he, Alex Williams, would be judge, jury and . . . immortalist.

Chapter Thirty-eight

"Jack, what the fuck are we going to do?" Oscar asked.

"I'm working on it," Jack replied.

"Well, work on this, too, bro," Oscar said. "I'm getting weaker by the minute."

"What?"

"I was shot, remember? Well, I've lost a lot of blood and I feel real dizzy. I can barely sit up."

"Can you hang on a little longer?" Jack asked.

"Yeah, man, I think so. But we gotta make a move anyway, *ese.*"

Then they heard new, louder, terrified screams.

Behind the naked hipster Johnny Z, two more crosses were being brought into the room. And just behind the crosses two women were being dragged by hooded, masked men.

"Is that who I think it is?" Oscar asked, peering shakily from his bloodshot eyes.

"I can't fucking believe it—that's Michelle and Jennifer," Jack said.

The girls had rags stuffed into their mouths.

The crosses were hastily raised, but there seemed to be some trouble with one of them.

"The crossbar is sagging," Oscar said.

"What's the fucking world coming to?" Jack asked rehetorically. "You just can't find a good crucifix maker anymore."

"You better show some respect," the guy in front of them said. "Or that could be you two assholes up there!"

The entire congregation seemed to be getting antsy now and their leader, Alex Williams, moved quickly to his pulpit.

"As you can see there have been some last-minute additions," he said. "But while my assistants are getting prepared there's no reason we can't start with our first trial."

"It's Williams, all right," Jack said, recognizing his voice. "He's been in with Lucky all along."

Jack looked to his left and saw a masked man just down from Oscar, staring intently at Oscar's feet. Jack looked down and saw blood dripping on the floor. Then he looked to his right and saw a couple of the men watching him, too.

He wanted to attack now, before the trial started, but Oscar was leaning on his shoulder and Jack had to hold him up. He'd have to wait. If he stood up now they'd both be caught, and maybe shot by the guards along the wall, before they even got out of their seats.

Alex Williams made a pyramid sign with his hands. A second later, everyone stood and made the sign as well, including Jack, but Oscar stayed in his chair.

After Alex lowered his hands to his sides, everyone sat down again.

"We are here tonight to accomplish a deeply serious task," the Blue Wolf leader said. "We must discuss the guilt or innocence of these three people who are accused of extreme crimes against the elderly. Some of us may be tempted to be lenient. We may say, 'Well, none of these people have been arrested, tried, and convicted of said crimes, and therefore who are we to play judge, jury, and executioner?' But that is the very attitude that has been the bane of our existence. Older people in our society, the very ones who created the best of the world we live in, are not valued enough for anyone to bother to arrest those who commit crimes against them. Do not doubt it. I will not bore you with statistics except to say that every model we have used has come to the same conclusion. Which is this: if the crimes of these three defendants had been committed against younger people they would have not only been arrested but put in prison for years, possibly even executed. But since the victims were senior citizens—and I use the phrase proudly—they were not taken seriously. We have tried to petition the powers that be but our earnest entreaties have been met with a silence that borders on outright ridicule."

The gathering in the cave suddenly came to life with cries of "No, no, no!" Many of them stood in their places and raised their fists in the air, screaming. Jack looked at Oscar, who was breathing deeply, trying to get his head clear.

The brethren in the cave sat down again and Alex Williams nodded his head as though he understood their anger.

"This is why we decided that we must make our own justice, a real justice, commensurate with the crimes committed."

The crowd went berserk. The people leaped to their feet and began to scream like madmen.

"Yes!"

"Justice!"

"We, who created the world we live in, the great modern world of Western civilization, will not go down defeated like the generations before us. We will not submit and we shall not be moved!"

The audience screamed again and Jack felt a deep fear in his soul. How in the hell would they ever stop this and live to tell about it?

Williams continued.

"First, we shall have the readings of the crimes. I bring to your attention the case of Philip and Dee Dee Holden, owners of the Evergreen Retirement Community in Columbus, Ohio."

Williams looked up at Dee Dee and Phil, each on their own cross, dripping blood. They looked down at him with eyes so filled with fear that they almost seemed comical.

But Williams didn't laugh or show any pity whatsoever.

"This supposed four-star retirement community houses over four thousand people. Their brochures and DVDs, their radio and TV spots, would have you believe that their community is a paradise for people over sixty-five."

Alex Williams picked up a brochure and waved it at the audience.

"Let me read a little of this to you. 'Evergreen is a virtual paradise for the elderly. The golf course, designed by Arnold Palmer, makes every day a great one for novices and old pros alike.' Interesting, when you consider twenty-three people were bitten by rats on the greens just last year."

The audience roared with disdainful laughter while Phil and Dee Dee groaned in agony.

Alex Williams's words continued to torture Phil. He had to hang there and listen as Williams read about the old people who had had strokes in the cafeteria and been left there to drool and spasm out on the floor until they expired. Why? Because Phil hadn't paid the money he owed to the insurance companies that indemnified the hospitals, so there was no emergency service at Evergreen. Phil twitched in agony as he heard case after case of neglect, of old people being left out in the snow to freeze, of a grandmother being robbed at gunpoint by her own nurse, and of the case of a feeble old minister who had objected to his treatment and was therefore injected with the wrong medicine and died of shock before the ambulance arrived.

Phil squirmed in guilt and pain. There were so many crimes documented that he had forgotten most of them. A woman who had been raped by an attendant, another woman who had been shaken down to get cable service and, when she refused to pay, had been thrown out of an upstairs window. On and on they went.

Of course, Phil did recall some of them. Why? Because he had paid for them to go away. Had paid so many people he scarcely thought it fair to bring them all up again now. He'd paid inspectors from welfare, from Medicare, lawyers hired by people who had barely survived the impossibly harsh treatment they had received from the jerks he'd hired. He had paid cops, doctors, teachers, and the sons and daughters of those who had been injured and killed at Evergreen.

He had paid them and made most of them go away!

He was great with such negotiations. He had a real knack for it. And the ones he couldn't handle Dee Dee had taken care of, playing the sweet and innocent wife, opening her heart to people who had suddenly lost their mothers because they had accidentally fallen from a cheapo balcony that had collapsed.

Dee Dee had the human touch, one of the things he loved her for.

But look where all his talents had gotten him.

Strung up on a cross, with nails in his hands and feet.

And he hadn't even been convicted yet!

Chapter Thirty-nine

Oscar slumped against Jack. Jack turned and looked down the row at the true believers who were watching him.

"Osc, what's up?"

"I'm going to be okay," Oscar said. "Feeling better. Just gotta get my balance. Another few seconds, amigo."

"Good. But if we just run up there with our guns out, these fucking fanatics will mob us."

"We need a distraction of some kind, *ese*."

In front of them, though a little off to the side, the carpenters were repairing the broken cross. Jennifer Wu looked at her sister, who turned away in shame. Fucking Michelle, Jennifer thought. That crazy, greedy bitch. Jennifer looked at the cross and the big, ugly nails and wished they had just killed her when they were caught. If only Jack and his partner were here to save them. Where the hell were those guys?

Back at the pulpit, Alex Williams was coming to the end of his list of the terrible crimes committed by Johnny Z.

"And, finally, he killed two kindly old grandmothers in Fountain Valley, California, just last month. Killed them and took their antique butter churns, which he pawned in Desert Palms. This brings to the end the known crimes of Johnny Zaprado."

There was a cry of fury from the faithful.

Jack assumed that now that the list of charges had finally been read the trial would begin. Who knew how long that might last?

Oscar looked pale and wasted.

Alex Williams spoke again.

"You have all heard the documented charges against Phil and Dee Dee. How do you vote? Innocent or guilty?"

"Guilty!" the entire congregation screamed.

"Guilty it is," said Alex Williams. "And Johnny Zaprado. How do you vote?"

"Guilty!" they screamed again.

"Fuck him with a hot poker," someone yelled.

"The verdict is guilty," said Alex Williams. "And now we come to the penalty phase of the trial. Johnny Zaprado, the court finds you guilty of murder in the first degree, assault in the first degree, burglary in the first degree, and other crimes too numerous to mention. You are guilty as charged."

There was a roar of approval from the crowd.

Williams looked up at Johnny Z, dripping blood from his hands and feet. Johnny's eyes were wide open in panic mode, and he tried to talk through the gag stuck in his mouth.

His words came out a muffled mess, and sounded like, "Waittt . . . gribmeahhh a chgabgagaga . . ."

Williams smiled at him and turned to his audience.

"Doesn't sound too intelligent, does he?"

In unison the masked audience screamed back at Alex.

"Noooooo!"

Williams looked up at the bleeding Johnny.

"You know what he sounds like?"

"Whaaaaaat?" they all screamed.

"Like a stroke victim. He sounds just like the senior citizens he used to victimize, right?"

"Yessssss," they screamed, and this was followed by much laughter and general good fellowship. A few of the people on either side of Jack and Oscar pounded one another on the back.

Jack looked at Oscar and whispered.

"It's a ritual, man. They're working from a script."

"Yeah, bro. They've done this before."

Up on the podium Alex Williams looked to the corner of the cave.

"Will you please bring out the ladder?"

From a darkened corner of the cave two white-masked men carried out a stepladder, which they quickly set up just beneath Johnny Zaprado's cross. They stayed on the stage looking intently at their leader.

Alex smiled and spoke to the audience.

"Shall I ascend?" he asked into his lapel mike.

"Ascend!" they cried.

Alex quickly climbed the ladder until he was level with Johnny Z. He gave a quick glance to Phil and Dee Dee, whose eyes were bulging out of their heads.

Then he turned his full attention to Johnny.

"You have been tried and found guilty of multiple crimes against the aged. You have beaten, maimed, and murdered scores of older people. You have shown no remorse for these crimes. Quite the contrary, you have been quoted by reliable witnesses as being proud of your conquests of people who were older and weaker than yourself. And you have constantly bragged about your ability to outfox the laws. Why? Because you have intimidated all the living witnesses into silence. In short, you are a public menace, and we, the Blue Wolf council, have found you guilty of all the aforementioned charges. Have you anything to say for yourself?"

Johnny Z began to scream through his gag, "Guv me a changggg."

The audience went wild with laughter.

"I'm sorry," Alex Williams said. "Would you please say that again? Your diction left a little to be desired."

"Ah thed . . . gimme a chance to . . ."

But the screams of laughter from the audience drowned him out.

"Here, let me help you," Alex said. "Open your mouth, please."

The defendant did so.

Williams pulled out the gag, and everyone could see the relief on Johnny's reddened face.

"Is that better?"

"Yes . . . yes . . ."

"Now that we've made it easier for you to express yourself, perhaps you'd like to tell us why we should spare your life."

Johnny looked at him and nodded his head.

"You have no right. None of you. I have never been convicted of any these crimes."

There was a great mumbling of dissent among the group. But Alex waved them quiet.

"Forget that argument," he said to Johnny Z. "This tribunal has already found you guilty. Let me help you in your own defense. If you can tell us what you might do with the rest of your life to atone for the crimes you committed against the elderly, perhaps we might see fit to allow you to live."

Johnny Z looked vastly confused.

"Atone?" he asked, in what was close to a whisper.

"Yes," Alex said. "You do know the meaning of the word?"

A huge sigh mixed with laughter rippled through the audience.

"Yeah," Johnny said. "You want to know what I can do to make up for the stuff you say I did."

"Wrong!" Alex screamed.

"You still haven't taken responsibility for your actions. If you don't own your actions, how can we believe you'd ever *really* atone?"

The audience mumbled in agreement.

"Okay," Johnny said. "I'm sorry. I am. Really. Can I tell you something?"

"Please. Be my guest," Alex said.

"You see, when I was a kid, my dad was always out drunk, hustling people, and I was, like, a really sickly kid, and I cried all the time, and wet my bed and stuff, see?"

"Yes?"

"And so . . . so my mom used to try to sleep but she couldn't, you know, what with me bawling all the time. So she found a way to put me to sleep. She really did this. She would hear me screaming and she tried to walk me around and all but I still didn't sleep. So she walked over to my bed and she got this idea. She noticed that when I was bad—you know, threw my food and stuff—she noticed that when she spanked me I would scream really loud for a few minutes but then I'd fall fast asleep. So she began to beat me to sleep. I'm not kidding. She used to beat me until my baby ass bled into the mattress but when I reached the right pitch of hysteria I would be just like a light switch. Flick! I instantly fell asleep."

Johnny Z began to cry. The tears rolled down his face as he thought of his savage mistreatment at the hands of his mother.

Jack looked around at the audience. Even they seemed moved by his confession. There was a general sorrowful tone to their mumblings.

And this encouraged Johnny Z.

"You see how it was?" he said. "I began to hate all older people. And so I began to think that whatever I did to them was okay 'cause it was payback for what my mom had done to me."

"I see," Alex said. Even he was touched by the story.

"And so, like, I could atone by helping older people for the rest of my life," Johnny said. "I could start a school . . . yeah, a school that was for young criminals just like me and I could teach them to, ah, venerate their elders, ya know? I really could. I could use all the money I got, the money I ripped off from old folks to *help* old folks. I mean senior citizens. You see what I mean?"

The crowd seemed to mumble as one in assent.

"I mean who would be better at this kind of reeducation than me?"

There was a near reverent silence.

It was almost as though the crowd had been swayed by Johnny's sad tale.

Then Alex Williams spoke.

"That's very interesting, and even moving, Johnny. Really. I was personally touched, as we all were. But think of it, John. So you were spanked to sleep? Far worse things were done to people. Girls were molested by their fathers, kids were cut up by their mothers. A million transgressions far worse than yours were done to children and yet they managed to become useful members of society. But not you, Johnny! Not you!"

Johnny looked terrified.

"No, but wait. That was only the beginning."

But as he opened his mouth to list more of the terrible things his parents had done to him, Alex Williams stuffed the rag back into his mouth.

"Bullshit," he said. "You're a con, Johnny. Pure and simple. A man born with the criminal gene, a man no amount of schooling or counseling can help. You are condemned, Johnny. But don't worry. In death you will do good as you never did in life. We'll use your arms to help older people who need arms. We'll use your legs so that wiser seniors can walk. We shall harvest your eyeballs, your ass, and your cock. No part of you, so worthless in life, will be worthless in death. You will achieve a greatness and a generosity of spirit in death that you never evidenced in life. You shall be redeemed."

The entire congregation roared their approval.

Alex Williams reached down to one of his robed and masked assistants. The man handed him a portable chain saw, small but efficient. Alex nodded as if to thank him. Then, chain saw in his right hand, he raised both his arms like a choir leader.

"And now let us sing. Let's sing a song that will take us all back to those days of innocence when we were young. And remember, as we sing, thanks to this man here and others like him, we shall all be young again!"

"A sing-along?" Jack said, unzipping his cloak a little and feeling inside for the revolver and the makeshift flamethrower. "What's next, s'mores?"

Then, to Jack and Oscar's amazement, all the masked lunatics in the audience began singing an old camp tune that Jack hadn't heard since he was twelve years old.

"Oh, you can't get to heaven. Oh, you can't get to heaven. In Johnny's car. In Johnny's car. 'Cause the gosh darn thing. 'Cause the gosh darn thing. Won't go that far. Won't go that far."

Oscar looked at Jack and shook his head.

"The glee club from hell, baby."

The masked madmen were all shaking and jiving now, like goofy teenagers around a communal campfire.

And their insane leader was leading them in song by waving the chain saw in time to the music like a camp counselor.

"Oh, you can't get to heaven on Johnny's skates, 'cause they'll roll right by them pearly gates. I ain't gonna grieve my Lord no more."

As they sang the lunatic chorus, Jack whispered to Oscar, "When they finish singing, you know what's gonna happen."

Oscar nodded, and swept his index finger across his own throat.

"Yeah, amigo. It's now or never. Can you make it?"

"I'll try, compadre."

Up on his ladder, Alex Williams revved the chain saw.

He moved it under Johnny Z's neck.

"You shall play your part!" he said.

And the entire congregation began to make a high-pitched keening sound as they watched Alex Williams ready himself for the execution.

Oscar and Jack leaped up and headed for the aisle. The congregation was so set on watching the murder on the cross that they were caught off guard.

"And we shall use your brain as well. With it we will create nectar, nectar that shall infuse the most loyal members of the Blue Wolf brotherhood with the greatest gift known to man. Eternal youth! All from you, Johnny boy. All from you."

He moved the chain saw closer to Johnny Z's throat but was interrupted by a cry from Jack, who was now near the guards.

"Stop it, now! Drop that fucking saw! You're under arrest. FBI."

Alex Williams was stunned. He stopped just short of slicing through Johnny's throat. He stared down and saw Jack and Oscar being met by a hooded guard who raised his machine gun, but Jack chopped at his wrist and the gun fell to the floor. Jack quickly picked it up and threw it to Oscar, who, though wobbly, caught it and trained it on the other guards. They dropped their weapons. Jack look up at Alex Williams.

"FBI, pal. Come down from there, now. You're under arrest for homicide."

"I don't think so," Alex Williams said. "And don't think you can shoot me. Because all our members are prepared to attack anyone who interferes with our sacred ritual."

Jack turned his gun on the guests, some of whom were out of their seats and moving toward the two cops.

"All of you back the fuck up or I'll be forced to shoot."

Jack looked up at Alex, who was waving his chain saw around in a circular motion. He looked down at Jack and laughed.

"You are two against a hundred of us."

"That's right," Jack said. "You get twenty or thirty of your people to take a run at us and we're going to lose. But the first ten or so are going to be full of bullet holes. I wonder how many of your loyal legion want to end up bleeding out on the floor?"

Alex nodded his head and grinned.

"Let's find out," he said.

Jack gave his partner a quick look. This was not the reaction he'd expected. He'd used this old trick five or six times in the past and it always held back the mob. But then, as bad as those other mobs had been, they had been mere criminals, not true believers.

Alex looked down at the first row of his faithful.

"First row, up!" he yelled.

They were a spry old group of maniacs and, though on rickety pins, they stood up as a unit and readied themselves for battle.

Pointing to the three men in the middle of the row, Williams spoke calmly.

"Now, when I give the word, I want you three to charge these men, take away their weapons, and then hold them for me to punish. Do you understand?"

The three men nodded slowly, as though they were in some kind of dream state.

"Take him, now," Alex said.

The three men rushed Jack, who calmly shot the first two. Oscar shot the third, right in the temple.

The entire room made a deep-throated growling voice. They were ready for blood.

Alex smiled down at Jack and Oscar. He revved up the chain saw again.

"You see how it is, Jack?"

Alex smiled widely.

The room of old people growled their approval.

"I'll come down and when I do you both may as well hand me your weapons," Alex said. "There's no escape for either of you. But I promise we shall make good use of all your body parts."

"So that's how it is?" Jack said. "Their fear of you is stronger than their fear of death?"

"I prefer to think it's their love of me that makes them fearless against your bullets."

"I'm sure you do," Jack said, taking the Super Soaker out from inside his robe. "But in most behaviorist experiments there are certain primordial fears that trump conditioned responses."

Williams looked at the red plastic weapon in Jack's hand.

"You've lost your mind, Jack," he said. "But don't feel bad. Fear of being torn apart will do that to even the bravest of men. Still, this must be a first in the annals of hopeless cases. Attacking an army of angry men with a child's squirt gun."

He began to laugh and the entire room laughed with him.

As they did, Jack pumped the gun.

"I give you one last chance to give up and be arrested. If you don't, I can't guarantee your safety, Williams," Jack said.

"You are an original, Jack," Alex said. "I'll have to give you that."

He turned toward the front row and almost regretfully said, "Tear this clown and his partner apart."

The nine remaining men in the first row made weird, simultaneous growling sounds and charged Jack and his toy gun.

Jack pumped the red flamethrower and a mass of flaming gasoline shot twenty-five feet down the line, immediately setting the first two men on fire. Jack aimed the gun at the second wave of men and they screamed and fell back as their eyebrows and hair went up in flames.

Their robes caught fire and they panicked. They turned and ran toward the exit, spreading the flames.

A second row of men started to run forward but Jack blasted them as well. They fell back into the third row, some of whom also caught fire.

The third row of men began ripping off their robes and used them to beat out the flames engulfing the men in the second row.

The others behind them seemed to be coming out of their trances. Some of them tried to help the burned men and others looked up at their leader, still high up on the ladder, for guidance.

Alex Williams was red-faced, furious, and not a little embarrassed by his minions' failure to overwhelm two measly federal agents armed with some kind of toy flamethrower.

He looked out at his suddenly timid, very human crowd, those who only seconds earlier seemed to be willing to die for him.

"Where is your resolve?" he screamed. "You are an army, and your cause is just! A few of you have fallen. Think what you are giving up if you let this man arrest you! You are giving in to a world where the old aren't valued. Where you will be shut up in old-age homes like the ones this other jackal owns."

He turned and pointed at Phil, who was watching the whole thing unfold in deep shock.

"Listen to me," Williams screamed. "All of you. Do your duty. Tear these two men apart, now! Before more police come and kill all our dreams. Do it! Now!"

He looked out at the men, his eyeballs bulging, his teeth pressed together as if he might physically will them to move as one large mass.

But the response he got was only a low murmuring, as if the men were talking to themselves. Many of them shook their heads from side to side, and some turned their backs to their leader in shame, for their failure to do as he commanded.

On the floor the burned and dying were moaning in pain, which further dampened the fanatics' ardor. It was hard to be a killing machine once you lost your group spirit. Only minutes earlier they had all been happy as one entity, singing the old camp song as though they were on a scouting trip with a revolutionary purpose. Now, some of them looked like charred pieces of meat on the floor while the rest were being told to kill federal agents.

Something that could only end in disaster for all of them.

They saw that now, and they suddenly felt every bit of their true ages. They were old men who were likely to spend the rest of their lives behind bars. But maybe not, if they didn't commit any more crimes. After all, they were all rich, connected, and they could probably blame Alex Williams for brainwashing them. More then one man reached into his pocket and tried using his cell phone to call his lawyer, only to find that service wasn't provided a hundred feet beneath the earth.

Only one man was truly anxious to continue with the work of the Blue Wolf brotherhood: Alex Williams. What he needed, he thought now, was to be a true leader, one who would do some outrageous act which would reinspire the faithful. Something that would show all of them their awesome power.

Yes, the situation was one that called for a revolutionary hero, and that hero had to be himself.

He looked down at Jack with a calculated hatred on his face.

"You think you've won now? You think you've broken our will?"

"Yeah," Jack said. "I couldn't have said it better myself. Now come down from there before I put a bullet in your leg."

"You want me to come down? You've got it!"

Alex Williams revved up his chain saw one last time and, as most of his army of ancient men watched, he turned and pressed it to Johnny Z's throat. Blood spurted out all over Alex's face, and then, as Jack shot him in the left shoulder, he leaped off the ladder like a man half his age, the chain saw screaming in his right hand.

He landed just in front of Jack, and though he wavered, he was able to stay on his feet. Jack stepped backward as Williams's chain saw smashed against his gun barrel. The flamethrower fell to the ground, and suddenly the older man was on Jack, clawing at his face with his left hand as he tried to press the saw's teeth into Jack's neck with his right.

Behind Jack, Oscar was of little help because some of the men had felt a revived spirit of twisted camaraderie and were moving forward with murderous intent.

Jack heard the screaming of the chain saw as it came close to his left ear. He tried to fight Williams off with his elbow, but even though wounded, the older man seemed to possess near supernatural strength.

The saw came even closer. In a second it would slice through Jack's neck. Jack felt his strength sapping. He couldn't hold the saw back for much longer.

Williams felt it, too. He would win this battle and then they would kill the Mexican and eat their bodies at the feast. And he would be a god again. He pressed the saw forward, felt Jack's muscles trembling as they became fully spent.

It would only be a matter of seconds now. He was stronger than the FBI agent. He redoubled his efforts, saw Jack pull his head away, and saw the sweat running down the agent's neck.

One more push.

But for all his strength Williams wasn't a practiced fighter. He was so intent on slashing the saw into Jack's flesh that he forgot an old rule of street brawling. You must fight with your feet and legs, as well as your hands.

A lesson Jack hadn't forgotten.

He kneed Williams hard in his groin, and Alex groaned and fell backward.

"You son of a bitch!" he gasped, the pain flooding through him.

As he fell, Williams lost his balance. Panicked by the sudden reversal, he tried to swing the power saw at Jack with a desperate hope that he could score a direct hit on his face.

But Jack leaned back and watched as the saw barely passed by him in a speedy, out-of-control arc that ended up embedded into Alex Williams's own flailing left arm. The blade cut through a tendon in the Blue Wolf leader's forearm and the ensuing geyser of blood splashed his shoulder and face. Alex dropped the saw and fell to his knees, howling in fear and pain.

Jack kicked the saw away, and quickly took off his robe, tearing off pieces of it to make a tourniquet for Williams's bloody limb.

As Jack expertly tied off the tourniquet, Williams tried once more to rise up and address his followers.

"Forget about me. Think of what we've accomplished. Attack these bastards!"

But the faithful, once wild, had too much to lose. Many of them were already thinking of plane tickets to South America, the last place that didn't have *America's Most Wanted* on DIRECTV.

Now the unrepentant leader looked up at Jack and held his ground.

"You have no idea," he said. "None at all. What we found is real. Real!"

"Right," Jack said. "Which is why you're so youthful. You found something, Alex, something that made you a little stronger, maybe gave you a couple of days' energy—but, when your time is up, that's the end of the show."

"No, no, you don't understand. It worked. I'm telling you, it's real. It's going to change the world and *I* am going to be the most powerful—"

"Right," Jack said, keeping one eye on the mob, which was still filled with anger. Oscar held a shaky gun on them.

"And you actually ate them?" Jack asked.

"Holy cannibalism," Williams said. "Like Jesus. The blood, the body . . . it's all one."

His eyes began to get cloudy.

"The ancient tribes knew. We had the answer. You can't understand. You're a reactionary creep."

He looked up at Jack with hatred, then gasped and died.

Jack watched the blood leak out of him and saw the crowd move forward.

He stood up and looked at them.

"Your leader is dead," he said. "And this little game is over. If any of you want a chance of getting out of this without life in prison you should give up right now."

There was some grumbling but within seconds the whole group had lost its nerve.

Jack and Oscar held their guns on them as they herded them toward the exit.

The roundup of the rest of the Blue Wolf crew went without incident. The FBI, the New Mexico State Police, and some local Santa Fe cops helped gather the now-depressed and embarrassed offenders.

"They look like a sad bunch," Oscar said as the medics strapped him onto his gurney. The two agents watched the perps shuffle along with their hands cuffed behind their backs.

"Crazy shit," Jack said, as he observed a bloodied Phil and Dee Dee being loaded into another ambulance. "But I understand the rage they must feel. At least some of it. The old *are* treated like hell."

"Yeah, man, but all that other stuff? I don't get it."

"Tell you who might know some of it. Jennifer and her very tricky sister, Michelle. Speaking of which, where are those two?"

Oscar looked around as a young medic tapped an IV into his left arm.

"I don't know, amigo. A minute ago I thought I saw them by the entrance but they're gone now."

"Par for the course," Jack said. "The hell with them. You go get stitched up."

Oscar laughed and groaned.

"I'm gonna be okay. But looks like that girl got you again, Jackie."

"Yeah," Jack said. "And right in the heart."

Jack watched the medics shut the door to Oscar's ambulance and suddenly felt very alone.

Chapter Forty

After finding out that his partner was going to be okay, Jack wanted nothing more than to fill out his paperwork and get back to Los Angeles.

But before he could leave the scene, his phone rang.

He looked at the caller ID and shook his head.

"Hi, Dad. How's it going?"

"Hey," his father said. "Well, it's fine now, Jackie. But where you been? I been trying to get ahold of you for two days."

Jack could hear the panic in his dad's voice.

"Sorry, Dad. Where I've been they have very poor reception. Is everything okay?"

There was a long beat of silence, then, "Yeah, sure, son," Wade said. "It all came out fine. In the end, I mean. But, well, we had us a little spot of trouble here. No, make that a darn big spot. Can you talk now? 'Cause I got a lot to tell you."

Jack felt his stomach turn. Then he got behind the wheel of his car and steeled himself for the bad news.

Chapter Forty-one

Back at La Fonda, Jack was still too wired and disturbed to go to bed. He left the hotel, walked over to the square, and sat down on a bench, the cold wind cutting through him.

He'd thought the case would be simple. He'd thought he'd clear it up quickly and, meanwhile, his son would be just fine with Wade. Kevin. His only son. Almost killed and who knew what psychological damage had been done by the freaking lunatic librarian and her homicidal husband.

And the whole time all that was happening, Wade was telling him that everything was just great.

"He's getting home a little late with the library lady. Other than that, everything's great. Don't you worry about a thing, Jackie."

What had ever convinced Jack that he could trust Kevin with Wade?

If Jack himself was a fuckup who only bluffed and staggered his way through cases, what was Wade?

A bigger fuckup, that was for sure.

And yet Jack had somehow convinced himself that it was fine for his dad to take care of his son.

How could he have talked himself into that?

Because he was just like his dad. A selfish bastard who put himself and his needs first. Not that he didn't love Kevin. He was crazy about him. But deep down he had to admit it. He didn't want the boy to get in the way of his adventurous life.

He felt a hot jolt of self-hatred sweep over him. He was a selfish adrenaline junkie. He put his love for a woman like Michelle in front of his own son.

He felt such a self-loathing that he wanted to blow his own brains out.

But that wasn't the way.

He had to think of Kevin first. Forget Michelle. Break whatever hold she had on him. She had helped him once, true, but this had to be the end. She had almost sacrificed her own sister to do what she wanted.

He had to realize that basically she was no good. His son needed him and that was it.

But even now, thinking of her hurt.

There was something deeply lonely inside of him, something that Michelle identified and sympathized with.

He thought of his time with her. The feelings he had just *looking* at her. Intensely sexual, of course, but something more important as well.

He felt like they completed one another. That both of them had grown up lonely and desperate. But when they were together they were fulfilled. Whole. One.

And this time he had almost been sure that she felt the same way.

But that was another lie.

She had tricked him again.

It could never happen again. No matter what happened in this crazy goddamned life, he must always put Kevin first. Michelle was history.

His son was his life. To hell with everything else. Silently, he made that pledge to Kevin and himself.

Exhausted, Jack stood up from the bench and headed for the hotel and, if possible, sleep.

Chapter Forty-two

Six months later . . .

Jack pulled into the driveway and looked for a light in Kevin's bedroom but there was none. The dark room worried him. It had taken a month for things to get close to normal. Jack and Kevin had been seeing a family therapist named Lake Hale together. They even brought Wade with them a couple of times and things had gotten very stormy. But now, after a month, all three of them had started to settle down. Jack was keeping his end of the bargain, coming home every night, making sure that Kevin had done his homework and that they had time together every day. The whole process was starting to work.

At least Jack had thought so, until now. It was eight o'clock and where was Kevin?

Jack told himself not to panic. The kid could be back in the bathroom, or the kitchen. But somehow he knew that things weren't right.

Jack walked into the house and called his son's name. No answer.

He called again. No answer.

Jack put the pizza down on the dining room table and walked to the back of the house. No sign of Kevin in the bathroom.

He wet a washrag and wiped his forehead. Don't panic. Don't expect the worst.

He stared at himself in the mirror. He looked tired, and his shoulder holster was a little tight. He felt a pain in his right arm.

Jack started to take the gun off when he heard something from his own bedroom.

What the hell?

He listened more intently as he crept toward his bedroom door. Now he could make it out, a narrator's voice like in a documentary film.

"Here they are. Two white mice of precisely the same age. Both of them are three years old, which is pretty old for a mouse."

Jack crept up to his bedroom door, his Glock in his hand.

"The mice are named Binky and Bobby. You can see now that they are very old."

Jack listened at the bedroom door. Yes, it was definitely coming from inside.

He aimed his gun at the door and slowly turned the handle.

Then he heard another voice. This one was a woman's. And one he had come to know.

"Come on in, Jack," Kim Walker said. "And put down your gun. You won't need it. Oh, and one more thing. Don't turn on the light. I have a surprise for you."

Jack walked inside, still holding his gun. Except for the light coming from a grainy, black-and-white video playing on a laptop sitting on the dresser, the room was dark.

The blinds were closed and Kim Walker was sitting on the bed. She was mostly hidden by shadows.

"Hi, Jack."

"Kim. Where's my son?"

"He's fine. I just sent him in a cab across town to meet you for dinner. Called him on his cell phone. He should be at Musso and Frank's just about now. He'll wait a while, then call you. And by that time we'll be all done."

"All done with what? What is it you want?"

There was silence like a canyon between them.

"I know you've been through a lot, Jack," she said. "And I can just imagine what you think of us."

Jack looked from her, lost in shadows, to the frozen image of the two aged, fat white mice.

"By 'us' I guess you're admitting your complicity in the Blue Wolf homicides."

"Yes, I guess I am," she said. "But let me explain, please. You see, when Alex first told me about it, I really didn't even consider being involved. First of all, it was immoral, and second, it was too wild to even believe. Injecting the liquid form of the pineal gland, add other new antiaging drugs, and you may be able to turn back the clock? Recapture your youth? That's crazy, right?"

"Yeah," Jack said. "That's crazy."

"That's what I thought, too, of course, but I was wrong. And so are you. I want you to watch this. It was made at a secret lab in London by gerontologists who worked with Alex. What they discovered is nothing short of a miracle. You may have trouble believing what you're seeing but I assure you it's all true."

Jack turned his attention to the laptop as Kim pressed the PLAY button. The British narrator began again.

"Here are our two subjects, white mice who are at the very end of their life cycle. Both Binky's and Bobby's coats are very shabby. Their fur has fallen out, much as hair falls out of humans when they get old.

And look how feeble they are. Here's Binky trying to make his way through a maze he used to dart through only a year and a half ago."

Jack watched the pathetic mouse limp through the starting gate, walk into a wall, and then look around, ever so slowly, for the doorway to the next room in the maze. But even though it was just to his left he couldn't find it.

"If you're wondering why the mouse is unable to find the doorway, it's a number of things. His sense of balance, once perfect, is practically gone. His eyesight is limited to one eye, so his left eye doesn't even see the open doorway. He suffers from anxiety just from having to make the decision. Yes, mice can suffer anxiety."

"Now let's watch Bobby. You can see the same things. The hesitancy, the panic, the inability to make a decision. All symptoms of old age in mice—and people, too. But now let's see what happens when our first mouse, Binky, is given D-35, a new drug developed from the pineal glands of freshly killed younger mice."

Jack watched as Binky was given an injection of a white, viscous liquid.

Bobby was given a placebo.

"After only two weeks of treatment, let's see our mice again. Bobby still has a gray, listless coat, and still can't get beyond the first room. But let's take a look at Binky. His coat is beautifully filled out. Why, it's almost as full and shining as it was two years ago, when he was still a young mouse. And what about his maze-running ability? Why, he runs right through the maze, as if he already knew where to go. And all his vital statistics have improved dramatically. Blood pressure, heartbeat, lung capacity, mood. Yessir! Binky is one happy mouse!"

The camera moved in on the perky, happy white mouse, which looked years younger than it had two weeks before.

"You see, Jack? It *is* real. All of it."

"If that's the same mouse," Jack said.

"Trust me. It is." Kim said.

"Even so," Jack said. "What works in mice doesn't always translate to humans."

"True. But in this case, it does," Kim said.

"I see," Jack said. "Then how come Alex isn't young and dashing? How about the others?"

"They had just started to take it," she said. "The results were amazing, but they wore off after a few hours. You have to take D-35 for about six months to a year to see really dramatic results."

Jack walked to the side of the bed.

"Don't come any closer," Kim said.

"Why not?"

"I don't know if you'll like me."

Jack came closer and put out his hand.

"Trust me," he said.

"Are you going to arrest me?"

"'Fraid I have to, baby," he said. "But if you play ball with me I bet I can get you a reduced sentence in a nice white-collar facility."

"Jack," she said. "It's been so long since I felt anything for anyone. I wanted things to work out between us. I really did. And I thought once you saw this video you would understand. I didn't know what else to do."

"I don't understand. Were you sick or something?"

"Not sick," she said. "Not really. I was just like this, Jack. The worst thing in this world."

She turned and grabbed the rod for the blinds and twisted it so that the slats opened all at once. The bright streetlight shone in and for a second it blinded Jack.

He saw spots in front of his eyes. He could see her pulling the covers back and then, finally, he could see her clearly.

"Your face," he said.

It was a mass of wrinkles and age spots, the skin as thin and translucent as wax paper. She opened her mouth and most of her teeth were gone. Her hair was dried out, and in the middle of her head was a pathetic bald spot.

Then she pulled the covers the rest of the way off her body. Kim's breasts were like dried-out prunes, and her stomach was a sagging mass of wrinkles that led down to her birdlike, stick legs. Her toenails were long, yellow, cracked, and curled up at the ends.

She gave out an anguished, furious cry.

"How do you like me now, Jaaaaaack? Aren't you going to tell me how great I look? Don't you want to fuck me now, Jackie?"

She got to her knobby, bony knees and reached for his crotch.

"How about a blow job, Jackie? I can really gum it for you!"

Jack fell back, too terrified and shocked to speak.

"What's the matter, Jack? You don't like me this way? Well, I wouldn't be like this if you hadn't interrupted the ceremony. It was my turn to get most of the new batch of D-35, but there wasn't any new brain syrup because of you. I thought I had to die, but then I realized there was another answer, Jack. Do you see?"

She reached beneath the covers, pulled out a long, pearl-handled knife, and using all of her strength, she slashed it into Jack's stomach.

The blood spurted out of him onto her face, and she let it flow into her dried-out old mouth.

"Ahhhhh, good," she screamed. "Goood. Fresh, young blood. When you die I'll take your pineal gland and I'll be young again. You see how perfect that is, don't you, Jackie? And how just. You owe me, Jack. You know you do!"

She stabbed at him again and he fell back against the wall.

He could feel the world turning upside down and somewhere in his mind the story of the happy mouse began to play again.

"Look at Binky now," the narrator said. "Why, all he wants to do is play! He's like a happy, youthful mouse again. A new mouse with a second chance."

"Yes," Kim said, as she knelt on Jack's stomach and lifted the knife again. "A new and happy mouse. That's all I ever wanted to be."

The knife came down, but slower this time, and Jack found his hand wrapped around the Glock.

He aimed and watched as the bullets blasted into her stomach. He felt dizzy, weak, trapped inside a nightmare.

She fell on the side of the bed and slowly pulled herself to her knees.

"You made me old," she screamed again. "You made me oldddddd, you son of a bitch!"

Then she plunged forward with the bloody knife but Jack shot her again, this time in the head, and blood and bone sprayed on him as she fell over sideways onto the floor.

He looked at her lying there. Her neck had runny sores on it, and her ears were laughably long, ancient donkey ears. He felt pity for her.

For her and for all of them.

They were Americans. The magic land where no one ever had to grow up.

And no one ever died.

He was no different from the rest. He found her old skin, her bones, her old-person odor revolting.

He never wanted to get old. Never.

Who knew what he might do when his time came? If he had the offer?

Who knew what he might choose?

He looked down at his stomach, blood pouring onto the floor and pooling now by Kim's head.

Like they were one. And maybe, in some ways, they were.

Jack knew he should get his cell phone. But where was it? Not in his pocket. Then he remembered. He had left it in the car. He fell back on the bed and watched Binky run through the maze again. Half-gone, he listened as the narrator intoned, "Yes, newly youthful Binky is running, jumping, and skittering through the maze once more. It's obvious to everyone: Binky is one young and happy mouse."

Chapter Forty-three

He dreamed he was with some friends at a party, a beautiful party in the desert. There were cacti, and armadillos, and cowboys with Spanish guitars. And hanging from the starry sky was the moon. It was bright and yellow and seemed to bask them all in romance. Some of the girls, Mexican girls with beautiful eyes, were starting to dance. And Oscar was there, too, wearing a festive sombrero and two antique pistols in his red satin sash.

It was all just great, except for one thing. Jack was bending over a trough, where the burros were tied up, and he was throwing up some stuff that looked like magma. It was red hot, and as it poured out of his stomach sparks shot from it, molten sparks that shot back up into his face and singed his skin.

He heard the guitars playing a rancho song, and he saw people dancing in the moonlight, and he kept throwing up this red-hot lava, and even after getting rid of a ton of it, his stomach still killed him.

It was no use. He was going to die from this red-hot pain in his gut. Even though he kept vomiting, there was always more.

And the screaming pain only got worse.

Jack opened his eyes and saw someone looking down at him. She was a crazy quilt of patterns. At first she seemed to have one eye, then two, then three. And he knew her name, knew it like he knew his own, only right now he couldn't recall either of them.

Then he felt a cool thrill in his stomach, which for a second stopped the horrible pain.

"Michelle," he said, blinking.

"Wrong sister, Jack," the voice answered.

Jack blinked again. It wasn't Michelle, it was her sister, her sister whose name was . . .

"Jennifer," she said.

"Jennifer," Jack echoed. "Of course."

"You gave me quite a scare," she said.

"Me, too," said another voice. Jack looked up and saw a broad, kind face. He felt a flood of warmth.

"Oscar."

"Jackie," Oscar said, and took his hand in his own.

"How you doing, Jackie?"

"Aside from this inferno in my gut, really great," Jack said.

"Yeah, "Jennifer said. "But the good news is you're going to get better. They got to you just in time."

Now Jack blinked and it all came back to him. Kim stabbing him, his Glock going off, her body hurtling back. The blood. The sound of the documentary. The oh-so-happy mouse.

"But how did you find me, Oscar?" Jack asked.

"It wasn't me, amigo," Oscar said.

Jack turned to Jennifer.

"You?"

"No," she said. "I came here after I got a phone call."

There was something in her voice. An insinuation.

"Michelle?" Jack asked.

"Michelle," Jennifer confirmed.

"But how?"

"Luck?" Jennifer wondered.

"Fate?" Oscar threw in.

"I don't understand."

Jennifer looked at him and shook her head.

"She said she had come around to see you. To explain why we got caught."

"Yeah?"

"The reason was that we went back. Michelle insisted on it. She wanted the serum. She knew it worked and she knew which refrigerator they kept it locked in. And she knew there was no lock she couldn't pick. So we went back to get it."

"And?"

"And we got it. We picked the lock and we were on our way back out with it when two guards saw us, overpowered us, and brought us back inside."

Jack looked at Oscar, who said, "Fucking Michelle."

Jack laughed and nodded. "Fucking Michelle."

"The guards didn't really see us in the lab. They caught us in the hall and had no idea why we were there. So they just brought us in to join the party."

Jack felt his stomach spasm and gasped.

"We better go," Jennifer said. "You need your rest."

"Wait a minute," Jack said. "You haven't told me how Michelle . . ."

"She said she just happened to come around when she heard shots. She broke in and found Kim Walker dead, and you almost dead. She called 911 and came with you to the hospital. Then she called Oscar and me on her way out."

Jack nodded. "Out to where?"

Jennifer smiled. "I have no idea, Jack."

Oscar looked at her in disbelief.

"No idea?" Jack asked.

"None," she said. "But she did say she'd get in touch with you when you get well. She loves you, you know."

Jack looked down and shook his head. "Oh, man," he said.

"Get well, Jack. You'll hear from her again. And thanks. I owe you." She lightly touched Jack's hand and walked out of the room.

Jack looked up at his partner. "Son of a bitch, Oscar," he said.

Oscar smiled. "Son of a bitch, Jackie," he said. "Michelle. She's like a bad dream, bro."

"Yeah, bro," Jack said. "But let's face it. She's my *best* bad dream."

Oscar smiled and squeezed Jack's hand tightly as he fell asleep.